Crazy Beautiful Love
(The Martelli Brothers)

J. S. Cooper

J.S. COOPER

ISBN: 1492338141

ISBN-13: 9781492338147

DEDICATION

For Grandma Flo, I hope heaven is as you pictured it. I miss you.

CRAZY BEAUTIFUL LOVE

Chapter 1

Logan

I like to clear my mind at night, so I usually go for a long walk down by the pier. It's not my favorite spot, but it's easy to blend into the crowds of people there. I'm unassuming in a crowd; no one looks at me too hard or too suspiciously. At the pier, I'm just another guy. No one's whispering that I look like one of the Martelli brothers. No one's pointing and saying, "I think that's Logan Martelli," in awe-struck tones as if I were Al Capone or some mafia boss. It's laughable how many people know me or know of me. I almost feel famous but not in the good way. That's the problem with living in a small town like River Valley. Everyone thinks they know you, but really they know nothing at all.

I stared out at the water and studied the moonlit ripples as they ebbed and flowed. There was a certain magic in the water that entranced me. Maybe it was because the water didn't lie. What you saw reflected in her murky, silvery depths was what you got. Like tonight, the moon glowed in all its ominous glory, and there was nothing hidden. The same thing couldn't be said of human beings. There were always so many secrets hidden inside that weren't reflected in the seemingly happy and perfect surfaces. I looked around at the couples holding hands and saw Roger Martin walking with his girlfriend Bella Casey. She was giggling up at him, and he was grinning at her lovingly. Anyone watching them would think that they were deeply in love, only I knew better. Roger was a barely-able-to-keep-it-together drunk, and Bella was in love with my brother, Jared. She called him and stalked him so much that she was lucky that he was a Martelli. Martellis didn't go to the police and file restraining orders; even if we did, the police would laugh in our faces.

I turned to look at the water again when I saw a glimpse of someone darting by me. And when I say dart, I mean running like lightning. I watched as the figure looked back quickly, and I was startled by the intense blue eyes that connected with mine for the briefest second. It wasn't the stare that shook me, but the fact that it was a girl. She winked at me and continued running, and I stood there and watched as two policemen rushed past me and ran after her. I wasn't the only one who noticed the chase that was happening; people everywhere were stopping and gaping, whispering ferociously. Everyone wanted to know what was going on, and I had to admit I was curious as well. Why were the police chasing a girl? She wasn't anyone I knew, and I knew most of the bad folks in town.

I saw Old Man Roberts hobbling up to a couple a few feet away from me, his face red and animated. "He tried to steal a cop car," he gasped out. "He got in the car and drove off, but he wasn't smart enough to—"

"Who, who?" The male of the couple was loud and excited. "Who was it?"

"Well, I don't know. But I bet it was Logan Martelli." Old Man Roberts's voice was loud. I clenched my fist; of course I would get the blame. If it wasn't me, it would be one of my brothers, Vincent or Jared. I wanted to laugh at the irony. I would love to steal a cop car for all their harassment against my family, but I'd never been brave enough. Not like this girl, whoever she was. *Poor girl.* I shook my head, as I walked back up the pier. There was no way she wouldn't get caught. There was no way she could outrun two guys. Especially on a night like tonight when the pathways were so packed with people. What a poor choice of locale. Didn't she know you needed to pick a place where you wouldn't be seen, and where you could have a clean getaway when you stole a car? I laughed to myself as I cut across the pathway and headed to the parking lot. Though I should thank her; she'd made it easier for me tonight.

I spotted the black Toyota Corolla and walked over to it slowly and casually, running my hands through my dark blond hair. I couldn't stop myself from grinning. Tonight's take was going to be easy. I pulled out my lock pick and glanced around casually to make sure no one was coming. I tried the different keys, almost laughing as the third one opened the door. I loved Toyotas. Always so easy to break into. I got into the car quickly and closed the door. I reached over to the glove compartment and opened it to see if my luck was going to continue. It was. I felt the spare key in my fingers and pulled it out quickly and started the car. I reversed and pulled out of the parking lot, laughing once again at my good luck. Thanks to good ol' blue eyes, this was the easiest car I had ever stolen. Nobody would be expecting it, not when they thought I was being chased down by the police at that very moment.

I turned on the radio as I pulled onto the main road and listened to the smooth sounds of Kenny G on the saxophone playing through the tinny speakers. I sighed as the speakers strained when I turned the sound up. That was the problem with these cheap cars; they just didn't stand up to the more expensive cars.

I never stole expensive cars with better stereo systems; it wasn't worth it. Expensive cars were too hard to pass on. People became more paranoid about buying a Mercedes or BMW without papers. I didn't mind, I still did well with the Toyotas and Hondas. I cruised down Main Street and thought about the girl who had tried to steal the cop car. I could still picture the look in her eyes, in the quick glance we had exchanged. She had looked excited and scared, and I could sense the exhilaration and adrenaline coursing through her body. It was the same exhilaration I used to feel when I started stealing cars with my dad ten years ago. The fear of getting caught mingled with the excitement of doing something bad was better than any drug. At least, it used to be.

I was distracted from driving as I saw something or someone running down the street. I pulled over to the side of the street and slowed down to see who or what was running. I knew I was being dumb. I couldn't afford to get caught in this car. I needed to keep going, but something in me had to know. A part of me thought it might be the girl again, but I knew there was no way it could be the girl from the pier. There was no way she could have run all this way this quickly. I heard the sirens before I saw the lights and I cursed as I saw the cop cars speeding down the street. I pulled over quickly, turned off the engine and the lights, and crouched down in my seat, hoping they were looking for the girl and didn't know about the stolen Toyota yet. I laughed at the irony as I crouched down. They probably thought they were chasing me anyway. Stupid cops!

Knock, knock, knock. The sound sent my heart racing. What the fuck? I looked over to the passenger side and saw the girl.

"Open the door," she hissed at me loudly. I stared at her in shock. What was she doing? Was she crazy? She didn't even know me. I pressed the unlock button and she jumped into the car. "Shit, took you long enough to open the door."

"What are you doing?" I couldn't take my eyes off of her. It was definitely the same girl. I would recognize her vivid blue-purple eyes anywhere. She was actually more beautiful than I remembered. She had long black hair and her skin was flushed red. She was wearing tight black jeans and a tight black tank top. Her chest was heaving and I could tell she was out of breath.

"I'm trying to escape the cops, duh."

"Oh?" I looked at her curiously.

"You were following me?" She turned to me with slanted eyes. "I saw you slow down, pull over, and turn off your lights."

"I don't even know you. I wasn't following you." I shook my head in disgust. "And why would you get in a car with someone who was following you? Are you dumb?"

"I tried to steal a cop car." She sighed and leaned back in the seat in shock. "I can't believe I did that."

"Why did you do it?"

"I don't know." She started laughing hysterically. "I am going to be in deep shit if my parents find out."

I stared at her, not sure what to say. I swallowed hard as I stared at the naked length of her neck and chest. I turned away, upset with myself for being turned on by this crazy, beautiful girl.

"What's your name?" I asked her finally, not sure how much longer I could stay in this weird situation.

10

"Maddie." She opened her eyes and looked at me. "You?"

"Logan," I bit out, waiting for the inevitable recognition. The widening eyes that would turn her half-smile into a frown, and the worry that would cross her mind when she realized who she was with.

"Logan?" She smiled. "You don't look like a Logan."

"I don't?" The words tripped out of my mouth in surprise.

"You look like a Brandon or something." She laughed and then rubbed her eyes. "Don't mind me, I'm rambling now."

"Why do I look like a Brandon?" I felt like laughing. This was turning into one of the weirdest nights I had ever had. And Maddie seemed to be living up to her name; she was quite mad to be sitting here in a car with me, a guy she didn't know.

" 'Cause you're hot." She giggled and leaned towards me. "I'm not coming on to you or anything. I'm sure plenty of girls come on to you and say that. But I'm not one of those girls. But you're hot. Like James Dean."

"James Dean?"

"He was an actor—"

"I know who he is, or was." I frowned. "I just don't think I look like James Dean."

"You've got that air about you." She nodded. "Definitely a James Dean look: dark blond hair, shimmering, hooded green eyes, slight stubble, and you look like trouble."

"I look like trouble?" I raised an eyebrow at this strange but honest girl.

"I know, right? It's ironic." She laughed. "Here I am, running from the cops, and you're here sitting in your car, and I'm saying you're trouble."

"Ironic is a fitting word." I nodded and tried not to smile. "Do you need a ride?"

"Yeah." She sat up, and I think the seriousness of the moment finally hit her, because her body froze and she looked at me carefully with an extremely worried expression. "Shit. Shit. Shit," she cussed under her breath, and she stared at me with wide eyes.

"No longer feeling like you made a good decision tonight?" I asked her softly. I knew that she was experiencing the crash. The adrenaline and excitement was fading now and she was starting to feel panicky and worried.

"I don't know what I was thinking." She bit her bottom lip. "I was just walking, and I saw the cop car, and something just came over me." She shook her head. "I'm going to be in deep trouble."

"Do they know it was you?"

"I don't know."

"Why did you do it?" I looked at her curiously. She didn't look like the sort of girl who would steal a car.

"For fun?" She made a face. "You probably think I'm a horrible person, right? I wouldn't blame you if you decided to call the cops on me."

"I'm not going to call the cops." I laughed.

"You have a baby?" She surveyed the car and I looked at her in shock.

"No, no baby." I shuddered.

"So why do you have a baby seat in the back?" She frowned and I turned to look in the backseat.

"Oh." I tapped my fingers against the steering wheel. "About the car."

"Yeah?" She leaned towards me. Her eyes looked even more purple up close. I could smell her minty breath on my lips, and I had

12

a sudden urge to kiss her. We stared at each other for a few seconds, and I studied her eyelashes. They highlighted her eyes and I wanted to feel them against my cheek, to see if they were as soft as they looked.

I leaned back away from her and gripped the steering wheel. "I don't own this car."

"You borrowed it from a friend?" She cocked her head at me, and I shook my head. "You rented it?

"No."

"Then what?" She looked puzzled and I watched as realization hit her. "You weren't following me, were you?" She sat back and looked dazed. "Shit, you pulled over because of the cops? You— you stole this car?" Her voice was amazed and loud. I didn't look at her because I didn't want to see the reproach in her eyes. I knew what people like her were like. It was okay for them to commit crimes because it was just for fun. But when it came to people like me, it was a big deal. It was a bad thing. A really bad thing.

"That is fucking crazy." She started laughing and I turned to look at her in shock. Was she insane?

"Did you escape from a mental institute?" I asked her seriously, worried that I had perhaps picked up a real crazy person.

"A mental institute?" Her eyes glittered as she stared at me. "Maybe." She laughed even harder and gasped out, "Maybe I should be in one, indeed."

"Why aren't you jumping out of the car? I'm a bad guy." I looked at her, unsmiling. This wasn't a joke. Maddie made me uncomfortable, and I didn't like feeling uncomfortable.

"I thought you were going to give me a ride home?" She buckled her seatbelt.

"Are you crazy? I just told you I stole this car, and you want to stay in here with me?"

"Why wouldn't I? I just told you I tried to steal a cop car."

"But that's different." I started the engine and sighed. "You did it for fun."

"This is your career?" She sounded surprised.

"Yes," I bit out and pulled away from the curb. "This is my career."

"Well, no wonder you're better than me at stealing cars."

"Where do you live?" I studied the road ahead of me. I didn't understand this girl. Why didn't she have more common sense?

"Are you attracted to me, Logan?" She pressed her fingers against my arm, and I turned to look at her quickly. She was giving me a sultry look, and I almost did a double take. What was going on here?

"Where do you live, Maddie?"

"I don't want to go home," she said softly.

"Where do you want to go?"

"To your place."

"I don't have my own place."

"Where do you live?" she asked.

"With my dad and two brothers."

"Do you have your own room?"

"Yeah," I replied.

"So let's go."

"Why?"

"Do I have to tell you why?" She laughed. "Isn't it obvious?"

"How old are you, Maddie?"

"Twenty."

"Let me take you home." I gritted my teeth and ignored the stirrings of lust in my pants. It would not be a good idea to take Maddie home. She was trouble, I could sense it in my bones. They

didn't come any crazier than Maddie. Yes, she was beautiful, and yes, she was fearless, but she was not someone I needed in my life.

"Come on, Logan Martelli, take me home."

My breath caught as she said my whole name and I looked at her with suspicion. Had she known who I was the whole time? "How did you know who I was?"

"Who doesn't know the Martelli family in River Valley?" She spoke matter-of-factly. "I mean, I only just figured it out a few minutes ago. You don't look like I pictured."

"How did you picture me? Like the big, bad wolf?"

"Something like that." She nodded. "You're younger than I thought. How old are you?"

"Twenty-five." I paused. "So, what's your address so I can take you home?"

"I don't know if I should give you my address. What if you come back to steal from my house?"

"I wouldn't—" My face flushed as I responded to her angrily.

"I'm joking, Log." She touched my arm again. "Can I call you Log?"

"No."

"I'm joking. I want to go home with you." She shifted in her seat and moved even closer to me. "Please."

"No." My voice was resolute, and I was saying that "no" to her and myself.

"Please."

"You don't even know me." I shook my head. "You shouldn't go home with strange guys."

"You shouldn't let strange girls into your car."

"I can take care of myself."

"So can I. Please." Her voice broke. "I don't want to go home tonight. I don't want to answer any questions."

"I can't take you back to my place." I shook my head. There was no way I was taking this girl back to my house. Not only would my dad and brothers wonder what was going on, it would go against my own rules. I never brought women back to our place. It was something I had never done. And I wasn't about to start with her.

"You think I'm pitiful, don't you?" Her voice cracked and I could barely hear her as her face was pressed against the window. "You think I'm just this beautiful girl, with nothing better to do than just steal cars for fun. And now I'm practically begging you to be with me, and you're disgusted with me. Do you think I'm crazy?"

"Yes."

"I can't believe you said that." She turned towards me, laughing. "I guess the pity act doesn't work on you, does it?"

"What do you want, Maddie?" I turned to look at her again. "I'm tired and…"

"Shhh." She leaned over to me and kissed my cheek. Her hand reached up to my face. She twisted my face towards hers and I felt her lips press down on mine. Her lips were soft and firm as she kissed me, and I felt a warm surge of electricity run through me. She pulled back after a few seconds, and I sat there immobile. She sat back in her seat and smiled to herself. "I live on Manor Road. You can take me there, or we can go somewhere else. Your choice."

I stared ahead and didn't answer her. My mind was spinning with questions. She lived on Manor Road? That meant she was rich, really rich. The sort of rich that made the Forbes' Richest People in the World list. What was she doing trying to steal a cop car? And what was she doing with the likes of me? And how brazen was she to kiss me? I grinned to myself as I thought about the kiss; I could still taste her on my lips. She was trouble, plain and simple. The only possible outcome to this evening was to take her home. Take her home and never see her again. I'd warn her that a life of crime wasn't the way to get attention from her rich parents. Obviously, she was crying out for attention. Maybe her daddy worked too many hours and her mom was too busy servicing the pool boy and getting her hair done. Maddie was lost and crying out for help. I couldn't do anything to help her. Not a damn thing. She didn't need to get messed up with a Martelli.

I stared straight ahead and pressed my foot on the gas, ignoring the thumping of my heart and the heat in my face and pants. Maddie was not the girl for me. I wanted nothing to do with some rich girl who was looking for a joy ride. I could sense the exact moment the grin spread on Maddie's face. As I passed Manor Road and kept driving, I wondered what I was doing. But I ignored the niggling thoughts in my mind. I'd worry about everything tomorrow. Tonight was special, it was crazy, it was beautiful, it was full of wonder. Tonight, I was going to just be with Maddie, and tomorrow, I'd worry about all the other shit.

Chapter 2

Logan

"I can take you back home if you want." I looked at Maddie as we walked across the grass. "It won't be comfortable."

"I see a blanket in your hand. Where did you even get a blanket from?" She laughed and pointed at the Disney Princess blanket in my hand. "I'm sure I'll be fine." She paused and said casually, "Do you bring a lot of girls here then?"

"No, and I got the blanket from the backseat." I shook my head and turned away from her. The truth was, I had never brought another girl here. It was my special place, the place I came to when I wanted to think and be away from my brothers and my dad.

"The stars look so close," she whispered in hushed tones. "I didn't think the sky could look any prettier than it does down by the pier, but it is gorgeous here."

"I think we're closer to the sky." I nodded in agreement.

"Really?" She looked surprised. "I didn't think the altitude was any higher here."

"I don't know if that's a fact, scientifically or anything," I increased my pace. "I just think we're closer."

"You may be right." She reached out and linked her arm through mine. "It's pretty here. Where are we going?"

"There's an old shack further down this path." I pointed in front of us.

She giggled. "Oh, it looks grand."

"You can see it?" I frowned. It was extremely dark, and while the stars and moon illuminated the field we were walking through, it wasn't so bright that I could see the shack.

"No, silly." She leaned her head into my arm and I tensed up. "I was joking."

"Oh."

"I'm glad you decided not to take me home."

"I figured you may as well continue your night of crime and debauchery." I tried to make a joke, but my voice sounded too serious.

"We're a regular Bonnie and Clyde, aren't we?"

"No, no, we're not. I had nothing to do with you and the cop car."

"I'm joking, Logan." Her voice was suddenly serious. "I'm sorry if you think I forced you to bring me here tonight. You can take me home, if you're scared I'm going to get you in trouble."

The irony of the situation hit me once again. She was worried she was going to get me in trouble? "Let's not talk about our crimes of the evening," I said lightly.

"Sounds good to me." She stumbled and I grabbed hold of her to make sure she didn't fall. My hands slid around her waist, and I brought her in close to me to steady her. She looked up at me in thanks, and I was overcome with an emotion that I was unfamiliar with.

"Be careful," I spoke gruffly as I let go of her. "I don't want you to get a twisted ankle."

"I'll be okay." She spoke lightly and ran ahead slightly. I felt slightly disappointed that she was no longer holding on to my arm. I missed the feel of her hand on my body.

"Where are you running to?"

"The shack."

"But you don't know where it is."

"I'm sure you'll tell me when to stop." She started running faster, and I watched as her long legs sprinted in front of me, and her hair flew behind her. Her strides were long and she had perfect form as she ran; I realized that she must have run track at some point in her life.

"Hold on." I ran behind her and tried to catch up. She paused for a second and looked back at me. I saw the same twinkle in her eye that I had seen earlier that evening.

"Catch me if you can!" She laughed and started running again. She increased her pace and I doubled up my efforts to catch her. It took about a minute of running for me to finally catch up with her. I grabbed hold of her waist and we both went crashing down to the ground, as I couldn't stop my momentum.

"Ow," she laughed into my face as we rolled around in the grass. "That hurt."

"Sure it did." I laughed into her face, panting. "You can sure run fast."

"Thank God! The police would have caught me if I wasn't as fast as a rocket."

"As fast as a rocket, huh?"

"That's what my dad says." She smiled into my face, and she rolled over on top of me. "You really do look like James Dean."

"Is that why you wanted to spend the night with me?" I said, only half joking. A part of me was sad at the thought.

"Nah." She leaned down, her hair framing her face and brushing against the sides of my cheeks.

"So then why?"

"Because you taste like sin." She winked at me and pressed her lips against mine softly. I reached up and pulled her head down and crushed her lips against mine. I rolled her over onto her back and straddled her, pushing my tongue into her mouth as I pinned her arms back so she couldn't move. Her eyes widened at the pressure of me against her and I grinned against her lips. She had no idea who she was dealing with. My tongue explored her mouth as she wiggled beneath me, and I kissed her harder, sucking on her tongue as she struggled to move her arms. I winked at her and finally released them, and she ran her fingers through my hair and down my back, allowing her fingernails to dig into my skin.

I ran my hand through her hair and down the side of her face, before removing my tongue from her mouth and licking down her chin to her neck. I allowed my tongue to trail down her neck to her chest and she stilled beneath me as my fingers ran up her stomach and settled on her right breast. I paused and moved my mouth over to her left breast. I bit down on her hard nipple through her tank top as my fingers played with her other breast. I could hear her panting beneath me, and she moved underneath me. I ran my fingers down from her breast to her stomach and then to her thighs. Running them lightly up her inner thigh, I then stopped and sat up.

I looked down at her, panting in the grass, staring up at me with eyes full of lust, and it took everything I had in me to not rip her jeans off and take her then and there.

I jumped up and reached down and pulled her up to join me.

"What just happened?" She looked at me with dazed and innocent eyes. "Why did you stop?"

"I'm not going to take you in the grass, in the middle of some field. And I don't have protection."

"Oh." She nibbled on her lower lip. "I would have thought someone like you would have protection at all times."

"Someone like me?" My heart beat rapidly at her words. I tried to ignore the hurt that coursed through my veins.

"Yeah, I figured a guy as hot as you would have hundreds of

women throwing themselves at him."

"Oh." I laughed, trying not to fall under the spell her eyes were casting up at me. "I don't generally get many girls throwing themselves at me."

"I'm the only one who has wanted you?"

"You're the only girl I know who has told me to take her in a field."

"Then you should do it," she grinned at me impishly. "I'm on the pill."

"I don't know." I shook my head, ignoring the urge to pull her towards me and take her then and there. She was one of the sexiest and most confident girls I had ever met and I was having a hard time resisting her. And it was about more than the hot lust I felt for her, there was something about her smile that was tugging on my heartstrings. And frankly, it was that emotion that had me scared and holding back.

"Why not?" She pouted.

"You don't even know me." I shook my head. "You're not very smart, are you?"

"I want to have sex with you."

"Me, or any guy?" I stared at her pointedly. As much as I wanted to take her, I knew that I couldn't. She didn't seem like the sort of girl who knew the score. And as much as I didn't care if she got hurt, I just couldn't go forward. I didn't bother asking myself why; I didn't want to know.

"I'm not a whore, you know." She stared at me with pleading eyes. "I don't just go around having one-night stands."

"So you want to use me for a one-night stand?"

"No, well, you know." She blushed and looked down. "You're

different from most guys I've dated."

"You wanted to know what it was like to be with a bad boy?" I ran my hands through my hair. "Time to experiment with a bit of rough?"

"No, no." She shook her head angrily. "What's your problem anyway?"

"I don't have a problem." I started walking.

"Are you mad at me, Logan?"

"No, why would I be mad at you?"

"I don't know." She sighed. "You're not how I imagined, you know?"

"Yeah, you told me earlier."

"Earlier, I was talking about your looks." She reached out and stopped me. "Now, I'm talking about personality. You say you're a bad boy, but a bad boy would have fucked me with no hesitation just now."

"Is that what you want me to do?" I looked at her through narrow eyes. "Do you want me to bend you over and fuck you and take you home?"

"Yes… no," she mumbled, and I laughed as I saw the hope and eagerness in her eyes, followed by the shock. "I mean, yes, I want to sleep with you, but I don't want you to take my home afterwards."

"Oh, you'd rather we talk about our dreams and goals after?" I cocked my head to the side and looked at her in consideration. "Shall we talk about our plans for the future after? Maybe about my goal to go to law school, and your goal to become President? Hmm, yes, that sounds like a good idea."

"You're a real asshole, you know that?" She glared at me.

"You don't know me."

"I know of you."

"Yeah, you know what everyone in River Valley knows about me." I shook my head, disappointed.

"You think I believe everything that I hear?" Her eyes shot daggers at me.

"I don't care." My voice was hard. "And you should believe it it's true."

"I don't think it's true at all," she said softly.

"You just hope it's not true."

"I want to get to know the real you."

"Maddie, we've barely just met tonight. You don't want to get to know me. You want a hot fuck in a field with the town's bad boy so you can go and tell all your friends."

"You think it would be hot if we made love?" she whispered up at me, and moved closer to me.

"I said fucked." I took a step back. This girl was stubborn and brave. And stupid. "I don't make love."

"That's okay, we don't need to make love."

"You're crazy. You know that, right?"

"Tell me you don't want me." She grabbed my hand and moved even closer to me. "Tell me, you don't want to feel yourself inside of me."

"You've been watching too many pornos, Maddie." I looked at her with a wry smile. "I've never heard anyone use those phrases in real life."

"I don't watch pornos." She leaned up towards me. "But I do want to feel you inside of me."

"Shouldn't I be the one saying that?" I could barely believe my ears. This girl was crazier than I had given her credit for. "I wouldn't go around saying that to every guy you meet."

"I don't want to sleep with every guy I meet."

"So why me?" I looked at her, and my heart skipped a beat. I knew I was falling under her spell. And I didn't want to. I wanted to be anywhere but here, with anyone but her.

"Because you're Logan Martelli." She smiled shyly.

"You say that like it's a good thing." I rolled my eyes. "Haven't you heard? Good girls like you are meant to stay away from me."

"I'm not a good girl." She licked her lips. "I'm a bad girl."

"Why are you here, Maddie?" I sighed as I stared at her lips. I wasn't going to be able to resist her much longer.

"I don't know." She stepped back, and I was loath to lose her closeness. "I like you. I'm attracted to you. I want to know the real you."

"There is no real me. The me you know about is the real me."

"I've always wanted to get to know you better."

"You don't even know me." I rolled my eyes.

"You're famous in this town." She pushed me in the chest slightly. "And you know what? I don't care what people say about you."

"It's true what they say about me."

"Who cares?" She shrugged nonchalantly.

"What do you do, Maddie?" I changed the subject, not wanting to talk about my reputation anymore.

"I'm a college senior. Well, I'm going to be a senior in the fall."

"I see." I nodded and turned away. "Back home for the

summer?"

"Yeah." She sighed. "I wanted to get a job, but my mother wasn't having it."

"She doesn't want you to work?"

"No." She shook her head. "But let's not talk about her."

"What are you studying?"

"History."

"Interesting."

"No, it's not." She laughed. "I know that many people aren't as inspired by history as I am. What did you study?"

"In college?"

"Yeah." Then she blushed. "Oh, sorry. I guess you didn't go to college?"

"No. I shook my head, annoyed. "I barely graduated from high school," I lied, not wanting her to know that I graduated with a 3.8 GPA and a number of college credits from dual enrollment classes.

"School's not all that."

"Yeah." We walked in uncomfortable silence. What was she doing with me here? What was I doing with her?

"Do you enjoy stealing cars?"

I looked over at her, annoyed and suspicious. What sort of fool was she? "Is that all you think I do?"

"No," She looked taken aback. "I was just curious, seeing as how we just met, you know." Her voice trailed off and I stifled a curse. Since when was she so sensitive?

"Look, Maddie, I don't know you and you don't know me. Let's just spend the night staring at the stars and leave it at that. I'm not down for any deep conversations. I don't need to be analyzed by some college girl."

"I think you have a problem with me." Her words were soft but I could hear the edge in her words. "You're pretending you think I have an issue with you because you're Logan Martelli. Woo, I'm scared to be with the big, bad Logan Martelli, eldest brother in a family of criminals. I'm so scared. You're going to steal a car and then have your wicked way with me. Uh oh. Even though I can't even get you to make out with me for longer than a few minutes. The issue we have here isn't what I think of you, which by the way is not much, and that has nothing to do with the rumors about you in town. The issue we have here is that I'm a girl, and I'm rich, and I'm college educated, and I'm forward, and you don't like that. You don't like that a girl like me is confident enough to tell you that she wants you. You're scared that I'm going to emasculate you. You're scared that I'm going to be a better thief than you. You're—"

I watched Maddie ramble on incensed and pulled her towards me. "Oh, shut up," I growled at her before pressing my lips down on hers again. "Just shut up," I whispered against her mouth, and this time it was she who pushed her tongue into my mouth first. We kissed passionately, as if it were the last kiss that either of us would ever have on earth. I ran my hands down her back and grabbed her ass and pulled her into me so she could feel my arousal against her stomach. I squeezed her ass cheeks and enjoyed the feel of her firm butt against my hands. She pushed her breasts against my chest and I felt her hands in my hair. I opened my eyes and saw her gazing into mine with a sparkly glint. She was loving every second of our encounter, and it crossed my mind that she had deliberately wound me up; she had wanted me to take control of the situation and just shut her up. All of a sudden, I felt even more aroused and I brought her down to the ground with me. If this was what she wanted, who was I to say no?

"Oh, Logan," she moaned against my mouth, as I slipped my hand up her shirt and cupped her breast over her bra. I slipped my fingers into her bra cup and pinched her nipples, delighting in the sound of her groan at the contact of my skin on hers.

"Sit up," I commanded her and pulled off her tank top as she sat up and stared at me. I then unclasped her bra and threw it on the ground.

"Take off your shirt as well," she whispered.

"What?" I stared at her, unsmiling.

"Take off your shirt."

"I'll take it off when I'm ready." I gave her a direct warning look. "If we're going to do this, we'll do it as I say."

"Yes, sir."

"Lie down." I watched as she lay back on the ground and smiled before leaning down and taking her naked breast in my mouth. I almost groaned as I tasted her. Her nipple tasted sweet, and I suckled on it as if it were the sweetest confectionary. Maddie shifted underneath me, and I saw her legs spread as if giving me the signal that she was ready for another area to be serviced. *All in good time,* I thought to myself. I moved my mouth over to her other breast and she cried out as I nibbled on her now extremely hard nipple. I felt her hands on my back, and I knew she was pulling my T-shirt up. I paused, not ready for her to take my shirt off. I shifted and grabbed her arms, pinning them back on either side of her head.

"I told you, I'm not ready to take my shirt off."

"I want to see your chest."

"Not now," I growled down at her, wanting her to be slightly scared, wanting her to pause and think for just a moment, *what the fuck am I doing here?*

"Okay." She smiled up at me sweetly. I couldn't resist her smile. This stupid girl had no idea who she was messing around with. Part of me felt sorry for her, and the other part of me felt sorry for myself. One of us was going to get really hurt. I could already see the heartache; there was nowhere for anything to go between us. It didn't matter if we were both drawn to each other like moths to a flame. It didn't matter that we had only met that evening. I knew she couldn't resist me, because I couldn't resist her. There was some magnetic pull drawing us together. I'd known it as soon as our eyes had locked earlier. But I wouldn't have pursued it or her. *Liar*, a voice in my head called out, *why did you pull over then? You were hoping to see her. You were hoping with every fiber of your being.*

"Logan," she whispered up at me, distracting me from my thoughts.

"Yes?" I blinked down at her, unseeing.

"Kiss me." She leaned up, and I blinked again and saw her staring up at me with beautiful, open, shining eyes. Shit, there was an emotion there that I didn't want to see. "Kiss me."

I reached down and pulled my shirt off and threw it on the ground. I saw her eyes widen in shock at the huge scar on my abdomen, and as she opened her mouth to talk, I reached down to kiss her. I didn't want to talk about the scar. My chest crushed down on her breasts as we kissed and rolled around. My fingers trailed down her stomach and I crept them down to the top of her jeans and unsnapped the button. I looked up at her to make sure it was okay, and she nodded. I popped the button quickly, and then unzipped her jeans and pulled them off. I stared at her in wonder. She looked like a beautiful angel beckoning to me in only a pair of black lace panties. I ran my fingers in between her legs and she gasped as I slipped them into her panties. I grinned as I felt her wetness; she was as ready for this as I was. I rubbed against her gently, listening to the sounds of her moaning as I brought her close to a climax with just my fingers. I increased the pressure of my fingers, and watched as she writhed on the ground beneath me, her eyes getting darker and darker. Just as I felt she was about to come I removed my fingers from her and she cried out in protest.

I didn't hesitate as I felt her hands on my button, and I allowed her to unbutton my jeans before I yanked them off and sat there in my boxers.

She reached her hand into the fly of my boxers and grabbed hold of me cautiously. She grinned as she felt my hardness in her hands, and I smiled at her before pushing her back down on the ground. I positioned myself between her legs so she could feel my hardness next to her. She moaned, and we rolled around in the grass, touching and exploring each other's bodies. Within a few minutes, her panties and my boxers were also off and I looked down at her with a question in my eyes.

"Are you sure?"

"I've never been more sure." She nodded and pulled me down. "Fuck me, Logan," she whispered in my ear seductively, as she arched her back up to me. I couldn't take it any longer, and I centered myself at her entrance and pushed myself inside of her. She cried out as I entered her. I moved slowly at first, but I just couldn't hold back, and I increased my pace so I could feel her enclosed tightly around me. I stared down into her eyes as I moved back and forth, and the intensity of the desire in hers turned me on even more. I leaned down and pressed my lips against hers again, wanting to taste her as I took her. My lips crushed down on hers and she kissed me back hard, as she wrapped her legs around my waist.

She scratched my back and I felt her body shuddering underneath mine as she came.

"Logan!" she screamed over and over again, and I felt my body spark with electricity before I burst into her and then slowly withdrew myself, collapsing next to her. I lay flat on my back and she leaned over and rested her head on my chest, her fingers trailing along my chest. I saw her staring at my scar, and she ran her fingers down and touched it gingerly. I saw her glance up at me to make sure it was okay, and I nodded and played with her hair.

"That was wonderful," she exclaimed breathlessly.

"I'm glad you enjoyed yourself." I smiled at her, too satiated to say much else.

"We should do it again."

"Not now." I laughed. "Unfortunately, I'm not Superman."

"Maybe tomorrow?" She looked up at me, and my breath caught. I looked away from her causally.

"I'm busy tomorrow."

"All night?"

"You should stay at home and out of trouble, Maddie."

"I don't want to."

"You shouldn't be sleeping with random men the first night you meet them." I turned to her, and caressed her breast as I told her off. "It's not safe."

"You're safe." She giggled. "That tickles."

"Why did you steal that cop car, Maddie? And why did you get in my car?"

"I just wanted to see what it would be like …" Her voice trailed off. "I needed a break."

"You could have gotten into serious trouble. You could have gotten arrested."

"It would have been fine." She shook her head.

"You don't want a record," I lectured her, but I realized the irony of my words. "You have your whole life ahead of you."

"If you hate crime so much, why do you steal?" She spoke earnestly, and I looked at this girl I had only known for a few hours and laughed. No one had ever seen me for who I was in my whole life. Or asked me such a question.

"Who says I hate crime?"

"It's obvious." She looked at me with sad eyes. "So why do you do it?"

"Why does anyone become a criminal?"

"You're not going to tell me?" She looked hurt.

"I don't know you, Maddie." I scowled. "We had sex, that's it. We didn't become best friends. I'm not going to divulge all my secrets in some post-coital bliss."

"Why are you so mean to me?"

"I'm not mean. And why do you care? You're a young, beautiful girl with the world at your feet. What does it matter to you what I do or say?"

"Logan Martelli, I wish you would get that chip off of your shoulder."

"I wish you would be smarter about who you get into cars with and sleep with right away."

"You weren't complaining ten minutes ago." She ran her finger down the side of my face. "And don't you dare call me a slut or easy."

"I would never say that."

"Sure, I know most girls say this, but this is the first time that…"

"Oh, my God, please do not tell me you're a virgin," I cut her off, aghast. "Shit."

"No, Logan." She laughed hard. "Though if I was, I would be devastated by your comments. I was about to say, this is my first one-night stand, or the first time I've had sex on the first night I met a guy."

"Really?" I looked at her with a disbelieving gaze. "I'm not calling you a liar, but you were pretty forward for someone who's never done this before."

"What can I say?" She laughed. "I knew what I wanted."

"You're crazy."

"You keep saying that." She stared at me thoughtfully. "Though, I suppose others would agree. I can see the headlines now: 'Mayor's daughter has sex romp with town criminal.'"

"What did you say?" My face paled at her words.

"Sorry, I didn't mean to be rude." She made a face. "I shouldn't have called you the town criminal."

"No, no, not that." I took a deep breath. "Did you say 'mayor's daughter'?"

"Yeah." She nodded and wrinkled her nose. "I know, I'm frightfully rich, and spoiled, and should know better, but…"

"No, that's not it. You're Mayor Wright's daughter?" I sat up and pulled away from her.

"Yes, what's wrong?" She looked worried. "Does it matter?"

"I need to take you home." I jumped up. "You need to go home, now." I picked up her clothes and threw them at her. "Get dressed."

"But, I wanted to spend the night—"

"I don't care what you want, Maddie, get dressed."

"What's wrong, Logan?" She jumped up and started pulling her clothes on and I turned away from her with my heart pounding.

"I have to take you home, now." I felt a headache coming on, and I avoided Maddie's gaze. I never should have pulled over. I knew it had been a mistake to bring her here. I just hoped it wasn't going to bite me in the ass. I grabbed my stuff, and ignored the slight pang I felt as I realized the reality of the situation. I could never see Maddie again. I had only known her for one night, but I already knew she was going to be someone I'd have a hard time forgetting.

Chapter 3

Logan

Maddie didn't say anything as I drove her back to her house. I was glad for the silence. I ignored her and the pounding in my head and concentrated on the street signs. My heart was also pounding, but I convinced myself that was due to my fear of the police catching up with me and not due to what had just happened in the field.

"You can just drop me off at the bus stop." Maddie's voice was low and pained and I kept driving without saying anything. "Are you going to tell me what I did wrong?" She paused and then continued after a minute. "Or was this just a bit of fun for you?"

"What do you think?" I kept my eyes straight ahead, wanting her to feel hurt.

"So this was just a roll in the hay? Or should I say, a roll in the grass?"

"You can call it whatever you want."

"You're an asshole."

"Then don't be so easy next time." I regretted the words as soon as they slipped off of my tongue. I heard her gasp and I knew I had hurt her. But I didn't want to let her know that I actually respected her for going after what she wanted. I liked that she wasn't the type of girl to play games. Unfortunately, I knew I couldn't tell her that.

"You were easy, too," her voice was accusing. "But let me guess, because I'm a girl, it's an issue. I'm a slut because I slept with you right away, but you're a saint, right? The criminal saint."

"I didn't call you a slut and I never said I was a saint." I shook my head and peeked at her. My heart trembled when I saw the confusion and hurt on her face. I felt horrible but a part of me was happy that she was hurt. She deserved it for what her father had done. I hated her because I hated her whole family. I just wished I hadn't gotten involved with her in the first place.

"Well, in case you didn't know, you're not a saint. I should call the police and tell them you stole this car."

"Yeah, you do that, wannabe cop car stealer." I rolled my eyes, though my stomach was a bundle of nerves. What if she said that I tried to steal the cop car, then stole this car and kidnapped her or something? Girls were crazy, and I didn't know her from Adam. I cursed under my breath as I felt my sweaty palms on the steering wheel. I had well and truly fucked this up. And then Maddie started laughing, and I looked over at her in surprise.

She grinned at me as she wiped tears from her eyes. "I guess I'm the pot calling the kettle black, aren't I?"

"Huh?" I frowned at her, confused at her sudden change.

"Me threatening to call the cops on you." She shook her head. "I wonder if I should tell them about my own attempted theft before or after I rat you out?"

"I guess that's the dilemma." I smiled at her reluctantly. Maddie really was different from any girl I had ever met.

"Are you going to tell me why you're taking me home?" she said softly.

I shook my head. "No."

"I like you, Logan Martelli." Her voice was sweet and she sighed before she continued. "You're a sexy, wonderful mystery."

"I'm not a mystery. You know who I am. Everyone in River Valley does." I paused and looked at her quickly. "Though you didn't go to school here, did you?"

"No, my parents sent me to boarding school in Boston." She made a face. "They didn't think that the schools in River Valley would prepare me to go to the best colleges."

"Ironic that the mayor thinks that the schools here are crap." I tried to hide the bitterness in my voice.

"Yeah," Maddie's voice was soft. "It says a lot."

"So why did you steal a car, Miss Wright? You've got more than enough money to buy a ton of cop cars if you so desired."

"I'm not going to say." She shook her head, and I frowned at the sound of her voice. It was a mix between humor and sadness.

"Wait, so now you actually know why?" I slowed down and stopped at the red light and then looked over at her hard. "I thought you didn't really know."

"You're going to think I'm crazy if I tell you."

"Oh?" I closed my eyes briefly in worry. Had this been some sort of sting operation? Shit, my dad would go crazy if I got busted, and especially because of Maddie Wright. I could just imagine how angry he would be, and Vincent and Jared would be worried and scared.

"So I'm not going to tell you," she continued childishly, and I squared my jaw and stared at her intently.

"What the fuck is going on, Maddie? I'm not one of your college beaus you can twirl around your little finger. You mess with me and I will make sure it's repaid. Do you hear me? Your parents warned you about the Martelli brothers, I'm sure. And they did that for good reason. You do not know what I'm capable of." My voice was low and harsh as I said the words I thought would scare her most. A part of me was sad that I had to play this role, especially with her. For some reason, I didn't want Maddie to believe the rumors about my family. I didn't want her to think I was capable of doing really bad things. But it was a bit late for that; she had met me on the night I had stolen a car. She would never believe I was a good guy inside; I didn't even know if I was a good guy inside.

"What are you talking about, Logan?" Maddie's eyes flashed with anger instead of the fright I had expected to see. "And the light just turned green, so you can go."

36

"I'll go when I goddamn please," I hissed, slightly unsure of myself. She wasn't reacting in the way I had expected.

"Logan, you've been watching too many John Wayne and Clint Eastwood movies." Maddie laughed and leaned back in her seat. "Or maybe *The Godfather* and *Goodfellas*? Did you watch a movie marathon recently?"

"What are you talking about?" I blinked at her in confusion, heart thudding again.

"That little talk just now, about me not messing with you." She laughed. "I've only known you a few hours, but I know you wouldn't hurt me."

"Are you stupid, Maddie?" I sighed as I pressed my foot on the gas. How could she trust me so easily? Didn't she know that there were real bad men around who could do her harm? "You do not know me, no matter what you think."

"I trust my gut instincts." She smiled at me sweetly. "You're not a bad guy."

"What sort of guy am I then?" I held my breath, waiting for her answer.

"You're the guy I'm going to marry."

I burst out laughing at her words and shook my head. She really was a Loony Tunes character.

"I think you've had too much time on your hands this summer."

"Have you ever seen *The Notebook* or *Love Actually*?"

"Nope."

"Well, have you ever seen any romance movies?"

"Nope."

"Well, when people are meant to be together, they just know."

"Maddie, I have no interest in getting married, and if I did, it would not be to you." I let the words linger in the air and felt her flinch at my words.

"I hope you don't think—"

"Look, Maddie," I cut her off and pulled over at the end of her street. "This isn't a romance movie or book or whatever. There is no happily ever after for us. I don't know what game you're playing. I'm sorry I slept with you. That wasn't fair to you. But listen to me carefully: we are nothing. I don't know you, and I don't care about you."

My eyes blazed into hers and I could see tears welling in them. I broke away from her gaze and looked at the tree-lined street of mansions. I stared at her house, with the colonial columns and the porch swing, and my blood boiled. There was no reason for me to feel sorry for Maddie; she had everything she could ever want. She was just some silly college girl, caught up in some fantasy of getting with a bad boy. I knew her type.

"That's how you feel?" Her voice was strong, and I was surprised that she wasn't crying already. I guess she inherited her backbone from her piece-of-scum father.

"Yes." I looked back at her and stared at her slightly trembling lips. They looked so pink and luscious, and I could almost feel them on mine; soft, moist, and sweet. I wanted to pull her towards me and hold her tight. I wanted to kiss her again. Shit, I wanted to take her in the backseat of the car. All I would have to do is throw the baby seat out.

"Well, I guess that's it, then." She opened the door. "It was nice to meet you."

"I wish I could say the same." I turned away from her harshly. Let her hate me. I needed her to hate me. I couldn't afford for the lines to be blurred. I was already feeling shitty, and I just needed to get away from her.

"I stole the cop car because I wanted to meet you," she whispered before she slammed the door.

"Wait, what?" I sat there in shock. "What the fuck is she talking about?" I cursed at myself as I opened the car door and jumped out. "What do you mean?" I called after her as I hurried to keep up with her. She was walking fast and I ran to stop her.

"Wait." I grabbed her arm and stopped her. "What do you mean you stole a cop car to meet me?"

She turned around slowly and my heart froze as I saw the tears streaming down her face. She looked up at me, and her cheeks were blotchy. I pulled her towards me subconsciously and held her in my arms. She rested her head on my shoulder and I stroked her hair and buried my face in her black locks. I felt her body pressed mine, and I ignored the stirrings of lust that grew in me.

"Why do you hate me?" She looked up at me with wide eyes, her irises cloudy and unsure. "I don't get why you're trying to hurt me."

"I don't even know you, Maddie. We just met. I'm not trying to hurt you."

"You're not a cruel guy." She shook her head. "You changed after we had sex." She sighed. "I guess it's my fault."

"I didn't change because we had sex." I shook my head and rubbed her lower back, pulling her closer to me. "We're two people who shouldn't have …"

"Shhh." Her eyebrows crept together. "I don't want to hear anything about being from opposite sides of the track or whatever. We're both adults here. Yeah, I know you're a criminal, a petty criminal. But I also know you're a smart guy. I know what you do to help others."

"I don't know what you're talking about." I looked away from her. How did she know so much about me? I thought I had hidden my tracks a lot more carefully.

"It doesn't really matter now." She pulled away from me.

"You're just a guy, and I'm just a girl. I know you like to go to the pier to steal cars at night. And you know that I like to watch romance movies."

"I see." I frowned. If the fact that I liked to steal cop cars at the pier was well known, then I had to choose another spot.

"I wanted to see what it felt like to be a car thief." She shook her head and frowned. "I wanted to be in your head."

"Why?" I looked at her in confusion.

"I don't know. I didn't think it through properly. I figured maybe you would wonder who the new thief in your territory was, and maybe you'd come find me."

"Now who's watching too many movies?" I laughed and ran my hands through my hair. "I can't say I really understand, but I guess I get it."

"I just wanted to …" She shook her head. "Oh, what does it matter? I'm too tired to explain."

"I want to know."

"Are you going to take me out tomorrow night on a date?"

"No."

"Are you planning on ever seeing me again?"

I looked at her and at that moment, I wished that I could give her a different answer. "No. No, I'm not," I replied honestly, I didn't tell her that I wished that the circumstances were different. It didn't matter what I wished; they weren't now and would never be.

"So it doesn't matter then. I was just a stupid rich girl." She let out a quick self-deprecating laugh.

"You're not stupid." I shook my head, wishing I knew what I could say to make her feel better. My intent had been to hurt her, but now, seeing her crushed and disappointed face, it didn't feel as good

40

as I had always hoped it would.

"Whatever. It was nice finally meeting you, Logan Martelli." She gave me a quick kiss on the cheek and pulled away from me. She walked slowly up to her house and I stood there in impenetrable silence as I watched her walking away from me. I saw her at the front door and then walked back to the car. I sat in the driver's seat and stared at the house, unseeing. I didn't even have to have my eyes open to picture every detail of that house and lawn. I'd been here so many times, sitting in a car, staring and listening to stories. I'd hated this street and this house for more than half my life. I'd hated the family that lived in that house for as long as I could remember. Even though I'd seen the mayor and his wife before, I'd never seen Maddie. We didn't even know she was called Maddie; we knew her as Maddison. I had hated Maddison Wright and her family with every bone in my body, and now I sat in my car with a ball of confused emotions. Because I didn't hate Maddie, not even a little bit. I didn't hate Maddie at all. But there was nothing I could do to ever let Maddie know that.

***

As I walked through the front door, it felt like I had been away for years, even though it had only been a few hours. I surveyed the mess in the house, and laughed to myself at the sight. I could only imagine the shock on Maddie's face if I had brought her here.

"Logan, what did you get?" My dad's gruff voice called out to me, and I saw him sitting on the large, scruffy brown leather couch, with a beer in his hand.

"Toyota."

"Highlander?"

"Corolla."

"Good for resale." He nodded and took a swig of beer. "We got worried. Why were you gone so long?"

"There was some drama on the pier, I had to wait it out."

"No one saw you, though?" He looked up through small eyes. "I don't need the police coming to harass me tonight."

"No one saw."

"Good." He frowned as he drank the last of his beer and threw the can into the corner. "Go and get me another beer from the fridge."

"Okay." I walked to the kitchen quietly, not bothering to ask if he was sure he wanted another. I no longer cared how drunk and obnoxious he got; he wasn't ever going to change.

"Hey." I nodded at Vincent who was sitting at the table with a stack of books in front of him. "Wassup."

"Trying to figure out these equations." He sighed and slammed the book shut and jumped up. "Where have you been?"

"At the pier. It took longer than I thought it would." I opened the fridge and grabbed a Bud Light. "Want one?" I lifted the can up to Vincent.

"Nah." He stared at me. "You should have told me, I would have come."

"I work best alone." I shrugged.

"You need a lookout, you know that." He sighed.

"You got an exam tomorrow." I walked to the kitchen. "You need to focus."

"It doesn't matter, I'll fail anyway."

"Hold on." I put my hand up, walked to the living room, threw the beer to my dad, who was staring at *The Simpsons* on TV and mumbling, and then I walked back to the kitchen. I looked around and resisted the urge to start shouting about the mess. The sink was full of dirty dishes, and there was food all over the counters and on the floor. "Where's Jared?"

"Dunno." Vincent sat back down and opened his book. I sat down at the table with him and studied his serious face. I wanted to tell him about my night. Not about the thrill of stealing the car; he knew what that was like already. I wanted to tell him about Maddie, and how she had lit my heart on fire, and how we had made sweet, hard, passionate love in the grass, and how I had thought I was going to explode from the sensations. I wanted to tell him how sweet the sound of Maddie screaming out my name had been. But I kept my mouth shut.

"You okay, Logan?" Vincent looked at me in concern, his blue eyes worried. He ran a hand through his spiky black hair and he leaned towards me. "Did something happen tonight?"

"No. Nothing happened." I faked a smile and hit him in the arm. "You don't know who I am? I'm Logan Martelli, the cops can't keep up with me."

"Ha, ha, I almost forgot you're Logan Martelli." He smiled and me and then sighed.

"What's wrong, Vincent?"

"I just don't think I can do this." He nodded at the books on the table. "I'm too stupid to understand this crap."

"You're not too stupid for anything." I gave him a stern look. "Let's have a look." I opened his book and saw the page on quadratic equations. "I can help you with this, I was pretty good in math."

"You were good in everything." He laughed and sat back. "Genius of the family."

"Well, you're the college boy, so I expect you're just as much of a genius as me."

"I don't know if I'd say I'm a college boy. More like a hopeful community college man."

"Community college is still college, you'll still get a degree. And then you can go on to a four-year university."

"I don't know about all that."

"You'll do fine. Now go take a five-minute break, let me look over the problems, and I'll help you, okay?"

"Okay, thanks, Logan." He jumped up. "You're the best."

"Yeah, yeah." I rolled my eyes and watched as he ran up the stairs. I sat back in my chair and closed my eyes for a second. I was worried that Vincent was going to drop out of community college and that everything would be for nothing. At twenty-two, Vincent was one of the oldest freshmen students at River Valley Community College, but I was so proud of him. Even though I had been pushing him for a long time to get a college education, he had ignored me. It was only when he got busted for smoking pot on the beach with some of his friends that he decided to enroll. Thanks to the judge, it was community college or jail. I hadn't told anyone, but I was glad Vincent had been caught that night. I didn't want a life of crime for him and Jared. I wanted them to go to school and get out of River Valley. They didn't need this life.

"Okay, back. You ready to teach me, Einstein?" Vincent ran back into the kitchen. "And I think Jared's back. I just heard a car door slam and then a car backing out."

"He got a ride?" I looked towards the front door, slightly annoyed.

"I guess." Vincent nodded and bit his lip.

"With Joey?"

"Dunno."

"Okay." I knew there was no point badgering Vincent about Jared. If there was one thing that was true about the Martelli brothers, it was that we weren't snitches.

"What's up, bitches?" Jared sauntered into the house and threw his fingers up in the air. I could tell that he was drunk right away, and I was pissed.

"Where have you been, Jared?"

"Out." He walked into the kitchen with bloodshot eyes.

"With Joey?"

"Yeah, and?" He glared at me, his green eyes daring me to say something. I stared into the eyes that were an exact replica of mine, and I counted to ten.

"I told you I don't want you hanging out with Joey."

"You what?" Jared laughed. "I'm twenty-one, bitch, and you're not my mom or dad."

"You know he's bad news."

"We're all bad news, that's the beauty in it." Jared stumbled to the fridge. "Any food?"

"He's real bad news, Jared." I walked over to him. "We don't get involved in that stuff."

"I know, I know." He sighed and turned around to me. "There's nothing to eat."

"What do you want?" I looked around the kitchen and realized that there was no space to make anything, even if I'd wanted to. "Let's just order a pizza."

"You sure?" Jared's eyes lit up and I pulled him towards me. He was my little brother but he was still taller than me, with his six feet and four inches. I patted him on the back and let him go.

"Yeah, go and call them."

"You the best, bro."

"Oh, I'm your bro now and not a bitch?"

"You're still a bitch." He laughed. "What up, Vincent?"

"Just trying to get ready for this exam tomorrow."

"Tell Logan to go and take it for you." He wiggled his eyebrows and we all laughed as we sat down at the table. I looked at my brothers and felt at ease; these were the guys I would give my life for. Even though I was only three years older than Vincent and four years older than Jared, I felt a huge responsibility for them. In fact, I often treated them like they were my sons. Ever since our mom died twelve years ago, we had been essentially alone. Dad had only been good for a few things: teaching us how to steal, how to drink, and how to not give a fuck about anyone else.

"Shh, Jared, Vincent can do this. And so can you." I looked at him pointedly, and he gave me such a glazed look, that I knew he wasn't going to remember this conversation in the morning.

"Vincent's going to become a lawyer so he can keep us out of jail." Jared laughed. "We only need one college boy in the family, Logan."

"Whoa, hold on. I'm a far way from law school." Vincent's voice was gruff, though I could see the hope in his eyes. Vincent's dream had always been to go to law school. He had this idea that if he got into the system, he could change it. I didn't really want him to go become a lawyer; I felt it would distance him from me. But I wanted the best for him. His dreams were important to me, more than my own worries and concerns.

"You'll make it, Vinny. And Jared, you get your ass working on that college application."

"Shit, Logan, I've got two months until the deadline." Jared rolled his eyes at me, and it took everything in me not to deck him.

"That's what you said last year and you missed it."

"How was the pier tonight?" Jared changed the subject, and I turned away from him with a shrug.

"Okay. I got a Corolla."

"I noticed, sweet ride." Jared laughed.

"Stay away," I warned him.

"You taking it to Marty?" he questioned me.

I shook my head. "Nah, not this one." I kept my voice monotone and jumped up to grab a beer. Marty was an old friend of my dad's. He ran a mechanic shop in River Valley and always took the cars we gave him. He either used them for parts or sold them through an auto dealer magazine. However, recently he had been paying less and less and acting shadier and shadier. I think it was because he didn't like dealing with me. He was used to my dad, who just took the money and shut up. By the end of the night, Marty would have most of the money back, either in his belly as free beer or as winnings from poker night with my dad and some of their friends. I didn't participate in either of those activities and Marty wasn't too happy about it. So now he offered less and less. In fact, the last time I had taken him a car, he had given me a veiled warning: take the cash offered or the car might make its way to a police parking lot in the middle of the night, and he'd hate to see them catch the thief due to fingerprints. I took the money instead of socking him in the jaw because he had his two henchmen next to him. But I knew after that, I couldn't take another car to him.

"Where you going to take it?" Jared questioned me.

"I'll have to see." My voice was rough and strained. "Anyways, I gotta help Vinny now. You go wait on the pizza and we'll talk later."

"Shit, I better go outside and wait before Dad goes crazy at the pizza guy for ringing the doorbell again."

"Yeah." I nodded in agreement. "Do that." I watched as Jared walked out of the kitchen, down the hallway, and out the front door, and I let out a deep breath.

"What's up, Logan?" Vinny's voice sounded worried.

I looked up at him with a weak smile. I had forgotten he was still in the room with us. "Nothing."

"Something going on with Marty?"

"Yeah, but it'll be okay."

"He's shady as fuck, isn't he?" Vincent sighed and I saw that his fists were clenched. "You let me deal with him, or all of us can. You, me, Jared, we should go down there and show him that the Martelli brothers don't play."

"We can't go down there and intimidate him, Vincent." I shook my head, trying to talk reason into him, even though his idea sounded good to me.

"I wasn't talking about intimidating." Vincent smiled a wicked smile. "I'm talking about using him as a punching bag and not stopping until he cries like a bitch."

"We're not going to do that, Vinny."

"Pussy."

"Watch your mouth." I laughed. "You can't afford to get caught for anything anyway, you know what the judge said."

"Yeah," he sighed. "What are we going to do?"

"I don't know."

"We got enough money for rent next month?" I could hear the concern in his voice and I was angry. Angry that we were in this position, angry that I hadn't been able to do anything to make our lives better.

"We got enough," I lied, not wanting him to worry. I knew what he would do if he knew I was worried, and the last thing I wanted was for him to go to jail.

"But not much more, huh?" He sat back, still worried but less stressed. "You think you'll be able to sell the Toyota?"

"Yeah." I nodded.

"We could always ask Joey …?" Vincent's voice trailed off, as I glared at him.

"We don't do business with Joey."

"It can't hurt to do it this once."

"No." I shook my head vehemently. "We don't deal with the likes of him."

"He's not that bad."

"I'm not going to discuss it again. I've told you and Jared already. We don't mess with Joey and his boys."

"Okay, okay."

"You wanna go over this math now or what?" I opened the book back up, and as far as I was concerned, the subject was closed.

***

I heard Vinny and Jared snoring as I walked to the bathroom. The TV was still blaring downstairs; it sounded as if my dad was watching Jerry Springer. I checked my watch and realized it was four a.m. It was more likely that he had fallen asleep on the couch with the TV on. I ran down the stairs so I could turn it off, but saw that he was sitting on the couch wide-eyed and staring, as if in a trance.

"Dad?" I walked into the room hesitantly. "You okay?"

"Just getting ready for the day." He looked up at me, but I couldn't tell if his eyes were really focused.

"You want me to help you up to your room?"

"I was just watching TV." He blinked at me and rubbed his eyes. "There was a lady that looked like your mom."

"Oh?"

"Yeah, same blond hair." He stared at me. "You're the only one who looks like her."

"I know. People always wonder if I'm really Vinny and Jared's brother," I joked about their dark hair and features. They took after my dad.

"She had such long blonde hair," he continued. "She was the love of my life."

"And you were hers." I gave him a wide smile. I knew the routine by now. We'd had this conversation hundreds of times since she had died.

"I failed her." He shook his head. "She should still be here."

"I know."

"They fucking killed her."

"I know." I sighed and rubbed my eyes, wanting to go back to sleep.

"Have you ever been in love, son?" His words sounded coherent and lucid and I looked up and saw the very real question in his eyes.

"No." I shook my head. Love was for fools. I was many things, but I wasn't a fool.

"I never wanted to fall in love," he laughed. "It just kinda hit me, like a deer in the night. Your mother was the most beautiful girl I had ever seen, and I just couldn't stop thinking about her."

"And she couldn't stop thinking about you."

"No." He shook his head. "She couldn't. She loved me when she shouldn't have. But she couldn't help herself."

"Yeah, some women are crazy." I shook my head, and an image of Maddie crossed my mind. "Some women are mad." I laughed at my joke, and looked up to see my father staring at me curiously.

"You've met someone?" He leaned forward and a beer can fell to the ground. I watched in dismay as the liquid seeped into the already-dirty, tattered, stained brown carpet.

"No." I shook my head vehemently.

"You've met someone." He laughed and sat back, his beer belly showing as his T-shirt rode up. "Who is she?"

"No one," I answered quickly, my heart beating fast. I was scared that he would figure it out. That somehow he would be able to read my mind and know.

"Must be someone special."

"She's not special," I retorted and then realized my mistake. "There's no one."

He peered up at me and gave me a sweet smile, a smile that almost reminded me of the man he had been when I was a child. The man my mother had fallen in love with had been a fun, handsome, wonderful man. And then the smile turned into a bitter look and he pointed at me. "You better not fuck around and let this chick take your mind off of what's important."

"There is no chick." I stepped back, not wanting to get into it tonight.

"I told you, women ain't shit. You got a family to take care of. Me and your brothers need you."

"I know."

"Go and get me another beer."

"It's late."

"Who you talking to like that?" He made to get up, and as I stared at his slovenly body, a shudder of distaste ran through me. How I hated this man who was supposed to be my father. It didn't matter that there were moments of sorrow and sympathy and that there were glimpses of the man he used to be. All he was now was a sorry old drunk. I just wanted to walk out the door and never come back. How I hated this place, this town, this house, my life. But it was all I knew. And all I could do, or try to do, was help Vincent and Jared achieve their dreams so they weren't stuck in this shithole forever, like I was.

"I'm going out." I looked at my father, who had fallen back against the couch, and I walked to the kitchen quickly and grabbed the keys to the Corolla. It wasn't smart for me to take this car. It had likely been reported as stolen already, and the police would be sure to be on the lookout. I got all the way to the car before I stopped myself. I couldn't take the Corolla. I would have to borrow Vincent's Mustang. I knew he would be pissed, and I knew I just didn't care. I ran back in, grabbed his keys, and headed back out and started the engine.

This 1977 red Mustang was Vincent's pride and joy. He had restored it himself and paid for all the parts with money he had made delivering pizza in high school. Most people couldn't believe it when Vincent got the job. They assumed he would just follow in my footsteps and be a thief, but I had made him get the job. If he wanted a legitimate car, he had to buy it with legitimate money. The cops were all over us as it was; there was no way he could drive a few weeks in his own car without having a money trail.

I started the engine and listened to it purr before quickly reversing off of the overgrown grass that made up our front yard. I revved the engine and peeled off down the road, rolling the windows down so I could feel the cold fresh air on my face. I didn't know where I was going and it didn't even matter. I just needed to be out of the house before I did something I would regret.

It had been a long night, and I felt anxious and angry. I hadn't felt this bad since my mom had died. I was so unsure and screwed up. And it wasn't because of my dad. It was because of Maddie: stupid, beautiful, wild and crazy Maddie. I didn't want to think about her, but the memory of her begging me to take her kept playing in my mind like some broken record. The feel of her skin next to mine, so soft and supple, aching for my touch, aroused my thoughts, and an image of her vivid blue-purple eyes flashed in my mind. My God, she was beautiful. Perhaps one of the most beautiful women I had ever met. And definitely the most unique. She was definitely a woman who was there to be admired and taken notice of, and she knew it. She was under my skin, she was in my skin, and I wanted to rip her out of me. I'd only known her one day—not even a day. One night. One night and already she was causing confusion in my life. And she was the enemy.

It was as if the car were telling me where to go. I felt like Michael Knight in *Knight Rider* as I drove towards Manor Road. I knew the way well as I had taken the exact route so many times. I pulled up to the street about twenty minutes later and parked in the same spot my dad had every time he drove us here.

I stared at the house for what seemed like the millionth time. It was so big that as a child, I had always wondered what people did with houses so big. Did they sleep in a different room every night? It was so different from what I was accustomed to. So grand and alluring. I wondered what it would be like to live in a place like that. To make enough money to afford a house that rivaled any Beverly Hills mansion. I sat back in the seat with the engine off and just stared. I thought about all the other times I had been there, and the vitriol my dad had spewed about the mayor and his family. The vitriol that had been the foundation of my hate for Maddie and her family. Only, as I sat there, I found it hard to hate her.

"That's what these worms do," I berated myself. "These parasites try and pretend to be someone else and then they fuck you over." I was mad at myself, I was mad that I was wondering and concerned about how Maddie was feeling. I didn't want to care about how she was feeling. She deserved everything that she got. She was a spoiled bitch. *Who tried to find some guy she didn't know and then sleep with him.* She was crazy. *She's not that crazy and she's not a bitch*, another voice whined inside my head. I jumped out of the car, confused and angry at myself.

I grabbed some gravel from the side of the road and ran up to the house, throwing it at the front door. My aim was off and I heard the sound of windows cracking as the small rocks slammed into them. I saw a light come on, and I stood there defiantly. I wasn't scared and I didn't care what happened. It was time for me to face the mayor. I needed to let him have it, and I didn't care if I was arrested in the process.

Chapter 4

Maddie

I heard the sounds of thunder against the windows downstairs and I sat up, slightly frightened. My mother's cat came running into my room hissing, and I jumped out of bed, unsure of what to do. I wanted to go downstairs to see what had happened, but I knew that was a bad move. I'd seen enough horror movies to know that only idiots went to see what was going on. But I also knew I didn't want to stay in my room, waiting for something to happen. I sighed and reached for my old tennis racket in the corner of my room. It wasn't a baseball bat, but it would have to do. Why had my parents chosen this week to go out of town? I was super pumped when they had told me they were going out of town and they hadn't made me go with them. I had almost been in shock; my dad was so overprotective that he usually liked to accompany me to the grocery store. It had taken me four months to convince him that I would be safe going to a college out of state, without a private bodyguard. It was so annoying and cloistering, and I hadn't known what I was going to do if he kept hovering over me as if I were some soon-to-be-extinct species.

The fact that they had chosen to let me stay home by myself was a huge feat, and I knew that if he knew what I had done the previous night, I'd never be let out again. But I wouldn't have changed a thing. It had been the best night of my life. I hugged myself as I thought of my time with Logan Martelli; it had been magical. He was magical when I got into the car to be with him, or maybe that feeling was due to the fact that my heart had still been racing after my attempted car theft. That had been crazy, and I still couldn't quite believe that I had done it. I hadn't planned on trying to steal it; my only plan had been to go down to the pier to *bump* into Logan. That was the best way to meet him; at least that was what I had been told. But then as I was walking and saw the cop car with the keys in the ignition, something came over me. I wanted to know what it felt like, but I panicked when the cops saw me pull away, and I jumped out of the car and started running. I knew I could outrun them; being the track star of your high school will give you that confidence. And then I saw Logan staring at me, and I paused for one brief second. And as our eyes connected, I saw the amazement, respect, and surprise in his eyes. And I felt like I was on fire. He was even more gorgeous than I had expected. I wanted to run over to him and kiss him, but I knew I couldn't stop.

My immobile body started shaking as I heard the sound of cracking down the stairs. My grip tightened on the tennis racket and I took a deep breath and crept through my open bedroom door and walked down the stairs slowly. I listened to the creaking of the stairs underneath my feet and cursed that my parents hadn't updated the historic mansion and put in a marble staircase. I tiptoed down and held my breath. I looked into the formal living room that was next to the entryway and realized that the windows were cracked and not broken. I peered through the windows and my breath caught as I saw the solitary figure standing by the main gate at the front of the house. It was Logan. What was he doing here? And why was he trying to destroy my house? Was he mad? I ran to the front door without thinking and ran outside in a hurry.

"Logan," I screamed at him, my heart beating rapidly. "What are you doing?"

"Where's your dad?" His voice was hoarse and he had a crazed look in his eyes.

"He's not here," I shouted at him as I ran down the porch steps. "Come inside."

"What do you mean, he's not here?" He frowned at me. "You told me you didn't want to come home right away because you didn't want to deal with your parents."

"I lied." I looked at him coolly, still mad at how he had treated me earlier in the evening.

"You lied?" His eyes narrowed and he took a step back. "What the fuck?"

"Would you have taken me to the field if you had known my

56

parents weren't home?" I shivered in the cool night air. I was only wearing a pair of short-shorts and a tank top. I saw Logan look down at me, and his eyes took in my whole appearance. I shivered again, but this time it wasn't because I was cold.

"You were in bed?"

"Yeah, it's still nighttime, you know."

"Actually, it's morning." He gave me a sarcastic smile, and I resisted the urge to kiss him and wipe the cocky smile off of his face.

"Actually, most normal people are still in bed sleeping at this hour."

"Actually, most working-class people are getting up at this hour because they have to get to their minimum-wage-paying jobs."

"Well, I guess that rules you out, then?" I lifted one eyebrow at him. "Or do car thieves make minimum wage these days?"

"Maybe car thieves get up early to steal cars before anyone else is up." He leaned towards me and my heart fluttered. "But you tell me, seeing as you joined the ranks yesterday, or at least, tried to join."

"Come inside." I grabbed his arm, and my stomach dropped as he yanked it back away from me. "I don't want people to see us standing out here."

"Scared to be seen with the town criminal?"

"No, but I don't want people to call the cops because they don't know what's going on."

Logan stared at me for a few seconds and shook his head. "I'm going home, have a good night, Maddie."

"Wait a minute." I poked him in the chest. "You're not going to tell me why you were throwing rocks at my windows?"

"I wasn't throwing rocks," he responded petulantly, and I almost laughed.

"Pebbles, rocks, whatever," I hissed and walked up to him. "But, I guess that's your M.O., just walk away when the questions start coming."

"Excuse me?" He glared at me. "I'm not walking away from anything. Just because you don't get your way every single time, it doesn't mean that I'm the bad guy. Maybe this will help you see what the real world is about."

I tried to ignore the hurt that coursed through me. I had been told he had a chip on his shoulder. It wasn't personal. I just had to remember that.

"Please come in, Logan." My voice was soft and I stared into his eyes, this time resisting the urge to touch him again.

"Why?" He laughed. "You want to fuck again?"

I turned away from him and felt my face flush. I wanted to slap him across the face, but I couldn't ignore the heaviness between my legs. He was right: I did want to sleep with him again. More than anything. But I also knew what he must think of me. What sort of girl sleeps with a guy on the first day they met? And what sort of a girl sleeps with a guy a second time after he treats her like shit? I didn't want to be that sort of girl.

"I'd like to chat." I looked back at him again. "That's it."

We stared at each other for a few seconds and I watched as Logan ran his hands through his dark blond tousled hair again. His eyes narrowed as he thought, and I could see that his shoulders were tensed. He looked back into my eyes, and as I stared into his deep, secretive green irises, I felt excited and scared.

"Okay." He paused. "I'll come in for a few minutes."

"Great." My heart soared and I walked quickly back up to the door with him right behind me. A part of me was a little scared. I really had no idea what I was getting into letting Logan Martelli into my house and my life. I'd had a small crush on him for a few years but that was based on a few photos and conversations about him with friends I'd gone to elementary school with, in the summers I'd come home from boarding school.

"Let's go upstairs." I closed the door behind him, not knowing if I was being too forward by taking him up to my bedroom.

"Okay." He looked around the house almost eagerly and I saw him soaking everything in. A part of me was worried that he was taking inventory of all of my parents' belongings. Maybe he was planning on coming back to steal everything. I ignored the brief hesitation and grabbed his arm. "Ready?"

"Your house is just as I imagined it would be inside." His tone was even and almost wondering. "It's grand, but it's warm as well." He stared at the antique grandfather clock next to the dining room entryway and walked over to it. "This is nice."

"It's heavy." I uttered the words without thinking and blushed. He turned towards me with a sardonic smiled and rolled his eyes.

"Thanks for letting me know. I guess I won't steal it when I come back."

"I didn't mean that." I walked to him. "I'm surprised you came back tonight, after what you said earlier."

"I came to talk to your father."

"Why?" I didn't really understand why he cared to talk to my father. Was he planning on telling him that I was on my way to becoming criminal and had slept with him in a field? It didn't make sense.

"Doesn't matter." He looked at me coldly. "Let's go upstairs."

"Are you mad at me?" I heard the pleading in my voice and hated myself. I wasn't this person. "Because if you are, you can just leave." *Take that*, I thought smugly. The ball was in his court now. I wasn't going to make him think he was doing me any favors.

"No." He walked towards me and grabbed hold of my waist and pulled me towards him. "I want to stay."

"Okay," I mumbled as I looked up into his dark gaze. His hands moved down to my butt and he pulled me into him roughly. I could feel his erection against me and I swallowed hard. "I just don't get you."

"What's there to get?"

"If you like me or not." I stared into his green eyes and saw the wanton desire and lust as he looked over my body. "Or if this is all about sex."

"Do you care?" His hand slid up my back.

"I don't know," I lied. *Of course I care, you stupid idiot.* I wanted to pound my arms against his chest.

"Exactly, so let's go upstairs then." His eyes issued me a challenge and I knew what he was saying. A spark of desire ignited in me and I reached up and brought his mouth down to mine to kiss him. He kissed me back hard and then pulled away from me, with eyes blazing.

"I didn't say you could kiss me." He shook his head, and a small smirk twisted his lips. "You'll pay for that."

"Oh?" I licked my lips.

"And for that," he growled at me.

"What are we waiting for?" I grabbed his hand and ran up the stairs excitedly. I paused at my bedroom door and turned to him hesitantly. "This is my room."

He peeked his head inside and nodded. "It's nice, but the bed's a bit small."

"It's a full." I looked at him and resisted the urge to bring him closer to me. "We'll fit."

"What size bed do your parents have?"

"King? Why?"

"Let's go in there." He stepped back and I realized that he was serious.

"Are you joking? There is no way we can have sex in my parents' bed." I looked at him like he was crazy. "Let's just go in my room." I pulled on his arm, and he stood still.

"Why not? You said they aren't here, right?" His eyes darkened as he looked at me. "If you're going to be a bad girl, then you may as well be as bad as possible."

"No, they're not here, but I just think that's kinda weird." I frowned at him. "And I never said I was a bad girl."

"I want to fuck a bad girl." He pushed me up against the wall roughly. "You have the house to yourself; wouldn't Daddy be mad if he knew you had a guy here?" His hands ran up my stomach until he was caressing my breasts, and my mind became even hazier with lust.

"I just think that…"

"You won't be thinking anything when I have you screaming out my name." His fingers played with my nipples and he licked his lips.

"Can't we just try it in …" My words died as he stepped towards me and his mouth replaced his fingers. My back arched as he sucked on my right breast and I closed my eyes.

"Which way is their bedroom?" he whispered in my ear as he replaced his lips with his fingers and they squeezed and pinched my nipples.

"I, uh, this way." I ignored the niggling questions in my mind and led him to my parents' bedroom. I opened the door and turned to him. "This is it."

"So, this is where the mayor sleeps?" He laughed as he took it all in. He walked away from me, and I watched as he walked around the room. He stopped at the closet and opened it, peering inside and then closing the door. He walked back over to me and grabbed my hands.

"I thought you'd be on the bed by now," he growled in my ear as he cupped my right breast again. "I thought your clothes would be on the floor and you'd be spread-eagle, waiting for me to devour you with my tongue."

"I don't know why you'd think that." I smiled up at him, my body shaking at his words. He wasn't smiling at me, and a hint of danger filled the air.

"Why are you smiling?" He grabbed me, pulling me towards the bed. He threw me down on the mattress and the small sense of hesitation left me. What did it matter what room we had sex in? I looked up at him as he gazed down at me with hooded eyes and a devilish look on his face.

"Are you going to punish me?" I batted my lashes at him, secretly turned on by his take-charge attitude. I wasn't sure what he was going to do and it thrilled me.

"You'd like that, wouldn't you?" He shook his head and his eyes were alight with laughter. "Do you want to feel my hands all over you?"

"Yes." I smiled up at him, and he laughed. He looked down at me with a huge smile and he sighed briefly.

"You really are a different one, aren't you, Maddie?"

"Perhaps." I reached up to him. "Is that going to be a problem?"

"What do you want me to do to you?" His eyes seemed to glitter as he stared down at me.

"Spank me," I breathed out lightly.

"How?" He stared at me and my heart raced.

"I want you to take me over your knee and spank me for being bad," I breathed up at him, hardly believing I had said the words out loud. But for some reason, I wasn't shy or scared. When I was with Logan, I felt like nothing was out-of-bounds.

"You want me to spank you?" He hovered over me. "Do you really want me to put you over my knees?"

I nodded, and he grabbed my body and placed me on his lap, facedown.

"Like this?"

"Yes," I moaned, and I looked up at his glittering eyes.

"You want to feel my hands on you?" His hands caressed my butt cheeks and his fingers slipped in between my thighs as he rubbed my ass. "Do you like this?" His voice was low and I could feel his erection hardening against my stomach.

"Yes," I moaned as he pulled my shorts down and slipped them off my legs.

"Do you like this?" He slapped my ass lightly and I wiggled beneath him.

"Hmm, yes." I closed my eyes, enjoying the feel of him touching me.

"Do you like this?" He slapped me a little harder this time, and my ass tingled a little bit.

I nodded, hoping he would do it again. I trembled in his lap, delighting in the deviancy of our actions. I had never felt so alive and aware in my life.

"And what about this?" This time his hand was even harder, and I yelped as his hand smacked my ass and then rubbed it gently.

"I'll stop, I didn't mean to hurt you." He removed his hand quickly and I looked up at his face wildly.

"Don't stop, it feels good," I gasped at him.

"You like me spanking you in your parents' bedroom?" He grinned at me, and I nodded, unable to say anything or think about anything other than his hands on me. "Do you like being a bad girl, Maddie? Is this what you've been wanting, to be with a bad boy like me?"

My eyes widened as he slapped me again. He slipped his hands between my legs, and this time his fingers pressed into my wetness. I thought I was going to come at his light touch.

"Have you been waiting on me all night? Hoping you could be a bad girl? Hoping that the bad boy would come and give you a good spanking?" His voice grew louder as he spanked my ass lightly and rubbed in between my legs. I felt myself growing wetter and I groaned. "Or do you want me to stop?" He started to move his hand and my body cried out for me to stop him.

"No." I shook my head and clenched my legs, trapping his hand in between my legs. He wiggled his fingers against me and I moaned as he slipped two fingers inside of me. "Oh my ..." I gasped as he played with me. "Don't stop." I begged him as he withdrew his fingers right as I felt my orgasm reaching a climax.

"Don't stop what?" He leaned back onto the bed and I turned around so that I was lying on top of him. I looked down at him and grinned before pulling my top off. He gasped as I leaned down and quickly unbuckled his belt and pulled his jeans down.

"Take your top off." I laughed at his surprised expression. Two could play this game. I dropped his pants on the floor and moved up so I was straddling him, his boxer shorts the only barrier between my sensitive mound and his pulsing erection. He stared up at me, taking in my nakedness, and I brushed my nipples against his mouth, moving back quickly as he tried to take one into his mouth.

"Take off your top first."

"Do you want me to spank you again?" he questioned as he pulled his shirt off. I stared down at his chest and ran my hands up and down his abs, trying to avoid staring at his scar. It had obviously made him self-conscious earlier and I didn't want to do that again. Though I wondered how he had gotten it. Had he been in a fight and someone had pulled out a knife? Or had he tried to rob a house and gotten cut on some broken glass? I ran my fingers over it thoughtfully, and he pulled me up to him quickly, rolling me over so I was on my back and he was in top of me. I opened my legs and wrapped them around his waist, and his mouth came crushing down on mine. I felt his chest crush against my breasts as his tongue sought out mine, our lips pressing against each other's urgently. I ran my hand through his hair and I felt his hand run down the side of my body, grabbing my leg and pulling me more tightly around him. I felt his hardness twitching against me through his boxers and I started moving back and forth slowly so I could feel him rubbing me up and down.

Logan gasped against my lips, as I increased my pace and he started moving his hips, rubbing against me harder and harder. I felt the tip of him against me and realized he must have slipped out of his boxer shorts. He was at my entryway so I reached up and grabbed his ass and pushed him into me so I could feel him inside me. He shook his head and laughed as he shifted slightly. I no longer felt him against me and I moaned in exasperation. My brain felt dazed with lust and I opened my eyes to see why he hadn't taken me.

"It's not going to be that easy," he whispered against my lips. "I told you that by the end of the night, I'm going to have you screaming my name, begging me to take you."

"I want you to take me now," I gasped and ran my hands down his body until I held his erection in my hands. "Take me now, Logan."

"Not yet." He shook his head. "Why ruin the fun?"

"I want you inside of me."

"You've had me inside of you."

"I want you inside of me again, now." I tugged at his hair. "Please."

"Have you ever fucked on your parents' bed before?"

"No," I moaned, needing to feel him inside of me.

"How does it feel?"

"Naughty." I blinked up at him. "Like I'm a bad girl."

"You are a bad girl." He laughed, and his mouth found my breast.

"Well, you're a bad boy."

"What would your dad say if he knew what you were doing?" He bit down on my nipple. "What would he say if he walked in right now and saw you naked on his bed, with Logan Martelli sucking on your nipples?"

"He wouldn't like it," I gasped as he suckled on my other nipple and bit down hard. "Ooh, that feels... oooh!" I cried out as he slipped two fingers inside of me as he continued sucking.

"What would he think if he saw me bringing you to an orgasm with my fingers?" He whispered in my ear. "His little girl being pleasured by the bad boy of River Valley?" My eyes shot open at the sound of venom in his voice, and I squirmed, slightly uncomfortable. Why did he keep mentioning my dad?

"I don't... oh my God," I screamed in ecstasy as Logan kissed down my body and his tongue replaced his fingers. "Oh my, Logan, ooh, don't stop." I grabbed his head and bucked under him as his tongue slipped in and out of me. "Please don't stop, I'm going to come." His hands grabbed hold of my hips and pushed my legs open even wider as he devoured me with his tongue and sucked on me. I felt my body tremble as my climax built up and then explode into a million pieces as I felt myself orgasm underneath him. Logan continued to lick me up after I had finished coming. I closed my eyes and lay there, delighting in the feelings that were still coursing through my body. Logan finally stopped and I felt his lips kiss up my body and stop on my mouth. His tongue traced over my lips and his hands grabbed mine and he pulled them above my head.

"Open your eyes," he commanded me and I opened them slowly, feeling slightly shy at what had just happened. "Did you like that?"

"Yes." I grinned up at him, thrilled at the look of desire in his eyes. As I stared up at him, I felt like I had known him for a million years, not just one day.

"Do you let every guy do this to you right away?" His eyes darkened and he looked at me furiously as if jealous.

"No, of course not."

"Then why me?" His grip tightened and he looked down at me. "You don't strike me as a girl who turns to a life of crime and winds up in my bed all in one day, just because."

"We're not in your bed," I replied impishly.

"What?" He looked at me in confusion, then his eyes sparkled as he got my comment. "Your mouth is going to get you in trouble, Maddie Wright."

"I'd rather trouble were to get into me." I winked at him and wiggled underneath him.

"You'd rather trouble get …" he burst out laughing as he realization dawned on him. "You are a bad girl, aren't you?"

"Only recently," I answered honestly. "But, I suppose my whole life has been building up to this moment." *And being with you*, I thought to myself. My whole life has been the opening to this main act. But I didn't voice my thoughts. I didn't want to scare him. I didn't want him to know that at first sight I had known that we were destined to be together. That I would do anything to be with him.

"Your whole life, huh?" He stilled and rolled away from me. "You've been watching too many romance movies, Maddie. This doesn't end in happily ever after."

"Who says?" I rolled over and looked at him, hurt.

"What part of this makes you think of happily ever after?" His fingers trailed down the valley between my breasts. "You're just a goodtime girl to me."

"Maybe you're just a goodtime boy to me." I tried to disguise the pain in my voice as best as I could. "Maybe I just want to be fucked by the baddest boy in town."

"Well, you already got your wish then, didn't you?" His voice was harsh.

"You're an asshole." I stared at him with hate. I didn't understand why he was so hurtful to me. There were times I felt he was just role-playing with me, and yet there were times I knew he was deliberately trying to hurt me.

"I never said I wasn't."

"You can leave." I rolled away from him, and closed my eyes. This had all been a mistake. I should have just left well enough alone. I hadn't intended for all of this to go down. I had just wanted to meet him and to get to know him, but everything had just spiraled out of control. I had acted wanton, crazy, and desperate, and now he had no respect for me. He probably considered me some sort of rich-girl whore.

"I haven't fucked you yet." He grabbed ahold of me and turned me around. His eyes surveyed my face, and I saw a glimpse of indecision in his glance before he pulled me towards him and held me in his arms. "Don't cry," he whispered against my hair.

"I'm not crying," I whispered against his chest, tears welling up in my eyes. I didn't know why I was so emotional. He was right; I was living in some sort of fairytale in my mind. And now I didn't know how to feel, and I didn't know how to tell him that I'd had a crush on him for years. He wouldn't understand and would definitely think I was a psycho then. A real psycho. I felt his hands running up and down my back and I bit into his chest, wanting to taste him, wanting to eat him, wanting to consume and be consumed. I needed this man. It didn't matter how long it lasted.

"What are you doing to me, Maddie?" Logan swore and pulled away from me. "I better go."

"No." I shook my head and held on to him tighter. "I don't

want you to go."

"I need to go." He looked at me and I could see that he was wrestling between two emotions. I just couldn't tell what those emotions were. "I'm sorry I threw gravel at your door, I shouldn't have done that."

"What, is Logan Martelli apologizing to me for something?" I gave him a small smile, trying to break the tension between us.

"We shouldn't be here." His eyes were dark as he looked around the room.

"Don't you want me to pleasure you again, Logan?" I leaned over and bit his lower lip. I didn't want him to leave.

"Why did you come to find me tonight?"

I shook my head, not wanting to tell him about my secret crush. I knew he didn't do relationships and I didn't want him to know how serious I had been with my comments about us falling in love and getting married.

"How did you know I would be at the pier?"

I sighed and looked away from him for a second. "I guess I'll tell you. I don't want you to think I'm a stalker."

"Tell me." He stared at me, unblinking.

"Joey Kennedy told me." I said the words I had been told to say and ran my hands down his arms and he froze.

"You know Joey Kennedy?"

"Yeah, we were friends in elementary school." I shrugged. "I guess he knows one of your brothers and they…" Logan's lips stopped my words, and he nibbled on my lower lip as his fingers went down to my sweet spot and explored again.

"Shhhh." His eyes blazed into mine, as he sat up and pulled his boxer shorts all the way off and threw them on the ground. "I think I'll stay. We don't want to waste this king-sized bed, do we?"

"No," I mouthed up at him, and I gasped as he slid into me, hard and deep. His eyes never broke away from mine as he thrust into me, and I cried out as he then pulled out and rubbed the tip of himself against me. "Please," I moaned as I gazed up at him, panting.

"Please what?"

"Put it back in."

"What?" He smiled down at me, and his green irises looked black.

"Please put it back in me," I moaned and reached up to pull him down to me.

"What?"

"Fuck me, Logan," I whimpered.

"What? I can't hear you."

"Fuck me, Logan!" I screamed up at him.

He smiled and cocked his ear. "What?"

"Fuck me, Logan Martelli!" I screamed so loudly that I swore the neighbors could hear me.

"Okay." He lowered himself onto me. He lifted my legs and pulled them over his shoulder and then entered me again. Sliding into me slowly this time, I groaned as every fiber of my being clung to him.

"Keep your eyes open," he commanded, and I stared up at him as his hardness pleasured me to my very core. He increased his pace, and before I knew it, he was slamming into me with no control, I could feel his balls slapping onto me as he took me without abandon. He held onto my legs and I felt his body shuddering as he came close to climaxing. I could see the sweat rolling down his chest and I wanted to lick it off of him.

"Oh fuck, I'm going to come." His voice was hoarse as he pulled out. I felt the warmth of his climax on my lower belly.

"You didn't have to pull out, I told you already I'm the pill," I moaned as he collapsed next to me on the bed.

"Shhh." He looked at me unseeing and took a deep breath. I felt his fingers in my hair and he combed through it softly. "You've got beautiful hair."

"Thank you," I said softly and curled into him.

"You're a fool, Maddie Wright," he whispered, and I wondered how he had read my mind.

"You're a fool too, Logan Martelli," I whispered into his chest, but he was silent. We lay there for a few minutes, and I felt him shift beside me. He rolled me over onto my back again and lifted my arms above my head. His grip was tight on my arms as he straddled me. I tried to move, but I couldn't. I looked up at him in confusion. He was no longer smiling and I stared up at him, with my heart thudding in fear. What was going on?

"Tell me why Joey sent you to track me down." He looked down at me with hard eyes. "Tell me why he sent you to fuck me. What does he want from me? And what does he have on you, to turn you into some sort of slut?"

I stared up at him in wide eyes, unsure of what to say. I'd never seen anyone so calm and controlled with such murderous eyes before. I swallowed hard and as I gazed up at him. I had no idea what I was going to say. There was no way I could tell him the truth.

Chapter 5

Logan

I stared down at Maddie's face furiously. Just when I had been willing to give her the benefit of the doubt, she had mentioned Joey. I felt murderous inside when she mentioned his name. Joey Kennedy was a snake, and as far as I was concerned, so was anyone who had dealings with him. I laughed bitterly as I stared down into Maddie's wide eyes. To think, I had almost felt guilty that I was going to fuck her in her father's bedroom as some sort of perverse revenge. For all I knew, she wanted this to happen. For all I knew, she had cameras taping the whole thing.

"Tell me what Joey wanted you to do," I growled down at her, trying to ignore the feelings of lust that filled me as I stared down at her body. Her eyes looked up at me unsure, and their purple hues called out to me like the siren that she was. I should have known not to trust her. She was too confident and too vulnerable, all at the same time. She was evil, just like her father. She wanted something from me, and I needed to find out what. "What's the game plan, Maddie?" I felt her try to move her arms and I laughed down at her. "You can't move. Trust me on that."

"I don't understand what you want me to say, Logan." She bit her lower lip, and I saw the worry in her eyes. And there was something else there, apprehension, and fear. There was a real fear in her eyes, and as I realized that I was the one who had put it there, I let go of her and moved away, jumping off the bed. I didn't mess around with women, and I didn't harm them. I had never harmed a woman, and I wouldn't start now. I reached down and grabbed my boxer shorts and pulled them on quickly.

"What's going on?" She sat up, confused. "Where are you going?"

"I'm leaving. I never should have come here." I shook my head. "It was a mistake."

"You're really confusing me, Logan. Why did you come here?" She stood up and I stared at her breasts, forcing myself to keep my hands to myself.

"I don't know." I shook my head and looked away from her. If I couldn't stop staring at her, I was going to bend her over the bed and fuck her again. But only after she begged me. I grinned to myself, there was something about hearing a woman beg me to fuck her that turned me on.

"You mentioned my dad." She frowned. "Do you know my dad?" She looked at me carefully. "Are you mad at me because of my dad?" She licked her delicious, juicy lips, and I stood still. "You got mad after I mentioned my dad was the mayor. And you said you wanted to speak to him when you got here." She paused. "And you wanted to sleep with me in this room."

I stared at her, unspeaking. To be honest, I was surprised it had taken her this long to connect the dots.

"And you said, 'What would your dad say if he saw us fucking on his bed?'"

"I don't believe I ever used those exact words." I smiled at her and she glared at me.

"What sort of sick fuck are you, Logan Martelli?" She shuddered and grabbed her shorts and top and pulled them on.

"You didn't have any problems with me earlier."

"I didn't realize you were sick in the head." She shook her head. "I just thought you were misunderstood."

"Misunderstood?" I burst out laughing. "You thought I was *misunderstood?*"

"I thought that maybe you weren't as bad as everyone said." She frowned and shook her head violently. "I'm a fool."

"Did you think you were the good girl who was going to fix the misunderstood bad boy?" I took her in and realized I was right. "So what did Joey have to do with it?"

"What the fuck are you talking about?" she screamed at me, and I stepped back in surprise. "Do you think everyone is after you? You're the big, bad wolf and everyone is tracking you down, is that it? My dad, Joey, me, fuck, everyone in River Valley is obsessed with you?"

"I never said your dad was after me." I walked over to her, and she pulled away from me, her eyes shooting darts at me.

"Don't touch me."

"Really?" I cocked my head and moved closer to her but stopped before our bodies were touching.

"Really." Her body trembled as she stared at me defiantly. "You're a fucking psycho."

"I'm the psycho?" I laughed at her. "Is that a joke?"

"I thought you were leaving." She lifted her chin up at me.

"I changed my mind."

"Don't stay on my behalf."

"I feel like seconds." I dropped my eyes to her breasts and back up to her eyes slowly. "Only this time I want you on top."

"You wish." Her voice trembled as she spoke.

"I think *you* wish." I stepped closer and pulled her towards me hungrily as I lowered my lips to hers softly, kissing her tenderly. Her lips were unmoving at first, but then I felt her hands in my hair, and I groaned and ran my hands up and down her back. I was mesmerized by this girl, this girl I wanted to hate. But she had flipped the switch on me, and I had been so scared that she was going to tell me to leave and never come back. I made to push her back on the bed and she shook her head.

"Not in here." She stared into my eyes, and I nodded. She held

74

my hand and guided me back to her bedroom. I felt my pocket vibrating and I reached in and grabbed my phone. Vincent's name was flashing up at me and I felt a pang of guilt.

"I have to go." I stopped at her doorway. "I have to get my brother's car back."

"Your brother's car?" She raised an eyebrow and looked at me in disbelief. "The Toyota is your brother's car now?"

"No, smartass." I smiled at her, trying not to laugh while loving how she made me feel light. "My brother Vincent has a Mustang, that he bought." I added in and she grinned back at me. "And I think he's pissed that I have it."

"You're telling me that a Martelli brother is pissed that his car has been borrowed?"

"Sshhhh." I laughed. "Ironic, I know."

"Will I see you again?" Her voice was unsure. I sighed. She looked so lovely standing there in front of me. I took in her long, dark hair, slightly swollen lips, and the curve of her breasts, and I felt a stirring of something that wasn't lust fill me.

"I don't know if that's a good idea."

"Because you hate my father?" She looked up at me unhappily.

"Yeah." I stared at her. "I do hate your father. And let's be real, he's not going to be delighted to find out you're dating me."

"Why do you hate him?" Her voice was soft. "He's a good man."

"Let's just agree to disagree about that." I shook my head and looked around me. I looked up and saw that she was staring at the scar on my body, and I could see the question in her eyes. "You can thank your father for this scar."

"My father did this to you?" She gasped in shock and her hand flew to her mouth.

"You could say that." I stared past her into the room and remembered the night my father had stabbed me. I had been sixteen and I was still heartbroken from my mother's death. I was also annoyed at our monthly trips to Manor Road. I had questioned my father as we had sat outside, staring at the mayor's house and he had grabbed his knife and lunged at me. I might have died if Vincent and Jared hadn't pulled him off of me. I could still remember the fear and the darting pain as the knife slid down my abdomen, slicing my skin. The pain was excruciating, and as the blood gushed out and my dad realized what he had done, he started crying. And we all sat there in silence, watching the mayor's house for another hour before my dad took me to the hospital. He had sat in the car, while Vincent and Jared walked into the emergency room with me. We said I had tripped while holding a knife. The doctors knew it was a lie, but they didn't ask me what the real story was. I suppose they didn't care. We had never spoken about that night again, and I never told my father that I didn't want to go to the mayor's house again.

My father was consumed by his hatred of Mayor Wright, and it somehow made him feel better when he took us there and told us the stories about his past. Stories that I hadn't heard in a few years. My father didn't bother coming out to Manor Road anymore; the alcohol controlled every part of his body and he didn't care about anything else now. He was never really lucid enough to think about anything other than his next beer.

"Will you tell me why, Logan?" Maddie's voice interrupted my thoughts and I looked up at her, trying not to let her see the pain in my eyes.

"It's not your problem." I stepped back. "I really do have to go now."

"Do you like me, Logan?"

"I don't know you."

"From what you know about me, do you like me?"

I stood there for a moment, not sure why she was asking me if I liked her. Was this some sort of trap? "I honestly don't know." Which was a bit of a lie. I did know. I did like her. I was drawn to her, I felt alive around her. I felt like someone other than Logan Martelli: criminal, brother, son around her.

"Will you be friends with me?" she asked hopefully. I looked at her in confusion.

"Did you just ask me to be your friend?"

"Yeah," she nodded. "I know you don't know me and you don't trust me, but maybe we can change that."

"I don't need any more friends."

"You have more than one?"

"Funny." I stared at her with my heart beating rapidly. This was a bad idea to be entertaining, but I didn't want to just walk away. "Do you mean friends with benefits?"

"No." She shook her head.

"What if I want friends with benefits?"

"I don't sleep with someone who doesn't trust me."

"What?" I gaped at her. "You've already slept with me on two occasions."

"I didn't know you didn't trust me then." She shrugged. "Now I do."

"I thought we were fated for each other?" I murmured. "I thought you wanted to feel me inside of you."

"I did, and now I have. And maybe both feelings have changed."

"Both feelings have changed already?" My voice rose. "Fickle, aren't we?"

"You know us rich girls." She winked at me, and I attempted a smile at her joke. I ignored the surge of anger that welled in me at her words. How could she go from hot to cold so quickly?

"No, not really." I felt like punching the wall. "So you want to be friends?"

"That seems like it would be best, right?" She looked away quickly. "You don't do relationships, and I don't sleep with guys who can't stand me or my family and won't tell me why."

"So you'll just find another guy to fuck, huh?" I glared at her, jealousy seeping into my voice. "I thought you weren't easy?"

"Give it a rest, Logan." She sighed. "You can't have it both ways."

"Whatever." I didn't need this shit. "I'm going."

"See ya." She walked into her room. "Close the front door on your way out," she called out to me.

"Fine." I glared at no one and ran down the stairs, pissed. I slammed the door as I left the house. The sun was rising and I ran to the car as annoyed as I had been when I had arrived a few hours earlier. What the fuck was Maddie playing at? Was this some sort of sick joke? I didn't understand girls and had never cared before. They were good for a night or two, but I had bigger worries than their feelings. And a girl had never gotten under my skin like Maddie had. I turned the ignition and pulled out of Manor Road as quickly as possible.

"I'm coming!" I yelled into the phone as Vincent called me again.

"Dude, I gotta go to take my exam soon." Vincent sounded annoyed.

"I forgot. I'll be back in fifteen minutes." I threw my phone on the passenger seat, and raced down the streets, not caring if a cop was waiting to pull me over for speeding. I sped home as if I was at the Indy 500, and when I pulled into the driveway, I was more upset than when I had left.

I ran up the stairs and to Vincent's room and pushed his door open. "Here are your keys." I threw them at him as he lay there in bed. He just stared at me with a worried expression. "Good luck with the test."

"Thanks." He nodded, and I left his room wordlessly. I ran into the bathroom and locked the door before turning on the shower. "Fuck you, Maddie Wright," I cursed her under my breath. "Friends." I rubbed the shampoo into my hair and closed my eyes. I needed to feel like I was in control or I was going to lose it. I stood there for a few minutes, letting the hot water beat down on me, and then stepped out of the shower calmly. I had bigger problems than Maddie Wright. I needed to come up with rent money in a little over a week or I knew we were going to get evicted. I walked to my room and sat on my bed, waiting for an answer to come to me. Praying that somehow I could figure it out. I'd always been able to figure it out before.

"Hey, Logan." Jared knocked on the door and walked in. "Sorry about last night."

"Don't worry about it."

"I wanted to give you this." He dropped five hundred-dollar bills on the bed next to me. "I thought it could help."

"Where did you get this kind of money?" I looked up at him and frowned. "Please tell me you haven't been dealing with Joey?"

"Joey didn't make me do anything." Jared's eyes flared at me. "I don't know what you have against him, but he doesn't control me."

"Joey is bad news, Jared." I shook my head as I held the cash in my hands. "I don't want to get into it, but he's not to be trusted."

"You know the only people I trust are you and Vincent." Jared sighed. "Joey is my friend. He does my bidding, trust me, bro."

"What are you doing to get this kind of money?"

"We bet on the horses."

"The horses? How old are you? Sixty?"

"Joey's old man does it. He knows a few guys that are trainers. We get some tips, who's looking good, who's not. What jockeys are excited, that sort of thing."

"I don't know about this, Jared, gambling's not a good thing to get into."

"And stealing cars is?" Jared's eyes bore into mine. "I love you, bro, but you can't do this much longer. Things are getting worse."

"It'll be fine. Vincent will get his degree and you will get your degree and we'll be fine." My voice held conviction; it had to be fine.

"And what about Dad?" Jared's voice was hoarse. "I want to leave, Logan. I don't want to deal with this shit anymore. He's a fucking drunk. He's not going to change and I'm not going to put up with his bullshit anymore. I've had enough."

"I'll take care of it."

"Until he hits you again or, God forbid, gets a gun."

"He's our dad, Jared."

"He needs to go to a facility or something. He needs to get help."

"I know." I sighed and stood up. "Don't you think I know that?"

"Where did you go this morning?" His eyes held a question, and as I stared at him, I knew I couldn't hold it in anymore.

"I went on a drive."

"To?"

"Manor Road." The words slipped out of my mouth bitterly.

"Why?"

80

"I wanted to see the house."

"It's been a while, eh?" Jared sat down on the bed and I sat on the chair in the corner. "Do you think Dad even thinks about it anymore?"

"I'm sure." We stared at each other for a while and we both thought back to our childhoods and our weekly drives out to Manor Road.

"Why did you go?"

"I met a girl." I sighed. "And I mean just met, so don't go getting any ideas. We kinda hit it off, I thought she was cool. Hot, but a bit kooky, you know how some girls can be."

"Trust me, I know." Jared laughed and I joined him. Jared was a player, but a charismatic one. Girls loved him on sight, and they never seemed to stop calling him, or wanting to be with him. I stared at my brother and his too-long wavy black hair and I shook my head.

"You need to get a haircut."

"Don't change the subject, tell me about the girl."

"I took her for a ride, we had some fun, but turns out she's a rich kid."

"Oh." Jared made a face.

"Yeah, exactly. And to make matters worse. It turns out she's Maddison Wright."

"The mayor's daughter?" Jared gave me a shocked look. I sighed inside. He was going to play the game with me.

"Yeah, she goes by Maddie, though."

"Maddie, as in mad in the head?"

"Yeah." I laughed and thought about Maddie and her forward nature. "I wouldn't be surprised if her name has rubbed off on her."

"So, you like her?" Jared cocked his head at me and leaned forward.

"Did you not hear me? Her name is Maddison Wright."

"Yeah? So?"

"Do you think I would date the mayor's daughter?" I rolled my eyes. "Granted, she's pretty and dynamite in bed." I laughed. "Do not repeat that."

"Maybe you should date her." Jared sat back. "Maybe this is the way."

"The way for what?" I squinted at him.

"Maybe this is how we can get vengeance for Dad."

"What do you mean?"

"So-o-o," Jared took a deep breath, "I met Maddie." He paused and looked at me.

"Continue." I held my breath. I had known as soon as she told me she had met one of my brothers with Joey, that it had to have been Jared.

"She knows Joey. I guess they went to school together at some point, and she is good friends with his sister. And every summer they hang out, and they go to college together somewhere in Boston." He looked at me anxiously, and I gave him a look to hurry it up.

"So anyways, we were hanging out at Joey's place one day, and Maddie was there. And Joey's sister was like, 'This is Logan's brother,' and she went all googly-eyed and asked me a bunch of questions about you."

"She did?" I frowned. "But why? She doesn't know me."

"I guess you were the pin-up boy of all the girls in River Valley. She had some crush on you. And so, I kinda told her where you'd be yesterday."

"Dude, why would you do that? What if she had called the police on me or told her dad?"

"She's way too into you to do anything like that. She has a serious crush on you, bro. Like, she could be a stalker. She was going on and on and on."

"That's weird." I made a face, but inside I felt a fire light up inside of me. So maybe she didn't just hook up with every guy she met.

"So anyways, I was going to tell her to fuck off, but then I thought, this was the perfect opportunity. She's the mayor's only child, and supposedly, he is really, really overprotective, and she's the apple of his eye. And I thought, what perfect retribution for Dad, if the mayor's daughter is caught up with a Martelli. You could date her for a little bit, and then just ditch her. It would devastate this girl. She thinks she is in love with you or something."

"She doesn't even know me to love me." My head was spinning with all the information he was giving me.

"I know, bro, she's psycho. Though, I mean, she is super hot." Jared grinned at me, and I resisted the urge to smack the smile off of his face.

"Why didn't you tell me about this before?"

"I wanted the two of you to meet naturally. You're a shitty ass actor bro, sorry to say, but you are. So I wanted your first meeting to be natural, and to see if you hit it off great." He laughed. "And it looks like you guys hit it off."

"Yeah." I looked at the wall, my heart racing. "We hit it off."

"So, what do you think? You willing to date her to pay her and her family back for what the mayor did to Dad?"

"I don't know." I was hesitant, even though that had already crossed my mind when I had been in her house. Hadn't I made love to her in her parents' bedroom as some sort of sick revenge? I felt my stomach knotting, and a dart of pain shot through me as I pictured the look of fear in her eyes as I'd held her down.

"We don't owe them anything, Logan." Jared stared into my eyes bleakly. "He ruined Dad's life, and ours. He cost us our childhood and our mother."

"I know." I nodded. "I just don't know that we can take that out on Maddie."

"We're paying for the sins of our father." Jared's voice was agitated. "She should pay for the sins of *her* father."

"I don't know." My voice trailed off. I no longer knew how I felt about Maddie, everything was so confused in my head, and the hatred that had existed for everyone in the Wright family was now hazy.

"He ruined our lives, Logan." Jared jumped up. "This is our chance to pay it back."

"Revenge isn't always the way." I sighed and stared at him. "Let me think about it."

"You want to think about it? Go downstairs and look at Dad; look at all the beer cans in the living room. Go try and have a conversation with him. He could have been something. You know that, I know that, Mom knew that. And it was all ruined."

"Yeah." I nodded and thought about my dad and his life. A life that had been diverted off-course because of Mayor Wright.

"Think about it, Logan." Jared walked out of the room. "And keep the money, use it to pay the rent."

"I, uh." I looked at him gratefully and sighed. "When did you grow up?"

"A long time ago, bro." He smiled at me. "A long time ago."

He walked out the door, and I sat back on the bed and lay back and closed my eyes. I could picture my mother's smile and the loving look in her eyes as she had played with me, Vincent, and Jared as kids. She had made sure to tell us she loved us every day. As we got older, we used to squirm and blush, embarrassed at her declarations of love, but what I wouldn't give for her to tell me she loved me one more time. She died within three weeks of getting diagnosed with cancer. There was nothing they could do. That's what the doctors had said. The cancer had spread, and even a mastectomy wouldn't have helped at that point. She should have been going for yearly checkups, they said. But we couldn't afford yearly checkups. My parents barely got by. The only income my dad could get was from the cars he stole, and that always depended on how much money Marty gave him and didn't win back in a poker game. My mom had died from cancer and nothing had ever been the same in our lives again. Not that everything had been great before then. It hadn't been, but there had been hope. Hope that my dad would get over his bitterness and try and make something out of his life. But his hatred of the mayor had consumed him. And he had every right to hate him. My eyes popped open and I stared at the ceiling as the bitter poison of hate ran through my veins.

Mayor James Wright, or just James, as he had been called back in the day, had gone to school with my dad. They were both in the same grade and they were best friends. James came from a rich, prominent family, and my dad's parents were hardworking Italian immigrants with little money but lots of ambition. Their greatest wish for my dad had been a top quality education and a job as a lawyer or a doctor. My dad had been really smart and had done well in school. He had been a handsome man as well, so he had done well with the ladies. He seemingly had the best life, aside from being poor, but that would have eventually changed, because he was smart and there was hope that he would get a scholarship to go to college. My dad signed up with James to take some college entrance exam and they both took it at the River Valley Library with about thirty other students. But the day after the test, it was discovered that some of the tests and answers had been stolen. Someone anonymously reported that my dad had stolen the exams. The school board and the colleges all believed the report because my dad had near perfect scores. So he was kicked out of school. But that hadn't stopped him: he had decided to get a GED so he could at least get into one college; even if he didn't get a scholarship, he could get financial aid. And he started tutoring students to make extra money, and that was when he met Mom. He had fallen in love with her right away, but so had James. James made a play for her, but my dad won her heart right away. Things were looking up for him; he got another opportunity to take a college entrance exam, but the night before he was to take the test, the police took him in for questioning. A car had been stolen, and he had been identified as the thief. My dad thought there had been a mistake. He didn't understand why or how two such huge and horrible incidents had been pinned on him. But then he found out it was James. It had been James all along. James wasn't as smart as dad, and he had stolen the tests. He had also been mad about being rejected, so he had stolen a car and left some of dad's belongings in it. He'd gotten his cousin to pretend to have seen dad stealing the car. Because James was from a prominent family, the police believed everything he had said easily.

So that had ruined dad's chances. He hadn't been able to go to college and get a loan or scholarship because he had a record, and no one in River Valley would hire him because of all the rumors saying he was a bad seed. Then one day Marty had showed up and presented him an offer: steal cars and sell them to him. And my dad took the offer. That was why he had never really spoken up to Marty. In some weird way, he thought Marty had given him an opportunity to make a living. I didn't see it that way; I felt that Marty had made Dad's life worse because after my dad turned to that life, nothing was ever the same again. He married my mom, and he had us kids, but he was never able to turn his life around. And he blamed it all on James Wright. And when James became mayor, my dad became obsessed. He took us to his house every week, and we would sit in the car and listen to the story of how the mayor had ruined his life, and our lives as well. And that it was us who should have been living on Manor Road. We just sat and listened and grew to hate the mayor, not only for what he had done to Dad in the past but what he had done to him now as well. We hated the mayor for making us grow up with a father who was a violent drunk, and for making us lose our mother, and for making our family the social outcasts of River Valley.

As I stared at the ceiling, I knew what Jared had said was correct: this was possibly the best way to get revenge on James Wright.

Everyone in town knew how much he doted on his daughter Maddison; there was nothing that was too much for her. I'd always wondered who Maddison was, and I'd always imagined she would be a big bitch. I hadn't ever pictured someone like Maddie. I'd never thought that someone like Maddie could come from someone like the mayor. She was too honest, too vivacious, and too sweet. I groaned as I thought about her. I couldn't allow myself to be swept away by her charm. She was no one to me. She was just some stupid girl, with a stupid crush and a James Dean, bad-boy fantasy. I was just someone for her to live out her schoolgirl fantasies with. I didn't owe her anything. Why shouldn't I get my revenge on her? I closed my eyes again and thought about her sparkling eyes. Did I really hate the mayor that much that I would want to hurt Maddie as well?

Chapter 6

Logan

It had been a week since I had stolen the Toyota, and I had finally gotten a call from someone in a town about an hour away. The offer had been low but they had been willing to take the car without the title, and so there wasn't much else I could say. The only problem was that he wasn't willing to come to River Valley to pick up the car; he wanted me to drive it to him. I was loath to drive a stolen car an hour away, but I needed the money from the sale. I had literally used all of my money up paying the rent and had about fifteen dollars to my name until I sold the car. I also knew that Vincent needed to get a textbook for a class, so I had to take the risk.

I ran down the stairs and grabbed a book to take with me for the bus ride back. My dad was in the living room watching Judge Judy, and I walked by the room quickly, hoping he didn't call out to me. I didn't have time to get into it with him.

"Hey." I nodded at Vincent and Jared as I walked into the kitchen. They were sitting together, whispering, and I frowned. "What's the big secret?"

"Nothing." Jared shrugged and looked away.

"Vincent?" I looked at my other brother and his face flushed.

"Nothing," he sighed. "We were just wondering if we needed to go get a car."

"What?"

"There's no food." He nodded towards the fridge.

"I'll get some today."

"With what?" Jared turned around and looked at me hard. "I know you can't have much money left, you haven't sold the Toyota yet."

"I'm taking it now."

"We can't continue like this." Jared looked at me and Vincent. "We need to make a change."

"It's not like we can get any other job." Vincent shrugged. "No one will hire us, the Martelli name is like death round here."

"We can all move."

"Where we going to move to?" Jared hissed. "We have no money."

"We'll get out of River Valley, and then we can have a fresh start."

"You've been saying that for years, Logan. And guess what? We'll still here." Jared slammed his fist on the table.

"We'll figure something out once you and Vince get through college."

"Stop calling it college." Jared's eyes narrowed. "He's a fucking freshman in a two-year school. He's not a senior at Harvard."

"It's better than nothing." I glared at Jared. "We got to break the cycle."

"It's not our fault that it's a cycle in the first place." Jared glared back at me. "The fucking mayor set Dad up, and he's had us stealing with him since we were old enough to walk."

"We don't want to steal forever, do we?"

"I don't know, do you?"

"Guys." Vincent stood up and put his hands on our shoulders. "Don't fight."

"Why don't you grow a backbone, Vinny?" Jared pushed him. "I'm fed up with this shit. Logan, you're not doing anything. Have you even thought about what we talked about?"

"I'm not going down that road." I shook my head. "Our issue is with the mayor, not his daughter."

"What?" Vincent looked at us, confused. "What are you guys talking about?"

"I'm talking about the fact that the mayor's daughter is in love with Logan, and he's not taking advantage of that fact, so we can get some motherfucking revenge on her dad."

"Huh?" Vincent looked at me, confused. "You met the Mayor's daughter? How? When?"

"Why don't you ask your smartass brother? The one who set it up?" My voice rose. "Don't try and play a punk with me, Jared."

"You wanna do something about it?" Jared stepped towards me, his nostrils flaring.

"You don't want me to do anything about it." I stepped towards him and stared into his eyes.

"Oh, yeah?" He pushed me, and I made to push him back when the doorbell rang. We all froze and stared at each other.

"Who the fuck is that?" Jared's eyes looked worried. "You paid the rent, right?"

"Yeah." I walked to the door slowly, fear in my heart. What if it was the police? What if they came to arrest me for the Toyota? What if this was the time they finally decided to arrest me? Maybe it was because I hadn't contacted Marty. Marty had some sort of deal with the police station and they never came to our house to look for stolen cars. It was like a safe zone for us. We had to worry whenever we were in the street with the car, but we never had to worry when we had it parked at home.

"Don't open it." Jared's eyes were full of fear, but I gave him a confident smile.

90

"It'll be okay." I nodded, took a deep breath and opened the door. "Hello?" I poked my head out, and my heart skipped a beat as I saw Maddie standing there with a huge smiled on her face.

"Hi," she beamed and pushed her hands forward. "I brought cookies."

"What?" I frowned and stepped outside the door quickly. "What the fuck are you doing here?"

"It's nice to see you again, too." She smiled again, though less confidently this time."

"What are you doing here, Maddie?"

"I brought you a peace offering." She pushed the plate towards me again. "Chocolate chip, I hope you like them." I stared at the plate in her hands and blinked. I then looked back into her face and she gave me an awkward smile. I noticed that her eyes looked bluer than usual today. Her hair was pulled up into a ponytail, and she looked like a younger and more innocent version of herself.

"I'm on my way out." I shook my head. "Sorry."

"Okay." She bit her lower lip. "I guess I'll be going then." She turned around and I watched her walk away from me quickly.

"Wait," I called after her. "Why did you come over?"

"Does it matter?" She turned to look at me.

"I guess not," I walked up. "But seeing as you're here, you may as well tell me."

"I wanted to see if you changed your mind."

"Changed my mind?"

"About being friends."

"Ha, friends." I laughed at her words but felt the disappointment in the pit of my stomach.

"I guess that's a no then." She turned away from me again.

"I guess it depends on the cookies." I reached out and grabbed her arm. "If the cookies are good, then we can be friends."

"So the cookies will make the decision for you then?"

"Yeah, problem with that?"

"I put Betty Crocker to shame, so no." She smirked at me as she handed me a big, gooey cookie and I took it from her slowly, allowing my fingers to graze hers softly. She stared into my eyes as I ate the cookie, and she laughed when I finished it off quickly.

"You're a messy eater." She laughed.

"Oh?"

"You have crumbs everywhere."

"I do?"

"Yes." She leaned towards me and her tongue darted out and licked the corners of my mouth. "There we go, all clean."

"Thank you." My breath caught as I felt her breath on my mouth, the corners of my mouth still tingling from her touch.

"No problem."

"It's nice to have friends who look out for you."

"I agree."

"I guess you just had a cookie as well, huh?" I smiled at her and raised my eyebrows.

She shook her head. "No, why?"

""Cause you have crumbs all over your mouth as well."

"I do?" She ran her fingers across her lips and then looked at them. "I don't see any crumbs."

"I think you're lying."

"Oh?"

"I think you just had a cookie."

"I'm sorry to tell you, but I didn't."

"I need proof." I said.

"I'm not sure how to prove that."

"There's only one way." I stepped towards her and grabbed ahold of her waist and pulled her towards me before leaning down to kiss her. My tongue pried her lips open and I explored her mouth, allowing my tongue to taste every inch of her. She kissed me back passionately, running her hands up and down my back. I ran my hands down the back of her hair and back and to her butt, pulling her even closer to me.

"Hey, what's going on?" Jared called out to me from the front door and I jumped away from Maddie quickly.

"Nothing." I shook my head.

"Hi, Jared." Maddie waved to him. "I brought some cookies over."

"Hi, Maddie." Jared grinned and walked towards us. He stared into my eyes as if asking a question, and I looked away from him.

"Maddie was just leaving," I said pointedly.

"Aww, I don't want to leave." She grinned up at me.

"Why does she have to leave, Logan? I'd love for her to stay."

"I'm afraid I have to go out of town today."

"Oh." Maddie gave me a disappointed look. "For a long amount of time?"

"Not really."

"Why are you going?"

"None of your business." I frowned at her and turned. "You should go home." My voice was unnecessarily harsh, but I didn't want Jared to get any ideas into his head that I had changed my mind.

"But I don't want to go home."

"No one invited you over. Didn't you know it was rude to just show up at someone's home?"

"I came with a peace offering." She glared at me.

"Why don't you take her with you, Logan?" Jared interrupted us. "I'm sure Maddie would love to join you, for a *ride*."

"Where are you going?"

"He's going to sell the car."

"Oh, you got another car?" Maddie looked at me in surprise. "What did you get this time?"

"I didn't get another car." I shook my head. "I'm selling the Toyota."

"Oh? I thought you would have sold it already."

"Well, obviously not."

"We had to switch guys." Jared smiled widely at Maddie. He was a good actor. Anyone would think he really liked her, to see the way he was treating her, but I knew differently. I know he was trying to ensure that I continued to see her, so that I could break her heart and exact some revenge.

"Guys?" She looked confused.

"Marty, the guy we used to sell to, well, let's just say we don't sell to him anymore."

"Marty?" Maddie looked at us considering. "My dad knows a

Marty, I wonder if it's the same guy."

"Doubtful." Jared smiled at her again. "A stand-up guy like your dad wouldn't know the Marty we deal with."

"Yeah, true." She nodded.

"It must be nice being the mayor's daughter," he continued. "Living the life of luxury."

"If you're asking if I'm daddy's little girl, then I guess I have to say yes." She laughed and groaned. "Though he can be a little out of control sometimes. It's like he thinks everyone is out to get me. He doesn't like to let me out of his sight." She shook her head. "He's terribly overprotective."

"Well, that must suck for you." Jared looked sympathetic. "I guess he knows that he's a target, being a successful businessman and all."

"Yeah, poor Daddy." Maddie sighed. "Oh well, he seems to finally be loosening the strings."

"That's good. Though, I'm sure it would break his heart if anything happened to you."

"Yeah." She grinned. "That's dads for you, you have to love them."

"Yeah, we love our dad too." Jared slapped me on the back. "Well, I better get back in and finish eating breakfast. It was nice seeing you again, Maddie. I sure hope you can convince Logan to take you with him. I think you'd both have fun." And with that he sauntered back up to the house with me glaring at his back.

"Your brother is so nice." Maddie laughed up at me. "And he is super cute."

"You have a crush on him as well?" I said harsher than I intended.

"What? No." She blushed, and looked away from me. "And what do you mean on him as well?"

"Well, don't you have a crush on me?" I looked at her arrogantly. "Haven't you had a crush on me for a while?"

"I— what? Who told you that?" Her face grew red, and a part of me was happy to have the answer confirmed.

"Joey and his sister aren't exactly the best people to keep secrets."

"Argh, I'll kill Lucy." She shook her head. "And it was a teenage crush, I don't have it anymore."

"Oh, no?" I smirked. "Really?"

"Really," she flung her hair over her shoulder. "I'm wiser now."

"Yeah, you're wiser." I laughed out loud and shook my head. "Well, are you coming or not?" I turned around and walked to the Toyota.

"Where are we going?" She hurried after me.

"To sell this car."

"You just sell it?" She looked shocked. "Don't they ask to see your papers?"

"They know there are no papers." I grinned at her, all of a sudden feeling lightheaded.

"Oh." She licked her lips and I could tell she was nervous. "Do you mind if I come?"

"Not if you don't mind taking the bus back."

"I don't mind."

"Then hop in." I jumped into the car and started the engine as she slid into the passenger seat. I looked over at her, and she smiled at me with her plate of cookies sitting in her lap. She looked beautiful and innocent, so unlike she had the first night she had gotten into the car. I stared at her, my eyes taking in the dimple in her left cheek and the way her lips had a natural curve when she wasn't even speaking. I looked further down her and tried not to stare at the swell of her breasts and the small rising of her chest.

"What are you waiting for? Aren't we going?" She grinned at me excitedly.

"One would think you'd never been in a stolen car before."

"One would think you'd never had a girl in a stolen car with you before."

"Then one would be thinking incorrectly."

"I see." She turned away from me quickly, and her tone sounded hurt. Good, I didn't want her to know that she was the first girl I'd had in a stolen car with me, and the first girl I had been on a drop with. It was crazy, and she was the last person I should be taking with me, but I couldn't help myself. *Bad move, Logan,* a voice in my head whispered. *Bad move.* But it wasn't a bad move if I listened to Jared and his suggestions. Maybe I was doing this because subconsciously I wanted to hurt her. I'd teach her a lesson, and she would be crushed. And then she'd be home and crying and the mayor would be beside himself. *But what would that do?* The voice whispered again, a little heartbreak wasn't going to do anything to the mayor. How many times had she cried over a guy before? I'm sure she'd had her share of dalliances and heartbreaks. She certainly wasn't some innocent little virgin, that was for sure.

"What are you thinking about?" She leaned towards the radio. "Can I put on some tunes?"

"Go ahead." I nodded without looking at her. I could feel my heartbeat racing, and I felt uncomfortable with her in the seat next to me. I didn't want her to be here with me, yet I felt so alive, so excited, so happy to have her here with me. And it had nothing to do with the fact that I could get revenge on her and avenge my family. The fact was, I didn't want to hurt her. I took a quick glance at Maddie and watched as her hair blew in the wind coming through her window. Her eyes were alert and happy, and she gave me a quick smile as she noticed my stare. I turned away quickly, as my stomach jumped. I wasn't sure I would be able to forgive myself if I hurt Maddie on purpose. And what was worse is that I didn't know if she would ever forgive me either.

"Do you like Maroon 5?" She bobbed her head to an unfamiliar song.

"I don't know them." I shook my head.

"You don't know Maroon 5? What?" Her eyes darted to me. "What about Adam Levine?"

"Who?" I laughed.

"From *The Voice*!"

"What voice?"

"The TV show."

"I'm sorry, Maddie, but I have no idea what you're talking about."

"Wow," she laughed. "Don't you watch TV?"

"Not really." I shook my head. We only had one TV in the house and my father was parked in front of it twenty-four-seven.

"That's crazy."

"Really?" I raised an eyebrow at her. "Out of everything you know about me, that's the craziest?"

"I mean, it's a surprise. I thought everyone watched TV."

"Even those who can't afford a TV or cable?"

"Oh, I didn't think …" Her voice trailed off and she blushed. "I suppose you think I'm just this privileged girl, huh? I guess I'm not helping my cause."

"I don't think you're a snob." I smiled at her gently. "But do you act like someone who comes from money? Yeah. But that's not unreasonable, because that was your upbringing, I'm sure."

"You're sweet to say that," she sighed, and I could see her twisting her hands. "I suppose I'm an utter bore to someone like you."

"You mean the big, bad wolf of River Valley?"

"No, I mean to someone who has so much excitement in their life."

"Excitement?" I laughed. "I think I have the least amount of excitement of anyone I know." *Aside from the night I met you,* I thought to myself with a grin.

"Really? I figured stealing cars would be like a drug."

"Not really." I turned onto the highway and checked the rearview mirror to make sure no cops were following me. "Maybe when I first started, yeah, there was a thrill of excitement, a hint of danger and exhilaration. Now it's mundane."

"Mundane, now there's a word." She looked over at me.

"I learned it when I was studying for the SAT." I laughed.

"You took the SAT?" She looked surprised.

"No." I shook my head, mad at myself for letting that slip. "I never took it. They made us study for it in school. I may have glanced at the words once or twice out of boredom."

"I see."

"So you're studying history?"

"Yeah." She rolled her eyes. "I don't want to bore you though."

"You won't bore me, I like history."

"You do?" I could hear the shock in her voice and I laughed.

"No, not really." I accelerated and switched to the left-lane of the highway. "I was more of a science guy myself."

"Oh, I sucked at all the science subjects."

"I doubt you sucked at anything."

"You would be surprised. My dad had to get me private tutors. It was awful. I was the only person in my dorm who had two tutors."

"Dorm?" I looked at her, puzzled.

"When I was in boarding school."

"Oh, yeah. What was that like?"

"Fun," she giggled. "At first it was weird, and I didn't understand why my parents wanted to send me away to school. But it was a small school, and there were only like fifteen of us who were boarders. We went from form to form together and became really close."

"I see. That must have been cool."

"It was okay, it was all-girls, so we didn't really have a chance to get up to anything too bad."

"No late night make-out sessions in the dorms?"

"Well, not really." Her voice was squeaky and I saw her turn her face to look out the window. Something about her tone piqued my interest, and I decided to press the subject.

"What do you mean, not really?"

"Well, we didn't have real live boys to kiss, but we had posters to practice on."

"Oh." I laughed. "Like Brad Pitt and Tom Cruise and stuff?"

"You could say that."

"Who were the actors you guys practiced on?" I asked curiously.

"I never said we practiced on actors."

"Oh, I just assumed. Who then?"

"You're going to think I'm a psycho." She shook her head. "I don't want to tell you."

"Now you have to tell me," I laughed. "And I already think you're crazy, so no need to worry about that."

"You're mean."

"Ha, ha, tell me, Maddie."

"Well, I really don't want to tell you this, but we used to kiss posters of you. Well, not all of us, but a few of us did."

"Posters of me?" I turned towards her. "What posters?"

"Okay, now I have to go into *Fatal Attraction* territory, but one summer I was over at Lucy's place and we were going through Joey's yearbook, and well, there was a photo of you in there."

"My high school pic?" I raised an eyebrow.

"No, there was a photo of you posing on a motorcycle, I guess it was a candid shot, and you had your shirt off ..." Her voice trailed off.

"Oh, when I was in eleventh grade?" I thought back. "I think I was deciding if I wanted to steal it." I laughed. "But then someone took a photo and I knew I couldn't, as that photo would definitely serve as incriminating evidence."

"Well, you looked super hot," she continued. "So I borrowed the yearbook and I took it to Walgreens and got it blown up, and then the girls and I ordered posters."

"The girls?"

"In my dorm, when I got back to school."

"Ah, ok. So I was your first kiss?" I grinned at her and winked.

"I guess," she laughed. "Though the physical honor goes to Matt Devoir."

"I see." Jealousy churned through me at the thought of Maddie kissing another guy.

"He wasn't as good a kisser as you, though." She reached over and touched my arm. "Who was your first kiss with?"

"Judy Hamilton," I answered quickly.

"Judy Hamilton? No way." Maddie laughed.

"Yup." I grinned over at her. "She was experienced and I was eager."

"Isn't she like five years older than you?"

"Something like that." I laughed. "What can I say, I like older women."

"I guess that's why you don't like me, then." She sat back in her seat with a wistful tone, and I was jerked back to reality. Maddie wasn't just some regular girl, and we weren't on some regular ride. If I took one wrong turn, this whole thing could explode on me.

"Hey, this is our exit." I quickly pulled back over to the exit lane and we sat in silence, as I navigated the unfamiliar streets. "So how was your first kiss?"

"Which one?"

"With Matt?"

"Oh, it was okay. Nothing earthshattering. I didn't tremble with passion or anything."

"Because you normally tremble with passion when you kiss?"

"When you kiss me." Her voice was sweet and confident and I wanted to shake her for being so forward. Didn't she know that girls were meant to play coy? Especially with guys they didn't really know.

"I suppose the poster knew a couple of tricks, huh?"

"No, but you do." Her voice was lower this time, and I glanced at her quickly, wondering if she was trying to seduce me.

"You're trouble, Maddie Wright." I shook my head. "You make me look like a good boy."

"What fun would a good Logan Martelli be?"

"Behave." I laughed and pulled into the Walmart parking lot where the exchange was meant to take place. I parked and turned to her with a serious expression. "Stay in the car when the guy comes. I don't want you getting involved with this."

"Do you have a gun?" She looked at me, slightly worried, but there was a glint in her eyes.

"This is not the movies, Maddie. I have no gun, and I don't want one either."

"What happens if the deal goes wrong?"

"I've never had a deal go that wrong. I'm dealing in Japanese imports, not diamonds from South Africa." Though maybe if I was part of something a bit bigger, my family wouldn't be so broke.

"Have you ever thought about getting a real job?"

"No." I lied to her, not wanting to get into it with her.

"I could ask my father if there was anything he could to do help." She looked at me eagerly. "Maybe he could get you a job at city hall and …."

"Enough." I held my hand up at her abruptly. "I don't need your dad's help."

"He won't judge you." She looked at me anxiously. "Not if I vouch for you."

"Would you vouch for me as the guy who fucked you in his bed a week ago?"

"Of course not." She made a face at me. "I would just say you were my friend."

"Of course, your *friend*. Don't you think he would want to know how we met? And would he be cool with us being *friends*?"

"My dad doesn't judge people, Logan. I don't know why you have something against him, but he's a good man."

"Yeah, he's a good man." My voice was harsh.

"I wish you would talk to me," she pleaded.

"What do you want to know, Maddie?" I shouted, frustrated. "Do you really want to know what I think of your dad? Your *perfect* dad? Do you want to know why I wish I could watch him getting run over by a semi truck?" I watched as her face contorted with pain and she shrunk away from me, but I was too annoyed to stop.

"I fucking hate his guts." I hit my fist against the steering wheel. "I am never going like him. I don't know why you just can't leave me alone. What don't you get?"

"Sorry." Her eyes flashed. "I thought you'd want to be friends."

"Why would I want to be friends?" I looked at her, agitated. I was starting to feel bad for shouting at her, and that was making me even more upset. I didn't want to care how she felt.

"I thought that we—"

"No, no, you haven't been thinking," I interrupted her. "I get it, you had a schoolgirl crush on me, but you move on, Maddie. You don't track me down to seduce me, and then tell me you want to be friends. I'm not going to change. You're not going to discover the other secret part of me. What you see is what you get. Do you understand that? I'm a car thief. I steal cars for money. I steal cars from people with kids." I nodded to the baby seat in the back and ignored the twinge of guilt in me. I couldn't afford to feel guilty in this business. "I'm not misunderstood, I'm not going to get a job in a fucking office, I'm not going to turn into some man who is going to

104

give you the safe life you've grown up in. Just because I fucked you, it doesn't mean I want anything with you. Yeah, you're hot. And yeah, I had a good time. But that was it. Stop trying to make this into more than it is. And don't ask me why I'm mean to you or hate you. I don't hate you. I just don't fucking care."

I took a deep breath and turned away from her. This time she didn't try to shield me from the tears streaming down her face. She stared at me with wide, hurt eyes, and I was taken back to my childhood when I had told my mother I hated her. The pain that coursed through me right now was the same pain that had coursed through me then. I had been about twelve years old, and my dad had been on his way to steal a car and I was going to accompany him. My mother had been upset that he was using me as his lookout, and she had pulled me aside and told me that I couldn't go. My father had been slightly drunk and had shouted at her. She stood her ground against him and had whispered that she couldn't put up with it anymore. She told him that she wasn't going to let him do this to the kids and that she was going to leave him. I had been incensed at her words and turned on her and shouted that I hated her and that she didn't understand. The look she had given me at that moment had broken my heart in two. The pain mingled with shock, hurt and disbelief as she stared at me. I could feel how my words had hurt her. The hurt that coursed through her had flushed through me and I hadn't known what to say. The anger and confusion in my own body had stopped me from apologizing in that moment. I knew that in that moment that my mother realized that the innocent and loving boy she had raised was gone. And as I stared at Maddie, in this instant, I knew I had also shattered her image of me. No matter what she had thought of me before, or what she were to think of me in the future, she would always be reminded of this conversation in this car.

"He's here." She bit her lip and turned away from me.

"What?" My voice was softer, and I didn't understand what she was talking about. I wanted her to shout back at me, to scream and call me an asshole.

"The guy you're selling this car to? I think he's here." She squinted and then doubled down in her seat.

"What are you doing?"

"I think I know that guy," she whispered up at me.

"Really?" I looked at her in surprise and then at the guy standing in front of the car. He looked somewhat familiar, but I couldn't place him. "Stay here," I hissed at Maddie again before I stepped out of the car.

"Hey." The guy nodded at me.

"Hey." I took in his dirty appearance and nodded. "You called me about the car?"

"Yeah." He looked it over. "It runs well?"

"Yeah, smooth as a Ferrari, only twenty thousand miles as well."

"You want five grand?"

"I want ten grand, but I'll accept five." I stared at him, and he stared back at me with a glint of something in his eyes.

"What about three grand?"

"No deal."

"You got no papers."

"So?"

"Two grand."

"I don't have time for games, five grand or nothing." My voice rose, and then I noticed his hands were full of grease. "I'm going to go."

"I wouldn't be so quick to leave, Logan." He stepped towards me with a menacing stare. "Marty's not happy that you didn't give him a call."

"Marty?" I held my ground as I stared at the man, as I realized where I knew him from. He was one of Marty's mechanics/henchmen.

"Yeah." His voice was menacing. "You get a lot of protection in River Valley because of Marty. I wouldn't like to think you were disrespecting him."

"I don't need Marty's help."

"Marty wants this car, and he's willing to give you a grand."

"You've got to be joking."

"You'll take the grand, and be grateful you're getting that. Next time, Marty won't be so nice."

"Forget about it." I turned away from him, angry.

"We don't want Vincent to get into any trouble now, do we? I'd hate to see his college dreams come crashing down as he sits in a jail cell."

"Leave my brother out of this." I turned around, heart racing. "What do you want?"

"I want you to give me this car, and Marty wants you to consider this a warning."

"Piss off."

"You think we're playing with you?" His voice was full of venom. "We know Jared's been messing around with Joey Kennedy. I'd hate for him to go down as well. Two brothers in jail? Well, how would that feel, Logan? No one would be surprised. In fact, everyone would just be waiting to see when the third and final Martelli brother made it to jail."

I stared at him with my blood boiling. If Maddie hadn't been in the car, I would have decked him, not caring what would have happened next. But I didn't want her to see the blood.

"You want the car, you can have it." I took a deep breath. I was pissed at myself for caving, but I needed the money.

"Here." He pulled out a stack of twenties and handed them to me. "Leave the car in the parking lot, we'll have it picked up and towed tonight."

"This is only five hundred." I glared at him.

"Be thankful you got anything." He came towards me and bent down and whispered in my ear. "I'd get out of the car business if I was you. Next time, Marty won't be so nice." He turned around and walked to his car. It took everything in me to not chase him down. I took another deep breath as I watched him drive away. I walked back to the car, opened the car door, and saw Maddie crouched over still.

"You can sit up, he's gone."

"Okay." Her voice was cold and she jumped out of the car. "Did he decide not to buy it?"

"He bought it, he'll pick it up later."

"Oh." She looked at me and then away again. "That's good, then."

"Yeah." I stared at her standing in front of me, clutching her plate of cookies. "Look, I want to apologize."

"Don't bother." Her eyes flashed in anger. "I'm glad you were honest with me."

"You're mad."

"Does it matter?"

I bit my lip as I stared at her. Damn, Maddie was making things hard for me. "We can be friends." I sighed.

She looked up at me in surprise. "You want to be friends?"

"I didn't say all that. I said we can be friends."

"I guess that's a start." She grinned and linked her arm through mine. "I knew you couldn't resist me."

"Well, you knew wrong." I shook my head at her. "Don't go getting any ideas."

"Did you get a lot of money for the car?"

"No." I turned away from her, frustrated. I needed to be alone. I needed to think about everything that had just happened and where I went from here. I knew that I was a threat to Marty now, and my brothers and I were his targets. Frustration ran through me, along with another emotion—I was scared. I had no idea where to go from here. And I had no one to turn to for help. There wasn't time for Vincent to get through college and law school anymore. Our lives were in the balance, and it was all the mayor's fault. I stared at Maddie, and Jared's words came crashing down on me. It was true; Maddie was the apple of the mayor's eye. If anything happened to her, he would be crushed. I knew that a simple heartache wouldn't do the trick, though. He had screwed my father over and ruined his life. If I wanted to get revenge for my father, mother, and my brothers, I had to make sure it would be something that affected the rest of his life, just like he had affected mine. Ideas crashed through my mind, and suddenly it struck me. What would make the mayor's blood boil more than anything? A baby. A Martelli baby in his family. And as I watched Maddie, smiling down at me, with her seductive purple-blue eyes, I knew exactly what I had to do.

Chapter 7

Maddie

I was so angry that I had a hard time looking at Logan. He was insufferable and I was fast losing my patience and the ability to just get over it. I hadn't expected my feelings to be so hurt at his words; I mean, I knew he had issues, and I had told myself that I could wait it out. I could make him fall in love with me if I had enough time. At least that is what I had told myself. I heard the sounds of a family walking towards us, and I turned to smile at them, needing to focus on someone else, if just for a few moments. I stepped away from Logan, glad I didn't have to pretend I was okay for a second. I smiled at the little girl skipping along and blowing bubbles, and I was reminded that I used to be that girl: innocent, carefree and happy. I could still be that girl if I wanted to, but I knew that too much had happened and I wouldn't change any of it.

"Let's go find a car." Logan grabbed my arm and I looked at his face. I couldn't read his eyes or the expression on his face, and I wondered if he was okay. There was so much going on with him, and I wished he would trust me enough to let me in. But I suppose that would all happen in good time.

"A car?"

"That's what I said."

"I thought we were taking the bus back." I paused. "Are we going to steal another one then?" I whispered and looked around to make sure no one was around to hear me.

"No." He grinned at me, and this time his eyes were sparkling with mirth. "We won't be stealing it."

"So then why are we looking for a car?"

"So we can window shop." Logan shook his head. "What's up

with all the questions?"

"Do you think you can just talk to me however you like and I'm just going to take it?" The words spurted out of my mouth angrily and I let out a deep breath. I guess it was harder for me to keep it in than I thought it would be.

"Huh?" He frowned at me, and I could see a brief flash of anger and respect in his eyes.

"You practically went off on me in the car earlier. Do you really think I'm going to just be *friends* with you and we could go look at potential cars for you to steal? I know you think I'm some silly girl who is kinda crazy and infatuated with you. But lookey here, mister, I'm not a doormat, and I'm not going to allow you to talk to me however you want. You want to go off on me because of something I've done to you, then fine. But to take out the issues that you have with my dad on me, which I don't even know about, well that's fucked up." I took a breath and looked at the shock in Logan's eyes and I grew even more incensed. "I don't know why you're so shocked. Did you think you were the only one who could get angry and spout off?"

"Are you done?"

"Look, if you just wanted to have some fun with me, then fine. We had fun. I'm not pushing you for anything else. I don't need you to be my *friend*."

"It was your idea to be friends." He looked at me in confusion, and I stared at his handsome face. How I loved his face, it was so expressive, so gorgeous. Even when I was angry at mad at him, all I wanted to do was kiss him and feel his lips against mine. Logan Martelli drove me crazy.

"I wanted to be friends because I thought that would be a good way to show you that you could trust me." I shook my head. "I don't need your pity friendship."

"My pity friendship?" He laughed gruffly. "You're the one that's—"

"Oh, shut up." I grabbed ahold of his shirt and pulled him towards me. I looked up at his handsome face and pressed my lips against him, relishing the feel of him as I kissed him lightly. He reached his hands around my waist and pulled me towards him, and his tongue darted into my mouth as his hands ran up and down my back. I reached my hands up to his hair and I kissed him back feverishly, wanting him to know exactly how he made me feel. I pulled back reluctantly after a few minutes, and he looked down at me with a dazed and dark expression.

"I have to have you now." He pulled me towards him and his hands ran up and down my back and shoulders as he kissed my neck. "What are you doing to me, Maddie?" He groaned and ran his hands through his hair.

"Driving you crazy." I smiled at him impishly, trying to suppress the sudden joy in my heart. There was a part of me that felt that maybe I was getting to him as much as he had gotten to me.

"That you are." He grabbed my hand again. "Come."

"Are we going to look for another car?"

"No." He shook his head. "I need to get you home."

"Why?"

"The car idea, it was a bad idea, sometimes I don't think I'm in my right mind." He grimaced and I wanted to ask him what was wrong, but I was scared he wouldn't tell me.

"You've got a lot going on." I squeezed his hand, and he looked down at me gratefully. His hands felt warm and strong, and I was delighted that he hadn't snatched it away from me.

"Why did you have to be a Wright?" he sighed as he looked at me regretfully.

"Does it really make that much of a difference?" I stared up into his eyes. I just didn't understand why he hated my father so much, and I didn't understand what he had said about my father being the reason why he had his scar. I was so confused, and all I wanted was for him to share everything with me.

"I can't think about it right now." His eyes were far away. "I have more pressing issues."

"Oh?"

"Like how I'm going to make money." He laughed manically.

"The offer is still open for me to talk to my dad," I said softly.

"Maddie, I'm not going to tell you this again ..." Logan pulled away from me and his voice was harsh.

"You don't know my dad like I do, Logan. He's a good guy!" I cried out, annoyed at him.

"Many times, we don't know the people closest to us, Maddie. Many times we'd be surprised at how many skeletons those we love the most have in their closet."

"So tell me." I held my breath and my heart was racing. "Tell me."

"You wouldn't want to know." His voice crushed me with its hollowness.

"I think you're just making it up. I bet you're just mad because my family is rich and yours is poor. That's not my fault. I'm so fed up with your shit, Logan. Why won't you give me a fair chance? I don't care if you're poor; I don't think that makes you a bad guy. Let me in, goddammit."

"You know why I wanted to go find a car?" Logan leaned in towards me with narrowed eyes. I shook my head. "I wanted to find a backseat to fuck you in." I swallowed hard as he whispered into my ear. "I wanted to take you in the backseat of a luxury car and fuck you on the seats of some brand new leather." His eyes looked into mine, searching for my response. "I wanted to fuck you like some easy slut, in broad daylight. Do you still think I'm a good guy? Do you like it when I'm honest?"

I bit my lip as I stared up at him. I hated it when Logan became this guy, and I found it really hard to give him the benefit of the doubt. If it wasn't for the brief hesitation in his eyes and the nervous throb in his throat, I would have slapped him hard and told him where to get off. As it was, I knew this wasn't the real him. For some reason, he was trying to get me to hate him, and I didn't understand why he was fighting the mutual attraction we both felt. An attraction that was about more than sex.

"I, uh, I don't know what to say." My eyes widened at him as he pulled me towards him again.

"I told you before, Maddie, I'm not the typical guy you meet. I can do bad things to you, very bad things."

"Maybe I like it when you do bad things to me," I breathed into his ear and he stopped still. "Maybe I want you to take me to that backseat right now. Maybe I'd like to choose the car." I wanted him to know that I wasn't scared of him, and that I could take it. He wasn't going to scare me away, and if anything, I was slightly turned on. I didn't want to analyze what that said about me.

"Come away with me." He looked into my eyes.

"What do you mean?"

"Let's go away somewhere, just the two of us." His eyes issued me a challenge. "If you really want to be a bad girl, if you really want to get to know me."

"I can't just go away." I bit my lip, thinking about my parents. They were back in town and I knew my dad would flip a switch if I just left town. "But maybe if I go home and tell them I'm going to a friend's place for a week."

"No, you can't go home." He shook his head. "You can call them and let them know you're going out of town, but you can't go home."

"But I don't have anything on me." I stared at Logan with my heart pounding with excitement; did I dare go with him? I wanted to,

114

but I was scared about the reality of just leaving with him.

"Neither do I. If you like me like you said, then come away with me. Forget about everything and everyone else."

"But my dad will be so pissed," I mumbled, not sure what he expected from me. Did he think I could just up and leave? "And what about your brothers and your dad?"

"I'll call them." He stood there, tapping his feet. "We can just leave and really get to know each other, without thinking about anyone else."

"How long will we be gone?"

"I don't know." His tone was serious. "A week? A month? Whatever we decide."

"A month." I swallowed hard. My dad would freak out if I was gone a month. He would get the FBI involved! "Where would we go?"

"Wherever."

"Where would we stay?"

"Wherever." His eyes lit up and he grinned at me. "We could break into empty houses."

"What?" My voice rose, and I wasn't sure if he was being serious or not.

"So, are you in?" His tone was light but I knew everything depended on my answer. I was freaking out inside from excitement and worry. But I had to put the worry aside if I wanted to show Logan that I was in this for real.

"Yes." I spoke loudly and confidently. I was shocked at how sure I was about this decision. Part of me knew it was foolish. What smart girl in her right mind would agree to just take off with a guy she barely knew; a guy she was just screaming at a few minutes ago?

"Good." He smiled and ran a finger along my cheek. "I'll have you screaming my name all night long."

"All night? Are you sure about that?"

"It can be all night and day if you want." He laughed and his fingers traced the lines of my lips. I opened my mouth and his finger slid in past my lips and I nibbled on his finger delicately and then sucked on it hard, watching as his eyes grew darker as he stared at me.

"Or I may have you screaming out my name." I winked at him and leaned towards him and whispered against his lips. "You don't know who you're dealing with either, Logan Martelli."

He stared into my eyes and we stood there for a few minutes, not saying anything. I studied his face and noticed the small mole on the left side of his cheek and reached up my hand to touch it lightly. I then ran my hand along the stubble on his jawline and across his upper lip. He reached up to my face and ran his fingers across my eyebrows lightly, and then down the curve of my nose. Running his fingers through my hair, he tucked it behind my ears carefully.

"You're beautiful, Maddie. You will have beautiful babies." His smile was light and he turned away from me quickly and I heard him whisper something under his breath, but I couldn't quite hear what he had said. My stomach had butterflies as he talked about babies. Was he now envisioning a future for us?

"I should call my dad." I fumbled around in my bag looking for my phone, trying to think up something to tell him that wouldn't make him completely lose his mind.

"That would be a good idea."

"He's going to flip."

"That's a shame." Logan cracked a smile, and he turned away. "That's not going to be the only thing he's flipping out about."

"What?" I looked at him curiously. "What do you mean?"

"Nothing." He looked back at me and laughed. "I was just thinking about how crazy life can be sometimes. You just never know what's going to happen."

"Yeah, that's true."

"Who would have thought that the two of us would be going on a road trip together? Logan Martelli and Maddison Wright." He laughed. "It's almost too good to be true."

"I guess." I paused as I stared at him. There was something in his voice that made me shiver. "Are you going to call your brother?"

"Yeah." He pulled out his phone and pressed some numbers. "Hey, Jared, it's me. I thought about what you said, and I've got it sorted." He paused and gave me a small smile. "I won't be home for a few weeks. Take care of things, okay?" He hung up and stared at me. "Your turn."

"Yeah." I took a breath and dialed my dad's number. I almost fainted with relief when his answering machine picked up. "Hey, Dad, it's me Maddie, ha, ha, your daughter. I, uh, I just met up with Brittany and Ellen, and they, uh, surprised me with a, uh, surprise trip, to Brittany's dad's place in Martha's Vineyard, ha, so, I, uh, am going to just hang out there for the next couple of weeks. See you soon. Love to you and Mom." I hung up quickly and saw Logan staring at me quietly.

"Your dad is going to be pissed, huh?" Logan's eyes were serious but there was a glint of a smile in them.

"Yeah." I nodded. "But he likes Brittany and Ellen, and this is the sort of thing they would do, so he should buy it."

"You don't have to come, Maddie." He shook his head as if clearing it. "I can get you home if you want." He paused and ran his hand down my arm. "But I would rather you stay."

"Logan, you change your mind more than a contestant on *The Price is Right*. I'm cool, I'm coming. I want to come."

"You want to come?" He licked his lips.

"Yes." I rolled my eyes, not taking the bait.

"How badly?" He kissed my lips lightly.

"How badly what?"

"How badly do you want to come?" His tongue traced the line of my lips and he gazed into my eyes.

"As badly as you want me to," I whispered softly, and my tongue darted out to meet his. I watched as he inhaled, and desire darkened his eyes.

"You're going to be the undoing of me, Maddie Wright." He leaned back away from me, and I could see a mixture of emotions in his eyes. "What are you doing to me?"

"The same thing you're doing to me." I laughed, happy that I was having this effect on him. Jared had been right. I only hoped that everything else went as according to plan.

"It's not all about the sex you know." His eyes took me in and his hand caressed my hair. "I want you to know that whatever happens, it's not about the sex."

"I know." I nodded. "I know." I knew what I was getting into, I knew from the beginning. If I got burned, it would be my own fault, I knew the score going in. But it was worth it to me; the possibility of having more with Logan was worth it.

"I can't believe you just did that. Your dad is going to be pissed." There was a new respect in his eyes as he stared at me. "You're pretty fearless, aren't you, Maddie?"

"Not really." I shook my head in wonder. "I honestly have never been this way before," I continued on, as I pondered his comment to myself. I'd never been the rebellious type. I'd never been the one who snuck out of the dorms to meet up with boys. I'd never given my parents any headaches. I wasn't really even a wild one. I'd only slept with two guys before, and both of them had been guys I'd been in relationships with. And we'd never had sex out in the open before.

I almost didn't recognize the girl I was becoming, and I wasn't sure if that was a good or bad thing.

"You're more fearless than me."

"No way," I scoffed. "You're Logan Martelli, you steal cars for a living, you are way more fearless than me."

"Not really." He shook his head and we walked towards the main road. "This is the life I was born into. I do what I know and what my father did."

"Do you regret that this is the life you were born into?" I wasn't sure if my words were too prying, but I couldn't stop myself from asking.

"No, I don't have any regrets about anything. Life is too short for regrets."

"That's a great attitude to have."

"My mom always used to say that." His voice sounded sad. "She used to say that not everyone was born into a family with a silver spoon but everyone could change their circumstances. There just had to be one brave person in the family willing to ignite the change."

As Logan talked about his mom, I hesitated. I wasn't sure how much he knew about our shared history, and I wasn't sure if he would be mad if I told him. "Your mom was a wise woman."

"Yes, yes, she was." He turned wistful eyes upon me. "Every day, I try to be the man she would have wanted me to be."

"Who did she want you to be?"

"She wanted me to be kind and compassionate; she wanted better for me and my brothers. She really wanted us to have a better life. Better than my father was able to give us. She even tried to leave my dad once." He sounded as if he were remembering something. "But then she found out she had cancer, and she knew she couldn't take us boys and deal with the diagnosis at the same time."

"I'm sorry." My heart broke listening to Logan talk.

"She knew she was going to die." His voice was hoarse. "She hoped her death would get my father to change, but he just drank more and more, and he got worse and worse. And I had to help him more and more, and then there came a point where I realized this was my life, this was who I was. But, it didn't have to be Vincent's life and it didn't have to be Jared's life. Her death wouldn't be in vain if I made sure they took different paths."

"They don't steal cars?" I bit my lip nervously as I questioned him. I had always heard that it was a family business and that all the Martelli brothers were involved. In fact, when I had met Jared with Joey, I was fairly sure they were up to no good.

"No, sometimes they come to be a lookout, but I try and keep them away from this life as much as I can." He looked at me with a weak smile. "Vincent's in college. Well, two-year college, but we are hoping he will transfer to State in a couple of years and then go to law school. And Jared is trying to get into school as well."

"Wow, that's awesome."

"I know it's not some fancy Ivy League school like you go to, but we're trying."

"Ivies are overrated."

"That's easy for you to say."

"Yeah, I guess it is." I sighed at his harsh words. But I knew he was just being honest. How many opportunities had I been afforded because I had been born into a well-to-do family? I had never had to want for anything, and yet I knew I didn't feel as if my life were complete. I had still never had love, and to me love was everything. I stared at Logan in his faded blue jeans and black T-shirt and he looked even better in person than he had ever looked in photographs. It was weird, this connection I had with Logan, the closeness I felt to him.

"But yeah, my goal is that my brothers don't have to go down this road as well."

"So you would give it up if you could?"

"Maybe." He shrugged. "But what else would I do?"

"What else would you want to do?"

"It doesn't matter." Logan cleared his throat. "This is my fate or curse. My life was dictated by another. It seems only fitting that I do the same." He clenched his fist and his eyes avoided mine. "I see a Lincoln Navigator over there. Wanna go check it out?"

"To steal?" I had a weird feeling in my stomach. Something didn't feel quite right and I wasn't sure what it was.

"No." He turned to me and winked. "To borrow for an hour." He grabbed my hands and pulled me close to him, and I felt his lips against my hair before he pulled back and looked into my eyes.

"An hour, huh?" I winked back at him. "I guess I'm a lucky girl."

"Hurry." He walked quickly. "We have to make sure no one sees us."

"What if the owners come back while we're in the car?"

"They won't." He laughed and grabbed my hand and started running. He let go of it as soon as we got to the car. I saw him pull something out of his pocket and he started fiddling with the lock.

"What are you doing?"

"Shhh." He put a finger to his lips. "Don't alert the world."

"What should I do?" I asked excitedly, and he smiled at me.

"You're such an eager beaver. Just stand there and be cool." He pulled me towards him and kissed me passionately, and my body melted at his embrace. I felt his hand squeezing my ass and I moaned into his lips.

"Not yet, Maddie." He grinned at me and pulled away. He started working on the car door again and I watched him work with admiration in my eyes. His biceps flexed as he tried to get the door open, and I took the time to admire his muscular body as he worked.

"Is everything okay here?" a deep voice asked behind us, and we both froze. I turned around slowly and saw a police officer behind us, and I thought I was going to faint.

"Good day, officer, I was just helping this young lady get into her car. She left her keys in the ignition." Logan's voice was cheerful, and the officer looked at him with narrow eyes before turning to me.

"Are you okay, ma'am?"

"Yes, officer, I locked my keys in the car by mistake." I beamed at him. "I'm such a ditz."

"This is your car?" He looked at me suspiciously and grabbed his radio from his belt.

I felt the blood rushing from my face as I stared at the officer and nodded. "Yes, of course this is my car. What do you think?"

"Do you have your license on you, ma'am?" His face softened a bit but he still looked suspicious.

"Uh, yeah." I opened my purse and pulled out my wallet. "Don't mind the photo, it was a bad hair day."

"You from River Valley?" He looked down at my license, and I nodded. "Far away from home, aren't you?"

"Well, I came to get some items from Walmart." I smiled weakly. "They didn't have them in my home store. And you can't beat a rollback bargain."

"Maddison Wright, hmm, any connection to James Wright?"

"Yes." I smiled outwardly but groaned inwardly. "Mayor James Wright is my dad."

"Oh, why didn't you say?" He grinned at me as he handed back my license. "We love Mayor Wright around here."

122

"Thank you."

"He's a great guy, takes care of his people, he does."

"Yes." I smiled at him. "He sure does."

"Well you have a good day, Ms. Maddison Wright. You let me know if you need any help, you hear?"

"Yes, officer, thank you."

"Oh, you can call me Tommy." He nodded. "I'll be up at the garden center if you need any more help."

"Thanks, Tommy." I blushed at his changed demeanor and he grinned back at me before walking away and back to his parked car.

"What do we do now?" I made a face at Logan, who was staring at me thoughtfully.

"What do you mean?"

"Isn't he going to expect me to leave in this car?" I groaned. "And now he knows my name as well. What if he tells people I was with this strange guy and word gets back to my dad? He'll know that I was lying in my voicemail." My voice trailed off as I saw Logan's lips twitching. "I sound like a mess, don't I?"

"A little bit." He smirked at me. "You're not even close to a bad girl, are you, Maddie?"

I ignored his words and glared at him. "Are you going to get us into this Lincoln or not?"

"Calm down, sweet pea." He rolled his eyes at me and went back to doing whatever he was doing before to get the door open. "This time please be a good lookout and tell me if anyone is coming."

"You were the one who kissed me and distracted me."

"Excuses, excuses." He laughed and then I heard a click, and he opened the door. "Go around the other side and hop in."

"I thought we weren't going to steal it?"

"We have no choice now. Now hurry up and get in."

I ran around to the passenger side and he opened the door for me. I jumped in and he was looking in the glove compartment for something. He looked up and saw my curious stare and smiled. "Spare key. You'd be shocked at how many people leave their spare key in their car. Aha!" He grinned as he pulled a key out. "Here we go." He put the key in the ignition and the engine purred smoothly. "Buckle up."

"Where are we going?"

"Wherever we want."

"No quickie in the backseat?" I pouted and his eyes darkened as he stared at me.

"No," He shook his head. "No quickie and no trip either."

"What?"

"You're going back home tonight."

"What? Why?" I stared at him, and my stomach did a double flip. Was he done with me already? What had I done now?

"It wasn't a good idea." He shook his head. "I wasn't thinking properly when I suggested us being a modern-day Bonnie and Clyde."

"I *want* to go, though." I frowned. "You're not making me."

"Just now, what you did, it was great. It was brave, and you saved my ass, but you also put your own ass on the line. You could have been in a lot of trouble."

"I did it for you." I shook my head in confusion. "I didn't want the cop to arrest you."

"He could have arrested both of us if he hadn't believed your

124

story."

"But he did believe it. And if he hadn't, well, I would have just had to deal with the consequences."

"You didn't have to do that." He pulled out of the parking lot, and glanced at me quickly. "You had my back."

"Of course I had your back." I looked at him in shock. "Did you think I would turn you in?"

"No." He shook his head. "You're not that kind of person." His voice was full of wonder and regret. "You're a good person, Maddie Wright, you deserve better than to be messed up with someone like me."

"What are you talking about, Logan?" I was worried. He sounded like he was second-guessing everything again. "Are we going down this road again?"

"I want to take you somewhere, and then we'll go home."

I felt tears well up in my eyes at his words. It seemed that no matter what I tried to do or say, something always popped into his head that made him back away from me.

"I already told my dad I'm going away; what do I say when I get home?"

"You had a change of plan."

"I don't want a change of plan." I wanted to scream, I was so frustrated.

"Trust me, Maddie. It's for your own good." He shook his head. "You're a good person. You make a good friend."

"So, I'm just your *friend* again?" I sighed.

"It may be for the best." He nodded. "I do like you, Maddie. It's just complicated."

I wanted to ask him what was complicated, but I knew I just had to be patient. If I really wanted to be in his life, I just had to accept what he was willing to give me. Friends wasn't bad; in fact, it was pretty darn good. It meant that he was on his way to trusting me and letting me in, and that was all I could ask for. A part of me was relieved that I was going home, not because I didn't want to spend time away with him but because a part of me was still a little unsure of exactly what he wanted from me. I didn't want to be his goodtime girl who he just used and threw away. I wanted more than that. I needed more than that. And I also needed to make sure I knew what I was getting into as well. Everything had been so fast and so dramatic already. I was putting everything on the line for a guy I didn't really know. And so even though my heart told me I was on cloud nine whenever I was with him, my brain sometimes begged to differ.

Chapter 8

Logan

I was ashamed of myself. For the first time in my life, I was ashamed of who I was as a human being. As I drove, all I could think about was how I could have even entertained the thought of getting Maddie pregnant for revenge. That wasn't who I was; I didn't just ruin people's lives. Especially not Maddie's. I snuck in a quick glance at her as I drove and I was struck at the intensity of emotions running through me as I looked at her. I had well and truly fucked up this whole situation; I wasn't even sure what I was going to do now. I couldn't stay in her life. I didn't trust myself or my brothers around her. She was safer without me in her life. There was nothing I could do to help make her life better.

"Where are we going?" Maddie's voice was open and I wondered how she could be so trusting. I guess that was one of the negatives of sheltering your kids: they didn't truly know what danger looked and smelled like.

"I want to take you to a field."

"Oh." She laughed. "I suppose since we didn't get to make love in the backseat."

"No, this isn't about sex." I shook my head and reached over and grabbed her hand. "Don't get me wrong, I love having sex with you, but that's kinda all we know about each other. If we're going to be friends, we need to …"

"Okay, stop right there." Maddie turned to face me. "You surprise me every single day, Logan Martelli. I knew you were a great guy."

"I'm not a great guy." I denied her words. If she knew the truth about what I had been thinking about doing, well, I'm not sure she would be so gushing then.

"So why are we going to a field then?"

"It's a special field." I smiled at her briefly. "Just be patient."

"Okay."

I looked at the familiar surroundings as I drove and I could almost smell the pollen in the air. The fields we passed were lush and green with dashes of colors, the flowers were in bloom and they brightened up the otherwise dull fields. I got excited as I pulled off of the road and down a street with a *Do not pass* sign. I stopped the car and jumped out.

"Come on, we have to walk from here."

"Can we leave the car here?" She jumped out of the car and looked worried. "What of the police see it?"

"It'll be okay." I laughed. "If you didn't notice, we're on a private road, pretty far from the main road. The police won't be coming."

"Okay." She looked up at me with bright eyes. "So where are we going?"

"Follow me." I reached over and grabbed her hand and she smiled at me happily. For a moment, everything almost felt normal. I felt like a regular guy, on a date with a girl he liked, and everything was right in the world. The sun was shining, the birds were chirping, and Maddie and I were happy to be in this moment.

"So what is this place?" Maddie asked again, not able to keep her curiosity to herself as we walked down overgrown path.

"It's a special field my mom used to take me to as a boy. Just me and her." I didn't look at Maddie as I spoke, scared that somehow I would be too overwhelmed to continue on this journey. "I always loved nature, it's something I got from my mom. I love the smell of the grass, I love the feel of the sun on my face, I love to just be swallowed up by nature; it makes me feel like I'm a part of something."

"It kinda makes you believe in something higher, doesn't it?"

Maddie's voice was soft and thoughtful as she looked around. "When I go camping, I'm reminded that there is so much more to the world than whether I get good grades or a new top."

"Yeah." I dropped her hand and bent down to pick her a few flowers that were growing to the right of us. "Like, take a look at these. Have you ever seen such a bright pink before in your life? Look how vivid it is. It's a pink that could punch you in the face."

"They are beautiful," she agreed, and smiled at me, a delicious, wide, gorgeous smile and I felt a part of me melt inside. It was as if she had awakened in me something that I hadn't known existed. A part of me that was full of wonder and belief.

"And this one." I held the violet flower delicately. "This one reminds me of your eyes, it's purple, but when you look at it in a different light, it looks navy blue. So beautiful and deceiving. Yet so lovely and captivating."

"I hope you don't think I'm deceiving." She smiled at me searchingly and my breath caught as my heart constricted at the sight of her.

"I think the image of you is deceiving," I answered slowly, trying to explain it to her, as well as to myself. "I think when I look at you, I see a beautiful, wonderful, capricious girl. And all I can focus on is your impish smile. But then there are times I look at you, and I see Maddison Wright, and I see a rich, privileged girl. And I feel deceived, because how can I be falling for the girl with the purple eyes if she's Maddison Wright ..." My words trailed off and we stared at each other for a while. I think we were both in shock, not because I had voiced my inner turmoil but because I had admitted I was falling for her. I was really falling for her, and I knew that a relationship between us would do nothing but cause more trouble.

"So when I look at you, Logan Martelli," she began softly and then reached over to hold my hands. "When I look at you, I see the handsome boy I grew up daydreaming about. I see your dark blond tousled hair and green eyes, and I think, this man is too handsome to be here with me. I think you can have any girl you want. And you're cocky and self-assured, and you don't mind throwing punches. And I think, he's a player, he's all about one thing. But then I see that hint of a smile in your eyes, followed by an even quicker hint of sadness and a whole lot of anger. And I think, this man, this man is trouble. He's secretive, and he doesn't trust, and he's a thief, and I know he hates my father. And I think, what am I doing here? What do I hope to get out of this? Am I just looking for a heartache?"

"I don't want to cause you a heartache, Maddie." Her words cut my heart and I didn't know what else to say.

"I slept with you on the first night I met you." She shook her head, slightly laughing to herself. "I tried to steal a cop car to get you to like me. I've cried and almost begged you to be friends." She leaned in towards me. "I've been slightly crazy, and I told myself that it would be worth it, that it had to be worth it. And just now, you made it all worth it."

"I did?" I wanted to step back from her. My head was starting to feel overwhelmed with emotions and realizations.

"Yeah, you did." She grinned. "You just told me that you're falling for me, too."

"Too?"

"Well, you know," she laughed. "I've already fallen for you."

"Oh, Maddie."

"We deserve to give this a chance, Logan." She bit her lip and leaned in and pressed her lips against mine. Her lips tasted like sweet mint and I closed my eyes as I kissed her back sweetly. I pulled away from her and grabbed her hand again.

"Come, we still haven't gotten to the field as yet." I didn't want to continue talking about us. I wasn't ready to delve any deeper into our feelings. It was all too new for me, and I needed to think. We walked for another ten minutes in companionable silence and then I saw the familiar two rocks on top of each other and stopped. "My mom and I put those rocks there." I pointed over to them. "We wanted to make a marker so we wouldn't forget this spot."

"Did you guys come here a lot?"

"Maybe four or five times." My eyes glazed over. As I had gotten older, it had been harder and harder for my mother to take me anywhere with her, especially once I became a teenager. I had not wanted to come and visit fields with mother anymore. I could still remember the last time she had asked me. I had been playing videogames with Vincent, and I had been feeling particularly proud of myself because I had bought the newest game out of money my father had given me for helping him steal a brand new Toyota Camry. I had heard her arguing with my father about letting me go with him, and she had told him she didn't want this life for her sons. She then came to my room and asked if I wanted to go on a drive with her. I hadn't even looked up from the game; I was still annoyed with her. "I thought we could go to our field," she had said, but I ignored her. She left the room silently and had never asked me again before she died. That was a memory that still pained me, and I felt my muscles tighten as I stared at the rocks.

"It must have been nice to come here with just your mom," Maddie continued and squeezed my hand as if she realized how hard it was for me to be here.

"It was nice." I nodded. "Let's go." I pushed through the bushes next to the rocks and held them open for Maddie as much as I could. She squeezed through and we took a few more steps and then I stopped and stared. There in front of us was the largest field of sunflowers I had ever seen in my life, it seemed to go on and on, and each sunflower seemed to shine even brighter than the next.

"Wow, this is amazing." Maddie's eyes shone with appreciation. "This is so beautiful." She gazed around and gingerly touched the petals of a sunflower in front of her. "I understand why Van Gogh painted sunflowers now."

"They all look so similar, but if you study them, they are all so unique. The yellows in their petals, the oranges of the florets, all so unique if you stop to study them carefully."

"I don't really know much about flowers."

"Me, either." I laughed. "Sad, really, but I couldn't name half of them for you."

"So are sunflowers your favorite flower then?"

"Why, of course. What about you?"

"Is it cliché if I say roses?" She blushed. "Red roses are my absolute favorite."

"They are the flower of love." I grinned at her.

"No one has ever given me roses before."

"Not even a boyfriend?" I teased, trying to ignore the slight stirring of jealousy inside.

"Not a one of them," she laughed. "And I gave them plenty of hints as well."

"What sort of hints? Maybe they didn't understand. You know how you girls can be."

"Hints like, oh, it's my birthday coming up. I'd love it if someone got me roses."

"Oh." I laughed.

"Yeah, exactly. Anyone who was listening should have known I would have loved to have received some roses."

"Good things come to those who wait."

"I sure hope so."

"So," I asked casually. "Are you dating anyone right now?"

"Is that a joke?" She gave me a weird look.

"No." I looked away from her. A part of me was wondering why I was going down this road of questions. I didn't want to go down this road, because I knew where it would end up. It would end up with her asking where we were going, and what did I want, and I didn't want to answer that. Though I did want to know more about Maddie. What was it about me that attracted her? What guys had she dated before? Did she have a history of choosing bad boys? Was she one of those girls whose goal was to fix her man? I knew I didn't want to be that guy to her, though I didn't know exactly what role I wanted to play in her life.

"Well, no, Logan. I'm not dating anyone. I certainly wouldn't be sleeping with you if I was sleeping with someone else."

"So, you don't sleep around?" I knew the words came out wrong. I knew she may interpret my tone as disbelief that she wasn't easy. Even though that wasn't what I meant, I really wanted to know if she was interested in anyone else aside from me, but I didn't want to voice it that way.

"I know it's hard for you to believe, but no, I am not sleeping around."

"So there's no one."

"There's no one." She rolled her eyes. "I'm just a single girl, having some fun."

"I see."

"You're such an idiot." She pushed me slightly. "I like you, Logan. Don't you understand that?"

"What?" I couldn't stop the smile on my face. "You like me?"

"Like that is really news to you."

"Well, you know," I laughed, "I'm a guy, I'm a bit slow."

"Just a bit?"

"You know how it can be sometimes."

"So what about you?"

"What about me?"

"So do you like me as well?"

"Hmm, that's a bit of a hard question."

"Logan Martelli!"

"I think I can say that I like you." I smiled at her warmly. "I think I can say that I like you quite a lot." I laughed at the words. If my brothers could see me now, telling a girl I liked her like some pussy.

"A lot, huh?" She grinned back at me. "Even though you were shouting at me just a few hours ago."

"Well, you were shouting at me as well."

"Only because you were shouting at me."

"I'm new to situations like this, Maddie."

"Have you been in a relationship before?"

"Of course. I'm not a monk." I laughed at the disappointment in her eyes. "I'm sure you appreciate the benefit of sleeping with a man with experience."

"I don't want to think about you sleeping with anyone else." She wrinkled her nose.

"Just think about me sleeping with you, then." I pulled her towards me. "Just think about the feel of me as I fill you up and pound you so energetically that you can think of nothing other than the feel of my cock in you."

"Logan." She laughed delicately against me. "Are you trying to turn me on?"

"Did it work?" I winked at her and watched as she licked her lips. I wanted to feel her tongue on me, and I groaned as I realized how turned on I was.

"I'm not going to tell you." She shook her head and stepped

away from me.

"I see the way you are." I adjusted myself and stifled another groan. "So tell me about your last boyfriend."

"Are we going to do this now, then?" She looked at me with a question in her eyes, and I wanted to tell her no. I didn't want to think about her with anyone else. I didn't want to picture her lips kissing another man's cheek, her hair trailing along another man's face, her fingers running through another man's hair, her eyes adoring another man's presence.

"Just curious, but if you don't want to," I shrugged, "no skin off my back."

"It's fine. I'd like to share with you, if you'll do the same."

"So who's the last guy you dated?"

"Brandon Howell III." She laughed. "His father was from Texas and in oil. And he loved steak. Like, really loved steak. Every date we had was in a fancy steakhouse."

"Nice." I smiled weakly, not wanting to hear about Brandon Howell the Third, jerkoff of steakhouses.

"He was tall, about six feet, with a really nice body. He went to the gym a lot. He had blond hair and blue eyes. His mom was from Sweden." She babbled on and I already regretted getting into this conversation. I really didn't want to hear about her perfect ex. "He just graduated from UT Austin, and he is starting the MBA program at Penn in the fall. He's not that smart, though, so I'm not really sure how he got in, but I wouldn't be surprised to hear that his father donated a few million to ensure he was accepted."

"Nice." I knew I sounded irritated, but I couldn't help it. The more she spoke, the more I realized that this could go nowhere. I couldn't take her anywhere fancy, I'd never be able to buy myself into a grad program. Shit, my brother wouldn't even be able to go to community college next semester if I didn't come up with a plan to make some money.

"Sorry." She looked at me, worried. "I know that was too much information. Basically we dated for about two months and then I found out he had a cocaine problem and I dumped him."

"I see. Did you sleep with him?"

"We messed around." She looked down. "Though we never had intercourse."

"Do you still talk to him?"

"Not really, but he does call me every now and then to hang out."

"Okay." My voice was short and I turned away from her to look at the sunflowers. The warmth of the sun on my face soothed me a little bit as we stood there in silence, and I was thankful Maddie didn't try and ask me what was wrong. I was overwhelmed with unfamiliar emotions, and I was already worried enough as it was. I really didn't need this additional stress. But somehow standing here calmed me. I felt like my mom was looking down from heaven, telling me to just relax and take it one day at a time, like she used to when I was a kid. I turned to Maddie and smiled. "When I was a kid, my mom always used to tell me that I looked like I had the weight of the world on my shoulders. And that one day, if I wasn't careful, the load was going to be too much to bear and I would collapse. She always said if it starts feeling like it's too much, just look around you, Logan. Just stop and go somewhere and look around you. And then, for a moment, everything will seem manageable."

"Is that why you like going to fields?"

"And to the pier." I nodded. "I love the ocean, it reminds me of myself."

"Oh?"

"The ocean is deceptive. Some days it looks calm and peaceful, and other days it looks dark and murky. Yet you never really know what's going on underneath. What are the currents like, the undertow, the waves? I feel like I'm the ocean to a lot of people, they don't really see me. They see what they want to see."

"What do most people see?"

"People see me as dangerous and stay away, and I don't mind that. Sometimes, there are people who see me as dangerous but like the thrill of danger."

"You mean girls?"

"Yeah." I nodded, thinking of all the girls I had dated who liked me just because of who they thought I was. How I hadn't cared how they saw me, they were disposable and weak and stupid.

"But what about those who see you the other way …"

"There aren't any people who see me that other way." I laughed harshly. "Aside from my brothers."

"I see you the other way."

My heart stilled at her words. The words I knew to be true. Maddie saw me as someone other than the town's bad boy. But I didn't feel as overjoyed as I had earlier. There was nothing I could give Maddie.

"All I will do is bring heartache and trouble to your life, Maddie."

"I can deal with trouble."

"You don't need to be involved in trouble."

"You don't know everything about me, Logan."

"And you don't know everything about me. This will never work between us."

"I thought we were just friends."

"We are just friends." I sighed. "But that's all we can be."

"Even though we both like each other?"

"Like is a fickle emotion, it will fade."

"Can you tell me why you just won't give me a chance?"

"I'm not good for your life, Maddie. Nothing good can come of this."

"Can't I decide that?"

"If it was just you and me," I sighed. "But we have a history. There's a history that none of us can shake, I'm sorry."

"Do you trust me, Logan?"

"Yes." There was no hesitation in my answer. I trusted Maddie as much as I trusted my brothers.

"I trust you as well. I'm not going to ask you again about what my dad did and why you hate him. I think you'll tell me when you're good and ready. And that's fine. But I'm not cool with the hot and cold game. You can't tell me you like me in one instant and then tell me that you're no good for me and we're never going to work out. Do you hear me? That's not going to fly."

"I don't know what you want from me, Maddie."

"Let's give it a fair shot, can you do that?"

"I don't understand why you care so much."

"If you don't have any interest in me and you don't want to see me, then fine. I'll move on. You're not the only guy in the world. I'm sure there will be someone else I don't have to beg to date me ..."

"Are you asking me to be your boyfriend?" I cut her off, not wanting to think of her with another man. "Aren't I a bit old for you?"

"You're twenty-five, not thirty-five."

"I'm a twenty-five-year-old loser, and you're a twenty-year-old with the world at your feet. You can do anything you want, Maddie.

You can be anyone you want. Go explore the world. Go save orphans. Go and become a feminist for women's rights. You don't get stuck with someone like me, I've seen what it does to someone."

"Are you talking about your mom?" she asked softly and I nodded. "Can we sit down?" She grinned. "My legs are a little tired."

I turned around and crouched down. "Get on my back."

"Wait, what?"

"Get on my back, I'm going to give you a piggyback."

"No way, Logan. I'm too fat for you to carry me."

"You're not fat."

"Well, I'm not a little kid."

"Shut up and get on," I commanded her. "I'm going to take us to a clearing so we can sit or lie down."

"I can walk there."

"No, you're tired. Get on my back and don't say another word." I felt her arms slide around my neck as she gingerly got onto my back. I stood up and she wrapped her legs around my chest.

"Are you sure, Logan? You can put me down if I'm too heavy."

"You're not heavy at all, you silly girl." I started walking and continued back with our conversation. "And yes, I was talking about my mom. She had her whole life ahead of her before she got caught up with my dad." I sighed. "She wasn't rich like you or anything, but she was smart and beautiful and she could have done anything she wanted."

"I know." Maddie's voice was soft and I stopped walking for a moment.

"What do you mean? You know?"

"My mom told me that your mom was the most beautiful girl in school. And that she had the longest blonde hair she'd ever seen in her life."

"Your mom knew her?"

"Yeah, they were friends." Maddie's voice was hesitant. "Best friends, I think."

"I didn't know that." I frowned at Maddie's words. How could I have not known that?

"My dad was in love with your mom for years," Maddie continued. "I don't know if you knew that. He was heartbroken when she dumped him."

"What?" I almost dropped her as the words ripped out of my body. "What do you mean, she dumped him?" I was frozen inside. How could my mom have dumped him? They had never dated before.

"Your mom and my dad dated for a few months before she dumped him for your dad." Maddie sounded surprised. "I thought that was why you may have been annoyed with my dad."

"That's not why." I continued walking until we came to the clearing and Maddie slid off my back. She had a slightly worried expression on her face.

"Maybe we shouldn't talk about this. I thought you knew."

"I had no idea. Tell me more." My eyes focused on her face intently. "Please."

"Well, there's not much to tell. Our parents were best friends. My mom loved my dad, but my dad loved your mom. Your mom loved your dad. When she dumped my dad, my mom and dad started dating, but my mom was so jealous she stopped talking to your mom. And basically that was the end of the friendship. My mom says she has always regretted the friendship ending like that, but she never really knew what to say. When your mom died, she cried for a few weeks straight, and she told me everything."

"I never knew." I shook my head. Had my dad known that mom had been dating the mayor before he had stolen her away from him? And why had Mom never said anything? She knew about the trips to Manor Road, yet all she had ever said was that people paid for their sins.

"That's when I started looking for photos of you and stuff," she paused. "She wanted to see what you guys looked like. They had always talked about when they got married and had kids, but they never got to share it together. My mom felt responsible for trying to make your mom see reason about your dad."

"See reason about my dad?" I frowned.

"Well, you know. Being a criminal and all that."

"My dad was a good man." My voice rose. "My dad wasn't born a criminal. He was going to go to college. He was going to be someone. My mom didn't make the wrong choice. Your…" I was shouting and Maddie placed her hand on my arm.

"Please, Logan." She bit her lip. "I didn't mean to upset you. I'm sorry. I don't know your dad. I'm just saying that my mom regrets what happened with your mom when they were in high school."

"My dad loved my mom."

"I'd like to meet your dad."

"That's not a good idea." I shook my head vehemently.

"I'd like you to meet my dad as well."

"Another bad idea."

"I think he'd like you."

"I'm sure he would love to hear that you're dating Logan Martelli."

"So we're dating?" Her eyes blazed into mine and I nodded.

"If you're willing to give it a go."

"I'm willing." She laughed and grabbed ahold of me. "I've been willing since the first night I met you." She grabbed my face and pulled me towards her, however, she surprised me by falling to her knees instead of kissing me. I looked down and watched her unbuckle my jeans and pull my zipper down.

"What are you doing?" I asked stupidly.

"I want to show you how happy I am." She winked up at me and I only hesitated slightly before pushing her back into the grass. "Ow."

"Shh." I sat down next to her and reached over to her. "Today is not about sex."

"We don't have to have sex." She pouted.

"I don't want this moment to be about sex." I shook my head as her hand worked its way into my pants. "But you're making this very hard on me."

"Is that a pun?" She laughed as her fingers circled my hardness.

"I want you to know that I …"

"Or is this about you liking to be in control?" She removed her hand and I resisted the urge to grab it and stick it back in my pants.

"Who says I like to be in control?"

"Well, that first night you wanted to be in command, and then when you spanked me, and now."

"And now?" I raised an eyebrow at her as I reached over to cup her right breast. "Do you think I'm saying no because I like to be in control?"

"Yes." She nodded as she squirmed on the ground beneath my fingers. "I think you prefer a more passive girl."

"Really?" I laughed aloud. How little she knew. I was delighted that she was confident and aggressive. I felt like she was a real match for my more dominant side. I knew I was dominant, but I also wanted a girl to give as good as she got from me.

"Are you attracted to me, Logan?"

"Oh my God, is this a joke?" I groaned. "We are not going to have this conversation already, are we?"

"You've had this conversation a lot?" She looked hurt, and a part of me was happy to see her jealousy. I felt a twinge of guilt at my happiness but ignored it.

"Not a lot, but why do girls always think you're not into them if you don't want to fuck? I mean, really, Maddie? I can barely keep my hands off of you. I just told you we can try dating and you want to know if I'm attracted to you?"

"Well, you just turned me down for sex." She looked away. "That doesn't really happen a lot."

This time my jealousy kicked in. "Save it, please. I don't need to hear about every guy you tried to give a blowjob to."

"What?" She looked at me angrily. "That is not what I was saying."

"Do you think I want to hear about how many guys were delighted that you were willing to have sex with them?"

"I didn't say that." She rolled away from me.

I pulled her towards me again. "I can't believe we're arguing about this."

"Well, believe it, ass."

"Fine." I jumped up and pulled her up with me. "Let's go."

"What, where are we going?" She stood up reluctantly, and stared at me with a dazed expression.

"Do you want to know something about me?" I leaned towards her and whispered in her ear. She nodded slightly, and I continued. "I like having sex in public."

"Okay, and …" She reached over to me and reached down my pants again. I shook my head and gave her a smirk.

"I like to have sex in public, where people are around."

"You like them to watch you?" She looked at me with wide eyes and I laughed.

"No, I don't go to sex clubs or anything. But I do like the thrill of knowing I'm having sex and that anyone could find out at any moment."

"Why?"

"I don't know why, maybe it's the fear of getting caught. It gets my blood pumping." I shrugged, worried I had scared Maddie off. It wasn't every day that people shared the intimate details of their life, and I didn't want her to think I was a freak. Not with everything else she knew about me.

"I suppose that makes sense." She looked at me, considering. "I've never really had sex in public before; I mean aside from in the field with you, but no one was there."

"We could change that …" I let my words trail off as I tried to hide my excitement.

"We could." She turned away from me, and I saw a glimpse of a smile on her face.

"What are you thinking?"

"Let's go shop."

"Shop?" I tried to hide my disappointment. "You want to go shop?"

"Yeah. I'm in the mood for some new things."

"You want to go now?"

"Don't couples normally go shopping together?"

"Yes, I'm sure normal couples go shopping together."

"We're not normal?"

"Well, we're not from Mars or anything, but I don't think I'm the sort of person who can be in a normal anything." I laughed. "Ask any of my exes."

"I'd rather not ask them." She frowned. "What did you do with your exes for fun?"

"For fun? Do you really want to know?"

"I guess not." She started walking away from me and I hurried to keep up with her fast pace.

"You're mad at me again."

"I'm not mad."

"You'll have to be patient with me, Maddie. This isn't something I do every day."

"What's not something you do every day? Have a conversation or try to not talk about your exes?"

I smiled to myself at her surly tone. Maddie was well and truly jealous. I knew it wasn't funny, but her jealousy just didn't seem to fit in with her confident attitude. It made me feel like I meant something to her.

"Let's both of us not talk about our exes anymore."

"Sounds like a plan to me." She turned to me again with a small smile. "Now, can we go shopping?"

"I guess if you make me."

"Make you?"

"Well, I'm not the biggest fan of shopping."

"I think you'll like this trip."

"I doubt it."

"We'll see." She grinned at me as we made our way to the car. "I mean we don't have to go if you think they'll be tracking the car."

"We'll park the car at the mall. I assume we're going to the mall, right?"

"Am I that predictable?"

"You and all girls. Oops." I laughed. "I forgot I'm not supposed to be talking about other women right now, am I?"

"No." She rolled her eyes. "Though, I suppose as a guy, you can't help it."

"You know us guys."

"All you think about it getting some."

"Yup, you got it." We got into the car and I saw Maddie grinning at me teasingly. "Sex, sex, and more sex."

"Sex in the bedroom, sex in the bathroom, sex in the kitchen, sex in the field." She counted off on her fingers. "That's all that's on your mind."

"You know me so well." I checked to see if there were any cop cars coming before I pulled back out onto the highway.

"I know men." She winked at me and shimmied in the seat, and I put on a fake Spanish accent.

"Maddie, I think you are trying to turn me on with your sexy talk."

"Are you trying to pretend you're Italian?" She giggled.

"How dare you, I'm from Puerto Rico." I rolled my R and tried to keep a straight face.

"Puerto Rico by way of Rome?"

"I'm from San Juan." I winked at her. "And I'm going to show you how to salsa."

"Ooh, really? I'd like you to show me how to salsa. Maybe I'll get a dress at the mall."

"Oh, God. Me and my big mouth. I'm going to become one of those men who stands there looking tortured while he waits for his woman to try on clothes."

"I don't know that you ever don't look tortured."

"Are you calling me dour?"

"Dour?" She made a face at me. "I'm not sure you can call a handsome young man dour. I've only ever thought of sour old women as dour."

"Yay. I'm not a sour old woman."

"Thank God." She leaned over and whispered in my ear. "I wouldn't want to have sex with a dour or sour old woman in a changing room."

"What?" My eyes nearly popped out of my sockets at her words. "You what?"

"I figured that would get your heart racing."

"You figured right! Why didn't you tell me earlier? I would have taken you to any mall you wanted."

"You're such a guy."

"I think we established that already." I laughed and pressed the gas pedal excitedly. I turned on the radio and stopped at a song that Maddie seemed to know. She was singing along and bobbing her head and I laughed as she danced around in the seat. As I drove, I realized that I was happy. It was a weird feeling. A unique feeling for me, and I wasn't used to how good it felt. The worries and the stress were gone, albeit briefly, and at the back of my mind. But in this instant, I felt like I was in Utopia. I'd never realized just how wonderful it could feel to be with someone I liked who liked me. It was a different but entirely pleasant feeling. Right now, I was just Logan, a regular boy, and I was amazed at how good that felt.

***

"Let's go into Macy's." Maddie pulled my arm. "They have lots of changing rooms and they hardly ever have salesgirls around."

"Macy's?" I made a face. "That's not exciting."

"It's in a store, it's fine."

"No, no. If we're going to do this, it has to be somewhere exhilarating."

"This is the mall, Logan. Not Hedonism Island in Jamaica."

"Now, I wouldn't mind going there."

"Hell, no." Maddie shook her head.

"I'm joking. I don't have the money to take us there, even if I wanted to." I made a face and turned away from her, angry at myself for bringing up money. For a moment, I had forgotten the dire straits I was currently in. I followed Maddie distractedly, as I started thinking about what I was going to do. Five hundred dollars wasn't going to help the family much, and now that Marty was onto me not selling him the cars any longer, I knew I had to think of something else to do.

"Logan, earth to Logan." Maddie looked at me in concern, and I could see her violet eyes searching my face. It was funny how she always seemed to know when my mood has changed. I knew that people said women were in tune with emotions and stuff, but I'd never had anyone close enough to pay attention to mine, not since my mom had died.

"Sorry, was just thinking."

"Nope, I forbid it." She grabbed her hands. "No worrying and no thinking right now."

"You're a bossy boots."

"It comes from being an only child."

"Must be nice." I laughed, only half-joking. If I didn't have Vincent and Jared to worry about, I could have left River Valley and started a new life for myself. I could have reinvented myself and perhaps made something of my life. *But then you wouldn't have met Maddie*, a little voice whispered in my head. *And you wouldn't have your two best friends in your life*, another voice whispered. And it was true; I'd take whatever adversity came my way to ensure that I had Vincent and Jared in my life. They were my life; they were everything to me. They were my blood and my sweat. They were the only people I knew I could trust my life with. Until I met Maddie.

"What are your brothers like?" Maddie interrupted my thoughts, and I smiled at her, wondering if she had ESP or something.

"Vincent's the second oldest, he's a fighter, and one of the best men I know. He is also pretty reserved, but he would do anything for the ones he loves. Jared, well, you know Jared a bit, he's the baby of the family. Handsome, lovable, charming, quick-witted, and a big troublemaker." I tried to laugh as I talked about Jared. Between Vincent and Jared, Jared was the one I was most worried about. He was smart and rebellious, more so than me and Vincent. And he had a propensity to act first and think later. I was worried he was going to get himself into trouble so deep that there would be no saving him. That was why I was pushing so hard for him to start college. I felt if he had some real goals and a real routine, he wouldn't have time for Joey and the other troublemakers he hung around with.

"Yeah, Jared seems really cool." Maddie smiled. "He's very handsome and friendly."

"Do you have a crush on him as well?" I played with the money in my pocket, waiting for her answer. All I could think about is how badly I would want to beat Jared if she said yes.

"Oh, no." She laughed. "Not at all. You've always been the Martelli boy for me, though I've never met Vincent. And anyway, Lucy loves Jared."

"Lucy?" I grinned up at her in relief. I hadn't been looking forward to socking my own brother.

"Joey's sister. My best friend." She smiled. "Did you forget already?"

"Oh, no," I lied. "Sure, Lucy."

"You totally didn't remember her." She giggled and then ran her finger down my chest. "I'd like to meet him, too."

"Meet who?" My brain was distracted as she ran her fingers to the top of my jeans and then paused.

"Your brother Vincent." She leaned closer and looked up at me, batting her lashes cutely.

"What about your brother? I mean my brother. I mean Vincent." I gazed down at her juicy pink lower lip and licked my lips. All I wanted to do was lean down and tug on it with my teeth.

"I'd like to meet him." She moved even closer to me and I felt her breath against my mouth. "Can I?"

"Uh, sure," I said without thinking and she rewarded me with a slow, sensual kiss. I pulled her towards me and put my hands in the back pockets of her jeans as we kissed. I pushed my tongue into her mouth and she ran her hands through my hair. It was only as I heard a couple of kids giggling beside us that I remembered where we were, and I pulled away from her regretfully.

"Oh, Logan." She smiled up at me through eyes of lust and my stomach flipped as I thought about making love to her again. I grabbed her hand and we walked quickly through the mall, looking for a store that would fit the bill. "What about JC Penney?" She pointed to the store in the far corner, and I shook my head. "The Gap?"

"No, no." I laughed and then I saw the pink stripes of Victoria's Secret and my heart started racing. "Let's go there."

"Where?" Maddie followed my gaze and stopped still. "There's no way we can go in Victoria's Secret." She shook her head. "They have girls by the changing rooms all the time and there is no way they will let you in with me."

"Then we'll have to sneak me in."

"How can we sneak you in?" Her voice lowered as we entered the store and I was surrounded by panties and bras. I glanced around and grinned. Now this was a store to have sex in. I glanced at Maddie and pictured her modeling underwear for me: something lacy and see-through would be nice.

"Logan," Maddie hissed at me. "Pay attention."

"Sorry, what?" I grinned at her, trying not to look too excited.

"You're like a boy in a candy store."

"I do have to admit, this day has gotten a lot better." I walked over to the side of the store and looked at some teddies. "What about one of these?"

"Huh?" She looked at me, confused.

"Well, you have to go in and try something on, right?" I raised an eyebrow. "That's the point of a changing room. So what about one of these?"

"Are you joking?" She rolled her eyes. "No way."

"Aww, come on." I grabbed a black number that looked particularly sexy.

"No way." She shook her head. "Or should I say, keep on wishing?"

"Awww, I thought you liked me?" I laughed and put the number back down. "So what then?"

"I was thinking about these." She picked up a pair of shorts and a tank top, and I frowned. "What?"

I tried not to express my dismay, but I must not have been able to hide it well because she burst out laughing.

"You should see your face right now."

"I'm guessing it looks like *what the fuck is she thinking?*"

"No, more like *I can't believe I have to eat broccoli for dinner.*" She laughed and put the shorts down.

"Let's be real, Maddie, we need something with easy access." I laughed and watched as she blushed.

"Shhh, Logan." She pressed her finger against my lips and I tried to nip it. I laughed as she pulled away quickly and walked away from me. I watched her going through the different bras and smiled to myself.

"Find one yet?" I walked up behind her and ran my hands across her ass as I pressed myself against her. "I'm kind of liking this one here." I placed my hands over hers and touched the fine lace of the bra in her hand. "This one is soft, but I'd prefer a see-through pattern," I whispered in her ear and she squirmed in front of me. "Then you can do a striptease for me before I bend you over and slide my…."

"Logan." Maddie's face was red and she pushed back against me. "People might hear."

"I don't mind." I laughed and looked around. No one was paying any attention to us, and I was glad we weren't in River Valley.

"Look, I'm going to go now. Bring these to me in about five minutes. If the girl is there, tell her you went to get me a different size." Maddie handed me a bra.

"Okay." I nodded. "Sounds like a good plan."

"But try and come when you see the salesgirl go and help someone else, okay?"

"Okay." I nodded, not really paying attention to what she was saying. I was too busy picturing Maddie shuddering against me in the lacy underwear I was now holding.

"I'm going in now." She gave me a quick peck and her eyes were shining. "Pay attention, Logan."

"Yes, ma'am." I grinned and watched as she walked in to one of the changing rooms. I noticed a salesgirl staring at me and so I turned around quickly and pretended to study the thongs.

"Hi, can I help you?" A petite young blonde walked up to me with a big smile.

"I was just looking for a gift." I smiled at her weakly, trying to ignore the way she was pushing her breasts towards me.

"Oh?" She pouted and leaned in closer to me. "For your girlfriend?"

"No, I don't have a girlfriend," I answered automatically and felt slightly guilty. I didn't really know what I would call Maddie.

"Oh?" She grinned up at me. "I'm surprised to hear that. A hot guy like you."

"Well, no need to be surprised." I took a step back from her and looked away. I could tell she was interested and that it wouldn't be hard for me to take her out back and have my way with her. She was looking for it and offering herself on a silver platter.

"My name's Brittany." She ran her hand down my arm as she looked up at me and batted her eyelashes.

"Nice to meet you, Brittany." I gave her a perfunctory smile and looked back down at the thongs.

"I get off at eight," she said, getting right to the point. I gave her a quick smile. She was beautiful, and in any other instance, I wouldn't have hesitated to get her number. But now I wasn't interested. Her feminine wiles did nothing for me. All I could think about was Maddie in the changing room waiting for me.

"Awesome, will you excuse me please, Brittany?" I gave her a quick, regretful smile. "I hear my friend calling me."

"Oh, okay." She looked at me in disappointment and walked away quickly. I felt bad for letting her down, but I didn't have time to worry about her as I noticed that the salesgirl was no longer standing by the changing rooms. I hurried over and knocked on Maddie's door, and she opened it quickly, motioning me to come in.

"Where were you?" she whispered up at me with wide eyes.

"Sorry, I got caught up." My mouth went dry as I stared at her. She was standing there in a black lace bra and some black lacy panties. I could see her nipples through her bra, and before I knew what I was doing, I pushed her back against the mirror and ran my fingers across her breasts, squeezing gently.

"Oh my God," she breathed against my mouth as my lips sought hers. Her hands lifted up my T-shirt and she pulled it up over my head and threw it on the ground along with her clothes. Her fingernails traced the lines of my pecs and she bent her head and lightly bit down on my shoulder. I grabbed her ass and lifted her up against the mirror and she wrapped her legs around my waist. I bent my head and kissed down her neck, sucking hard as if I were a vampire, trying to draw blood. Her scent surrounded me, and she moaned against me as I kissed further down and took her breast in my mouth. I slid my hand in between her thighs and slipped a finger into her panties, groaning as I felt how wet she was.

"You're so ready for me, baby."

"So are you," she whimpered against my lips and moved her hips up and down so that she was grinding against my erection.

"Fuck, Maddie. You're going to make me come if you keep

154

doing that." I pushed her against the wall harder and she slipped a hand to my jeans so she could unzip my pants. She reached into my boxer shorts and pulled out my erection, and her hands felt cool against my hardness.

"You're so hard already," she gasped, and I laughed.

"I've been hard ever since you told me you were taking me to the mall so you could fuck me."

"That's not exactly what I said." She giggled, and I pressed my lips against her mouth to shut her up. I pulled her panties to the side, and we both paused as we heard the sound of the fine lace ripping at my rough touch.

"Oops." I laughed. "I guess we'll have to buy them."

"Or not." She grinned and winked at me. "You're a Martelli, you don't have to buy anything."

"Shhh." I bit her lower lip and positioned my erection against her slick opening. I rubbed the tip against her ever so slightly, and I felt her body shudder against me and the wall. I ran it up and down without entering her, loving the feel of her wetness against me.

"Oh, Logan, please," she moaned, and I moved my hands up to slip her breasts out of her bra. I bent my head down and sucked on her right breast as she played with my hair and whimpered against me. She gyrated against me, trying to get me to slip inside of her, but I let my erection rub against her slickness without entering her.

"Logan, please," she moaned in my ear louder this time as she wrapped her arms around my waist and placed her hands on my butt, bringing me in closer to her.

"Do you need any help in there, ma'am?" I heard Brittany's voice at the door after her slight knock, and Maddie froze, with her eyes wide with shock.

"Oh, shit," she mouthed.

"Are you okay, ma'am?" Brittany asked again.

"Yeah, I'm fi…" Maddie bit down on my shoulder as I slowly entered her while she was talking to Brittany.

"Sorry, what did you say?" Brittany raised her voice. "What did you need me to replace?"

"Nothing, ahhhh," Maddie groaned as I pressed her up against the wall and increased the pace of my movements. "I'm fine," she gasped out finally, and glared at me as I continued to move, in and out of her. I alternated my pace from fast to slow and watched her face as she came to a climax. The way she bit her lips, and looked at me wildly was turning me on, even more than being in the changing room. I grabbed her butt and pushed her onto me, so that the length of my erection was going deeper and deeper into her. I held onto her tightly to keep her from falling, and myself from losing absolute control as she brought me to new heights of lust and excitement.

"If you're sure." Brittany's voice sounded hesitant and I knew she had to be slightly suspicious of what was going on. "I'll be right here. If you need me, just holler."

"Okay," Maddie squeaked out and I stifled a laugh. Her eyes flashed at me and she gave me a naughty grin before my mouth came crushing down on hers. The sweetness of her eager lips beneath mine, combined with the sudden thrust of her hips meeting my powerful drive, took me to the edge and I cried out as I burst into her. It seemed as if Maddie had been waiting on me to come because all of a sudden she cried out and I felt her body trembling against mine as she convulsed against me. She bit down on my shoulder again and her fingernails dug into my back while I continued thrusting into her as she came. All of a sudden she went still, and she lay her head on me. I kissed her cheek and she looked up at me lazily.

"That was amazing," she whispered with a smile. "It's never felt like that before."

"So alive and tingly?" I smiled back at her, delighted to hear that I had brought her new throes of passion.

"Every nerve ending in my body enjoyed that moment." She

grinned at me shyly and ran her fingers down my chest, as she unwrapped her legs from my waist and slid back to the ground. "I can see why you enjoy having sex in public, the hint of danger and being caught really adds to it." She giggled. "And if you tell anyone I said that, I will kill you."

"I'll just tell my brothers, no one else." I laughed as she punched me and I leaned over to kiss her again. "Of course, I would never tell anyone."

"Good." She took the bra and panties off and I stared at her in lust, feeling myself grow hard again. "Don't even think about it, big boy." She laughed as I pushed myself against her. "There is no way that salesgirl will believe it takes this long to try on a few bras."

"Then why are you trying to tempt me?" My eyes were transfixed on her hands as she pulled on her panties and bra. I couldn't look away from her beautiful body. I was addicted to her touch and to her taste, and even though I had just had her, I wanted her again.

"I don't think they'd like it if I walked out in their stuff." She laughed. "I'd hate to steal a car but get busted for shoplifting a twenty-dollar pair of panties."

"Twenty what?" My eyes widened. "That much?"

"Ha, ha, I was actually saying the amount was small in comparison to a car," she giggled. "Though I'm not sure what I'm going to do with these now, seeing as you ripped them."

"I'll buy them for you." I held my hand out. "And I'll keep them as a keepsake."

"A keepsake of what?" She was grinning at me, and I could tell she was happy to see I had a sentimental side.

"A keepsake of my first time having public sex." I grinned.

"You mean *our* first time," she corrected me and shook her head.

"Actually, no. I mean my first time and our first time." I laughed and she looked confused. "So when I told you I liked public sex, I didn't mean I had actually done it." I grinned as her confused expression turned to one of shock and understanding. "I mean I've always wanted to. It's always been something on my to-do list."

"Oh my God, Logan. I'm going to kill you." She glared at me and I pulled her close to me.

"I'm glad my first time was with you." I stared down into her frazzled eyes and then kissed her nose. "I hope my second time will be with you as well."

"I don't know about that." She shook her head, but I could see the hint of a smile on her face. She had on all her clothes now and she turned around and gave me a small devilish smile. "I'm leaving the changing room now, see you outside." And before I had time to respond, she had left the room. I stood there shaking my head and paused as I heard Brittany talking to her.

"Did you see anything you liked, ma'am?"

"I'm still deciding, thanks." Maddie's voice was filled with laughter. "But you never know, maybe someone will surprise me and buy me a pair of panties and a bra."

"Sorry, what?" Brittany's voice sounded confused and I held back a laugh, as I picked up the bra Maddie had left hanging next to me. I looked at the price tag and saw it was sixty dollars. My head pounded as I realized I would have to spend eighty dollars to buy the bra and panties for Maddie. Plus tax. And I only had five hundred dollars and some loose change. And no prospect of making money anytime soon either. I stared at my reflection and wanted to punch the mirror. Who was I kidding? I was never going to be good enough for Maddie. I was still Logan Martelli, no matter how many fun afternoons we had or how passionate the sex was. I was never going to be good enough for her. And it didn't even matter that her dad was fucked up. I wanted better for Maddie because she was better. She wasn't him and she didn't deserve to pay for his sins. I'd figure out a way to get him without involving her. Maddie was special; she was my Maddie. And I was starting to think that I was falling in love with her. My breath caught as I realized the gravity of my thoughts. The emotions welling up in my heart were unfamiliar and I was scared. In less than a month, Maddie had come into my life and turned it upside down and I wasn't even sure who I was anymore. The even scarier part was that I no longer knew who I wanted to be, either.

Chapter 9

Logan

"You shouldn't have bought me both the bra and the panties." Maddie frowned at me as we waited on the bus.

"I wanted to buy you a present." I ran my hand through my hair and gave her a quick smile. "And I knew I had to keep the panties, so I wanted you to have the bra."

"Logan, you shouldn't have spent your money on me."

"It's okay." I tried not to think of how much my family needed that money. I didn't want Maddie to think that I was a loser, someone who couldn't even afford to buy her a small gift. I laughed at the irony of the whole situation—who ever heard of a broke thief?

"I had a good day today." She changed the subject and slid down closer to me. "I'm glad I came over."

"I'm sorry we left the plate of cookies in the car."

"Ha, ha, ha. I don't care."

"It was nice of you to bring them over."

"I wanted to see you." She grinned sheepishly. "I told myself I would try one last time, and if you still hated me, I would just forget about it."

"I never hated you." I shook my head, staring at her in disbelief. "You can't have thought that? I haven't stopped thinking about you since the first time I saw you."

"When I jumped into your car?"

"No," I laughed. "When you were running away from the cops."

"Really?" She looked surprised, but her eyes lit up.

"Yes, really." I grabbed her hand and held it in mine and we sat in silence waiting for the bus to come. There were so many things I wanted to tell her, but I just didn't have the words. My heart wanted to tell her about my newly discovered feelings, but my head knew that was foolish. This was nothing more than a summer romance, and it would just hurt both of us if I were to pretend otherwise.

"Here's the bus." Maddie stood up and we walked to the curb.

"I'm sorry you have to ride the bus with me."

"Hey, I'm not a princess, I'll live."

"Your dad would be pissed if he knew you were on the bus though, I bet."

"My dad can be a snob at times." She rolled her eyes. "It's fine. Like I said, I'm not a princess, no one is looking to kidnap me or do anything bad to me."

"I guess he's just worried about his little girl." I could have laughed at the fact that I was sticking up for the mayor. Today really was a day of firsts.

"Yeah, I guess." She shrugged. "I'm used to it."

"Yes, I suppose you are." I paid for our bus tickets and then we found a seat towards the back of the bus. I let her have the window because I noticed a few guys looking at her a bit too closely, and I didn't want them trying to cop a feel as they walked past us.

"So tell me more about Vincent and Jared." Maddie gazed up at me longingly.

"Why are you so interested in them?"

"I don't know. I like hearing about people's siblings. I guess it comes from being an only child. And I want to get to know you better."

"Okay." I leaned back and Maddie rested her head on my shoulder. I could tell she was tired because her eyes were drooping as I played with her long hair with my fingers. "I'll tell you a story from when we were kids, and you can relax."

"I'd like that." She smiled up at me sleepily and lovingly, and my heart melted for a moment as I realized that I had her heart and her trust completely.

"So you know my mom died of cancer. It was pretty quick and swift. Within a few weeks of her being diagnosed, she was gone." My breath caught and Maddie looked up at me with saddened eyes. "We were all pretty young, but we all knew that she was dying, and we were all devastated, but we didn't really talk about it. Around that time was when my dad made the turn to complete alcoholism. Please don't be sad for me." I frowned down at her, not wanting her sympathy. "His drinking had already been a problem, along with his gambling and paranoia, but we had all hoped it would get better. And me and the guys hadn't realized just how bad it was. Only my mom really knew, and there wasn't really much she could do about it. She loved my father, and she was his world, but he was so bitter and angry over things that had happened to him, that he never really got over it. He instilled that bitterness in me and Jared, but for some reason, Vincent never became as jaded as the two of us."

"Do you know why?" Maddie questioned me softly, and this time I noticed her eyes were completely alert.

"He was always a bit softer and a bit more sensitive than Jared and me." I laughed. "And I don't mean he's gay, though I wouldn't care if he was."

"Well, that's good to hear." She smiled briefly. I laughed.

"Yeah, so anyway Vinny, well, he's always looked at things on the more positive side. When Dad told us stuff, me and Jared got mad and wanted to get even. With Vinny, it was different; he wanted to think of solutions and ways to fix the problem." I could see that Maddie wanted to ask me what stuff my dad used to talk about, but I wasn't willing to go down that road with her yet. I didn't want her to know how evil her dad was. I had a feeling it would break her heart and I didn't want to be the one to do that to her. "Anyway, that's why he wants to become a lawyer."

162

"He wants to become a lawyer?" She looked surprised.

I nodded. "He thinks that if he can become a part of the system, he can advocate for those who have been let down by it."

"He wants to be a defense attorney?"

"No, though we tease him about that all the time. He wants to become a constitutional lawyer. He wants to take on cases that will help shape the way we construe the laws of the land."

"Wow." Her eyes widened. "That's pretty big."

"Yeah." I smiled down at her. "I tell him that one day, he'll become a Supreme Court Judge, and then for sure everyone in the country will know the Martelli name."

"Logan Martelli, car thief and brother to Supreme Court Justice." Maddie grinned. "It does have a certain ring to it."

"Yeah, it does." I felt sad for a moment as we spoke, and the reality of everything hit me once again. It all seemed like such a pipe dream. If something didn't change soon, there was no way Vincent would even get his AA degree, let alone make it to law school. I sighed as I remembered my mother's last words to me. "You can change your destiny, Logan. You must take care of Vincent, Jared, and your dad. You have to be there for them, Logan. Promise me that you'll be the man I know you are."

I'd nodded and cried, but her words had always stuck with me. My life was dedicated to making sure that Vincent and Jared weren't trapped in the same life I was. And that was why I had never left River Valley or left my dad to fend for himself. Even though some days all I wanted to do was run away and start a new life.

"You okay, Logan?" Maddie caressed my face. "You look deep in thought."

"Yeah, I'm fine." I grabbed her knee and squeezed. "So anyway, before my mom died, Vincent came up with this idea that we should perform a skit for my mom."

"A skit?"

"Yeah." I rolled my eyes. "Have you ever seen *The Sound of Music*?"

"The movie?"

"Yeah," I nodded. "Do you remember the lonely goatherd scene?"

"Hmm?"

"High on a hill was a lonely…" I started singing, and Maddie burst out laughing.

"I do remember that."

"So we performed that song for my mom in the hospital," I groaned.

"With puppets?"

"No." I laughed. "With GI Joes, and socks, and pieces of string."

"Wow, I would have loved to have seen that."

"It was pretty funny. None of us really knew the song, but it was one of my mom's favorite movies, so we tried." I laughed as I remembered her huge smile as she watched us messing up the song and dancing around her hospital room. "And then Jared decided that we should do the can-can, and we flung our legs up and down like a bunch of Vegas showgirls."

"While singing the lonely goatherd song."

"Oh, no, we had moved on to *do re mi* by that point."

"Oh, wow," she giggled. "I would have paid good money to have seen that."

"I'm sure you would have." I shook my head in mock

164

embarrassment and shuddered. "Holy hell, we must have been a sight to have seen."

"I bet your mom loved it, though."

"Yes, yes she did." I looked out the window and pictured my mother's face. "That's the only reason the nurses let us continue. My mom was overjoyed to see us all together singing and dancing. I think at that moment, she realized that we were three brothers who would let nothing part us. She was able to die knowing that while she was leaving us, we would always have each other and we would always be there for each other."

"You really love your brothers, don't you?"

"I'd die for them." I stared into her eyes earnestly. "I would do anything for them. They are everything to me, and my goal in life is to see them succeed."

"That's a pretty important goal."

"It's one I've dedicated my whole life to," I said seriously.

"At the cost of your own?"

"I don't know." I turned away from her, upset at myself for my answer. I was upset because things had changed now. I knew she would want to be my world if we became serious, but I knew that I could not give her that promise until I knew Vincent and Jared had their lives in order. I was mad at myself for wishing that it could be different, and that I could put myself and Maddie first.

***

"I had a nice day." Maddie leaned up and kissed me as we stood next to her car door. It was close to ten p.m. and we were finally back at my house and her car.

"So did I." I combed her hair away from her face. "I had a really nice day."

"Though I wish we had Bonnie and Clyde'd it for a week or so." She smiled wistfully. "That would have been awesome."

"Not so awesome if you didn't have your birth control," I joked lightly, not wanting to know how big a part that small fact would have played in our trip.

"Oh, yeah, oops." She slapped her hand against her mouth. "I totally forgot about that, I'm such a ditz."

"Good thing I remembered."

"You're my hero." She kissed me again.

"I wouldn't say that exactly." I shook my head, feeling uncomfortable at her words. I already felt ashamed of myself for even thinking about going along with Jared's plan.

"Logan Martelli, you never let me say anything good about you."

"When there is something good to say, I will let you."

"I hate that you don't see how great you are." Maddie looked sad. "Forget the fact that you're a car thief, which isn't really all that bad. You're a good person."

"A car thief isn't as bad as a murderer maybe, but it's still bad, Maddie. I could go to jail. It's not like I'm borrowing flowers from the park or something."

"You don't have to be a car thief." She pursed her lips. "I'm not going to say it again after this, but my dad could ..."

My blood boiled as she mentioned her father again. It was getting harder and harder for me to listen to her go on about her dad being this great guy, especially when she talked about him helping me. All it did was add salt to the wound. And I sure didn't want to start thinking about how much I hated her father right now.

"Let's not talk about it tonight." I kissed her hard. "Don't you

166

worry your sweet head about anything."

"Logan, no man is an island."

"And no woman can fix a man. I am who I am."

"Do you want to come over tonight?" She looked at me hopefully. I shook my head. "Can I stay over?" I froze at her words; there was no way I wanted her to come inside of my house. I was embarrassed at how shitty the house looked inside, and I was scared for her to meet my father, and I didn't really want her around Jared, either. There were just so many things that could go wrong if she came inside. "I guess your silence is a no." She pulled away from me. "Fine, call me when you want to see me."

"Don't be like that, Maddie." I grabbed her shoulder and she shook my hand off.

"Whatever, I'm going home." She yawned. "I'm tired, I need to go to bed."

"I wish I could be in that bed with you," I said softly and gave her a half-smile. She looked at me dismissively and got into her car.

"I'll see you whenever." She closed the door and started the engine with me standing there, staring with my mouth slightly agape. I wasn't used to Maddie treating me like this. I knocked on the window and she rolled it down slowly.

"Thanks for spending the day with me." I leaned in to kiss her cheek, and she turned to me with eyes flashing.

"I'm mad at you, Logan Martelli."

"I don't know what I …"

"Oh, shut up, of course you know why I'm mad. You don't trust me. You won't tell me why you hate my dad, you won't let my dad help you, even though I can tell you don't love being a thief, and it doesn't seem to be paying you that well. You won't let me meet your brothers. Maybe you're ashamed to be dating me? Or maybe you don't want to bring me into your small microcosm because you don't really like me that much. Maybe you just like having kinky sex with me, but you don't really want to date-me date me."

"That's not true, Maddie," I sighed as she glared at me.

"Well, why don't you think about it and decide what you want to do. Because this limbo isn't going to work for me."

"Wait, what?" I frowned, confused. Why was it getting so difficult already?

"I'll be seeing you, Logan." She reversed out of the driveway and I watched as she pulled into the street and left. My heart was pounding and I realized that I didn't have her phone number. Shit! I rolled my eyes as I walked into the house, I would just have to wait for Maddie to contact me. She'd likely call me in a few days anyway, once she realized that I didn't have her phone number. She couldn't stay away from me. I laughed as I opened the door and walked past the living room without thinking about my dad. I was about to walk up the stairs when I heard footsteps behind me.

"Whoa, Logan. What are you doing?" Jared slapped my shoulder and his eyes were burning into mine. "I thought you weren't coming home tonight? What happened with Maddison?"

"I changed my mind, and Maddie went home."

"What? You let her go home? Fuck it." He shook his head. "Tell me what happened, man. What's the plan?"

"There is no plan, Jared," I answered him wearily.

"What?" His eyes narrowed. "I know you're not going to let this opportunity go."

"There is no opportunity, Jared," I hissed at him angrily. "Maddie has nothing to do with this."

"Dad had a fit tonight." Jared placed his hand on the wall. "He hit Vincent."

"What?" My heart started pounding. "Why?"

"He told him to get some beer. There is no beer, and we have no money."

"Fuck, is he okay?"

"He's fine. He didn't even hit Dad back." Jared's face looked violent. "If he ever tries that shit with me, I'll punch him the fuck out. I don't give a shit."

"Where's Vinny?" I sighed, worried.

"In the kitchen. We've been talking about you." He looked down. "We're kinda hungry." His voice was low and his heated animation was gone.

"Why didn't you buy any food?" I frowned as we walked to the kitchen.

"I gave you all my money."

"What?" I bit my lip.

"I gave you all the money I won on the races, and Vinny threw in his last hundred as well. We knew you didn't have the rent money."

"How did you know?" I was mad at myself for not having hid it better.

"We just knew." Jared looked at me with concern in his eyes. "We're worried about you, bro."

"Why … oh, shit." I walked into the kitchen and saw Vincent's black eye. "You okay?" I stopped short of running up to him and checking it.

"I'm fine. He can still sock a man hard." Vincent made a joke, and I half-smiled back at him. My blood was boiling as I stared at my brother, and all I wanted to do was go into the living room and shout at my father.

"We need to talk, guys." Jared's voice was loud, and I turned to look at him. He looked like a man. I realized that his boyish charm was gone and he was now a hardened man. I felt disappointment seep through my body. I had failed my mother. Everything was shit. I had done nothing to improve our situation.

"What's up?" I frowned at him. I wasn't happy that he was now trying to take control of family situations.

"I want everyone to know that I can't live like this anymore." Jared looked at Vinny and me with a hard look in his eyes. "This is shit. Dad is a fucking drunk who thinks he can say and do what he wants, and we never have enough money for anything. We can't get jobs in this godforsaken town and Logan won't even make the man responsible for it pay. This is a joke." He shook his head and looked at me. "I love you, man, and I know you're trying, and I know you made a promise to Mom to look after us, but you need some help."

I stared at him silently, not sure what to say. I was upset that I hadn't been able to fulfill my mom's last wishes. She had trusted and believed in me and I was failing her. I looked over at Vincent to see what he had to say. He looked at me sadly and nodded slightly before speaking.

"We need to do something big." He stared down at the textbook in front of him. "And I don't mean calculus big, either."

"What are you guys thinking?" I asked pointedly. I knew better than to just assume they were just thinking about this for the first time. They had probably been plotting for a long time.

"Jared has an idea." Vincent nodded towards his brother, and I looked over to Jared, who was staring at me with a defensive look.

"Don't shoot me down right away." His eyes bore into mine. "Listen before you say no."

"Why do I feel like I already want to say no?" I groaned.

"I was hanging out with Joey, and he …"

"NO." My face turned red as I shouted. "Hell NO."

"Logan," Jared sighed. "Just listen."

"Joey is bad news."

"Let him talk, Logan," Vincent spoke up. "I don't particularly care for Joey either, but this sounds like a pretty good idea."

I glared at Vincent for being a traitor and then looked back at Jared. "Go on, then."

"There's some guy in town who has a Bugatti," Jared talked quickly. "A two-million-dollar Bugatti, and he's going out of town in a few weeks."

"So?" I shook my head annoyed. "You know we don't steal big money cars, we have no way to sell them."

"Here's the deal." Jared leaned forward excitedly. "Joey has a buyer, he knows someone who is interested in buying it. A million dollars in cash."

"But it's worth two million." I stared at my brother, starting to feel slightly excited.

"It's all cash and a done deal." He grinned at me. "This is the answer to our problems! One million dollars in cash. Can you even count that high, smarty-pants?"

"There's only one problem." Vincent ran his hands through his hair. "The car is in a garage and a keylock won't work."

"I can get in any car." I shrugged, thinking how I would break into a Bugatti. "But if it's in a garage, it's a no-go."

"All we have to do is break in to the garage as well." Jared looked annoyed. "I'm sure it can't be that hard."

"We don't break into houses." My voice was firm. "You know that, guys."

"It's not a house, it's the garage."

"The garage is part of the house." I shook my head and my voice was resolute.

"Maybe we have to start playing by some different rules." Jared turned away from me and looked at Vincent. "Who's ever heard of thieves with an honor code? And who only takes Japanese imports? Give me a fucking break, it's not doing anything to help us."

"Jared, this isn't the road we want to go down." My voice was soft as I walked up to him. "I don't want you guys involved in this shit. Let me think of something," I pleaded with him, hoping he would realize what a big deal it would be for us to break into a garage. Theft was a slippery slope, and I was scared that if we did this, they would think that it was okay to break into houses or even into stores. And that was when people started getting hurt. That was when knives and guns came out. I was scared and panicked. I didn't want anything to escalate. And I knew I was running out of time.

"Logan, listen to me." Jared turned around and looked at me with wild, passionate eyes. "I get it, I really do. I know you have always looked out for me and Vinny. I know that you don't want us involved in this life. And I understand. Bro, we both understand, but you gotta admit, it's not going so well for us. This is one deal. We steal this one car, and we're set. We don't have to steal anymore. Not one single car unless we want to. And we can move. We will finally have enough money to send Dad to rehab, pay for college for all three of us, and we can get the shit out of River Valley." He grabbed my shoulder and stared at me for a few seconds. "This town is toxic to us, bro. It's time we finally packed up and left."

"What do you think?" I looked at Vincent to get his opinion. Jared had a point. A million dollars was a lot of money. I'd be able to go clean, and I'd be able to ensure we all stayed clean. We could get help for Dad and move and maybe buy a small place so we didn't have to worry about rent. And then maybe I could find a real job somewhere, start to lead a somewhat normal life. I could be someone Maddie could count on. I could take her out on a nice date and do things with her that normal couples did.

"I think it's a good idea, Logan." Vincent looked at me seriously.

172

"We'd have to study up on how to get into a Bugatti and how to break into a garage, but I think we can do it."

"We would also have to figure out the mechanics of the ignition." My voice was firm. "We can't expect to just find a spare key, and something tells me that fiddling with a few wires is not going to do what we want."

"Joey has someone who can teach us," Jared interrupted me eagerly. "If we want to, of course."

"I just don't know," I sighed. The idea itself was attractive, but knowing Joey was involved made me very hesitant to get involved. I just didn't trust him. "You guys know how I feel about Joey. This just doesn't seem like the sort of thing we should get involved with."

"Joey is fine," Jared sighed. "Come on, Logan."

"What does he get out of it anyway?" I shook my head. "Why is he brokering this deal?"

"He gets a hundred grand," Jared mumbled. "But it doesn't come from our million. The guy buying the car will pay him."

"But we don't know who's buying the car?" I cleared my throat. A knot was beginning to form in my stomach. There were too many unknowns and I was starting to get a bad feeling about everything.

"Just trust me please, Logan. I trust Joey. I think it's going to be fine. We need this, bro."

"What do you think?" I looked at Vincent again.

He nodded slowly. "I think we should do it." His eyes looked calm and serious. "I say we do this deal and we walk away from the car theft business forever and never look back."

"Okay." I nodded and sat down. "Let's do it." I ignored the qualms and fears I had over getting involved in a deal like this. Jared was right, playing it safe and doing small deals wasn't helping the situation. We needed something big to happen, and we needed to get out of this lifestyle. I didn't want to be the guy who wasn't good enough anymore. I wanted to make a future for myself.

"For real?" Jared grinned at me.

"Yes," I sighed. "I hope this isn't going to be a big mistake."

"Trust me, bro. This is the best decision you've ever made. We're going to be set from here on out."

"I sure hope so."

"I think it is going to change our lives, right, Vincent?"

"I don't know." Vincent frowned. "There are some things I don't want to change."

"What?" Jared looked at him like he was crazy. "Are you fucking joking?"

"No." Vincent's voice was soft. "I hate that we're poor and that we worry so much, but we have each other. We've always had each other. We've always been close. I just don't want money to come between us. I don't want everything to change."

"Dude, it's one million dollars, not a billion." Jared burst out laughing. "We'll be set for now, but not forever."

"I don't want the money to come between us."

"It won't." Jared shook his head. "We just have to decide how we'll spend it."

"How do we decide?"

"Hey, guys," I interrupted them. "I agree with, Vincent. We can't let this money divide us. We all have to be on the same page as to how we are going to split it and spend it."

"I figure you can be in charge of the money." Jared's tone changed. "You're the eldest, you've always had our back. I trust you. Right, Vincent?"

"Yeah, that sounds like a plan. You'll be in charge of the money, Logan."

"Are you guys sure?"

"Duh." Jared grinned and sat down next to me. Vincent sat down as well, and we all just looked at each other for a few moments. This was the biggest decision of our lives and I think we all realized just how much our lives would change based upon this decision. We had all talked about the positive change, if everything went well. But I knew we all realized that maybe everything wouldn't go as planned. Maybe it would all go horribly wrong. Maybe one of us would get caught. Or all of us.

"We need to talk worst-case scenario." I pursed my lips and looked at them, feeling overwhelmed with emotion. These were my two baby brothers, and as I stared at them, the feeling of love washed over me, and I couldn't believe just how much they meant to me. "I don't want both of you in this with me."

"What are you talking about?" Jared frowned. "You can't do this alone."

"Jared's right. It's all of us or none of us." Vincent's voice was firm. "You don't have to risk your life for us anymore, Logan."

"What are you talking about?"

"We know everything you've done for us." Vincent leaned towards me. "And we appreciate it. We've been selfish. It's not fair to you. If we do this, it's all of us. I won't accept it any other way."

"You won't accept it?" I raised an eyebrow at him. I had never seen Vincent speak up like that before.

"I won't accept it." He grinned. "I'm second oldest and I'm usurping your command."

"Really?"

"Really! So deal with it."

"Okay, but we have to decide our roles."

"Joey said we should start the training right away. We don't have much time."

"I really wish Joey wasn't involved with this," I groaned. "I know you guys think I'm overreacting, but he's bad news."

"We don't have to deal with him after this." Vincent made a face towards Jared and he shrugged.

"Joey's cool, man, but, if it means that much to you, I won't hang out with him as much after this."

"What about Lucy?" Vincent laughed and gave Jared a teasing smile, and I looked over at Jared in surprise.

"You dating Lucy?"

"What? No, no, of course not." Jared made a face and turned away from me, so I didn't push the issue. There was no way I wanted him dating Lucy. That would make it that much harder to get Joey out of our lives. And if there was one thing I wanted by the end of everything, it was for Joey to be a distant memory.

"Fine, tell Joey that we will start the training as soon as his friend is ready. Also, I have a favor to ask you guys."

"Uh huh?" Jared and Vincent looked at me curiously.

"We need to clean this place up."

"Huh?" Jared made a face.

"We need to tidy up this house." I took a deep breath. "I want to invite someone over."

"What?" Jared's jaw fell open.

"I said we need to tidy up. This place is a mess."

"Uhm, I heard that part. I'm talking about the inviting someone over part."

"What about it?"

"You've never invited anyone over. None of us have."

"Well, I am wanting to invite someone over now."

"Who?" Jared stared at me through narrow eyes.

"Maddie."

"What the fuck?" Jared's face grew red.

Vincent looked at me in confusion. "Who's Maddie?"

"He's talking about, Maddison Wright, the mayor's daughter."

"The mayor's daughter?" Vincent's eyes grew wide. "What?"

"Exactly." Jared turned towards me again. "What are you thinking, Logan? What is Dad going to say if you bring her over here?"

"I don't care what he has to say." My voice was serious and I stood up. "She wants to get to know you both, and I think it's a good idea."

"What the fuck?" Jared exclaimed again and gave me a crazy look. "Are you fucking kidding me? Not only are you not getting her father back, but you're dating her?"

"She isn't responsible for what her father did." I spoke slowly, understanding why he was upset but wanting him to understand why I liked her.

"We're not responsible for what happened to our father, but we still got screwed. Is this a fucking joke? You're going to date the fucking mayor's daughter. The man who basically ruined our lives. He fucking turned Dad into an alcoholic and he killed our mother. And we can't even afford to pay the fucking rent. Do you hear me, Logan? He fucked up our lives and now … now you have the opportunity to exact revenge on him for all this shit, and you decide to date his daughter. And no, not to get the best revenge ever. But because you like her."

"I never said I liked her."

"So you just want her to come over because …?" Jared rolled his eyes. "And why do we need to get to know her? This sounds like a bad idea."

"She's not like her dad."

"How do you know?" Jared jumped up as well. "You barely know her. Dude, she was obsessed with you as a teenager and now she is having a summer of fun with you. Do you really think this could become something serious?"

"Stop it, Jared." Vincent raised his voice.

"You are not taking his side." Jared shook his head in disgust.

"I'm not taking anyone's side. I'm just saying stop it." Vincent ran his hands through his hair and looked thoughtful. "We need to support Logan. I'm sure he knows what he's doing."

"Thanks." I gave him a grateful smile and swallowed hard. I looked away and my brain felt like it was about to explode. The problem was I really didn't know what I was doing. I felt like I was spinning out of control. Everything just felt crazy, and it was all changing so fast. An image of Maddie's sweet smile flashed in my mind, and I felt my insides melt as I thought about her. I wasn't even sure when I had decided that she should meet Vincent and get to know Jared better. But I knew that I needed to give her something to show that I was serious about trying to create something special between us. I wasn't even really sure what we could create. How could her family ever accept me? How could I ever explain to my father that I was dating the daughter of the man who betrayed him? And what if all along the story my father had told wasn't exactly true? Why hadn't he told me that Mom had dated the mayor first? He had always said that the mayor had tried to date her but she had chosen Dad and been happy with him. Had she really dated the mayor first? Had Dad stolen her from him? And had that been why the mayor had set him up? Had it been some sort of sick revenge that had gone out of control? All of a sudden, I felt overwhelmed and dizzy. Too many things were coming up that didn't make sense or fit in with the life I had made for myself.

"Look, guys, I know how hard this must be for you. And Jared, I know you hoped that I would use Maddie's liking me to exact some sort of revenge on her father for what he did to Dad, but that's not going to happen. I am not going to do anything to her. I like her a lot, and she's a good person. And I want you both to get to know her. I want you both to see the woman that I see. Please give her a chance."

"Fuck giving her a chance." Jared turned away from me. "If I have to take matters into my own hands, I will."

"Leave her alone, Jared." My voice held a warning tone.

"Or what?" Jared scoffed. "What will you do?"

"You don't want to know." I grabbed his arm and looked down into his face. "Do not do anything to her or I will fuck you up."

"Ha, she's already got you threatening me. She sounds like a great catch. Not like her dad at all." Jared pushed me away.

"Guys." Vincent jumped up and stood between us. "Come on. We can't afford to get upset with each other right now. Not when we are about to do the biggest job of our lives."

"Whatever." Jared glared at me. "I can separate the two. I just didn't expect for Logan to betray us like this."

"Stop being so overdramatic, Jared." I glared back at him. "Fucking give Maddie a chance. Do you really think I haven't thought this through? Do you really think I would risk everything if she wasn't someone special?"

"Who knows?" He shrugged. "She's pretty, maybe she gave it up and she got you hooked."

"Shut the fuck up." I swung out to hit him and Vincent grabbed my fist.

"Come on, guys."

"You're not going to talk about her like that and not expect me to thump your sorry ass." I glared at Jared and he looked at me contemplatively.

"You're lucky you're my brother." He shook his head. "I would have fucked you up so badly."

"Really? You would have fucked me up?" I scoffed back at him.

"Yeah, I would have fucked you up." He laughed, and I laughed as well, as the tension in the room drifted away slightly.

"So, we all down to clean?"

"I guess." Vincent groaned. "When is she coming over?"

"I don't know yet." I looked at them with an embarrassed smile. "We kind of had an argument when she left, so I'm going to let her cool down and when she calls me I'll invite her over."

"It's already rocky, and you want us to meet her?" Jared shook his head in amazement. "This is going to be so ironic if she breaks your heart."

"Jared." Vincent looked at him in admonishment.

"Let's be real, it would be kind of crazy if she ends up breaking his heart. Talk about some sort of fucking poetic justice, right?" Jared gave me a rueful smile. "I mean, I hope it doesn't happen, but I just honestly can't see this going well."

"Let me worry about that." I stretched. "Anyways, I gotta go to bed. Talk to Joey, and let me know what's going on. We can start the cleaning in the morning."

"And can we get some food?" Vincent's voice was soft, and I nearly cursed myself. I had already forgotten we didn't have any food.

"Look, here's $400." I put the cash on the table. "It's all we got for the car, don't ask. We need to make it last."

"Soon we'll have the table filled with cash." Jared grinned and I smiled weakly, trying to ignore the gnawing feeling in my stomach.

"Yeah." I nodded. "Night, guys."

"Night, bro." Vincent sat back down and opened up his textbook. I looked over to Jared, who was staring at me with a slightly apologetic expression in his eyes.

"Night, Logan." He offered me a peace smile and I walked back to him and gave him a quick hug.

"I know you got my back bro, it's okay," I whispered into his ear before walking out of the room. I tried to hurry past the living room, but I wasn't fast enough.

"Logan, is that you?" my dad called out to me, and I opened the door and peered up.

"What's up, Dad?" I stood at the door and avoided eye contact with him. I didn't want to look into his vacant bloodshot eyes tonight. I didn't want to talk about Mom or hear stories about his life. Or be shouted at or questioned. I just couldn't deal with it.

"I was just watching this movie, and the actress, she looked like your mom."

"Yeah?" I nodded and looked at the TV screen. He was watching some old movie on AMC.

"She had long blonde hair like your mom, though she wasn't as beautiful."

"Okay."

"Your mom was the most beautiful woman in the world." His voice cracked and I finally looked over at him. He was lying down on the couch and there were tears streaming out of his eyes.

"She was beautiful."

"Why did she have to die?" He looked up at me with a pained expression. "She promised me we would grow old together. She promised me she would stand with me through thick and thin, good and bad. But she lied."

"She didn't lie, Dad." I ran my hands through my hair. "She died."

"It was my fault." He sat up, and reached to grab an empty beer can from the pile of cans at his feet.

"It wasn't your fault." I sighed. "She had cancer."

"Have you ever been in love, son?" He looked at me searchingly.

"No."

"When you're in love, that person becomes a part of you. What happens to them, happens to you, and you do everything you can to protect them." He crushed the beer can in his hand. "And I didn't protect her."

"It wasn't your fault, Dad."

"I wasn't the man for her." He shook his head. "Sometimes when you love someone, you have to know when to let go. Sometimes no matter how much you love someone, you have to let go, because even your best person is not the best person for them."

"She loved you, Dad." I tried to comfort him, but my mind immediately went to Maddie. She liked me a lot, and I liked her. I really liked her, more than I was willing to admit. And a part of me wondered if I was just fooling myself. Could any of this ever work? Even if we made the million dollars, I'd still be a Martelli and a thief. And she would be Maddie: beautiful, intelligent, wonderful, caring Maddie. I wasn't sure if I would ever be able to give her the life that she deserved. The life that I wanted for her.

"But where did that get her?"

"It got her three children."

"She wanted to leave me." He threw the crushed can at the TV. "She wanted to leave me and take you boys."

"I know."

"I told her she would have to kill me first." He picked up another can from the ground. "Turns out, it was she who died." He started sobbing. "What did I do, Logan? Where did I go wrong? I sit back and look at my life, and I don't understand. Where did I go wrong? How did this become my life?"

"I don't know." I bit my lip as I stared at him. But in my mind all I could think was, *it was the mayor, the mayor did this to you, Dad*. And a part of me broke all over again. How could we ever get through this?

"She was in love with someone else when she started dating me." It took a few seconds for his words to resonate in my brain, and I froze as I realized what he had just said.

"What do you mean?" I frowned and walked closer to him, so I could look into his face as he spoke.

"She was dating someone else. Someone she was in love with." He laughed. "But I loved her, and I knew she had to be mine."

"What do you mean?" My voice rose. "Who was she dating?"

"It doesn't matter." He frowned as he took me in. "Get me a beer."

"There is no more beer."

"What the fuck do you mean?" His tone changed and his face grew red. "I need a fucking beer, you fucking idiot."

"You need to go to rehab, Dad."

"I don't need to go to fucking rehab. I need a fucking beer."

"Dad." I took a deep breath. "Who was Mom dating when you met her?"

"James." He laughed. "She was fucking dating James. But I got her in the end." He smirked. "Serves his pompous ass right. The rich guy doesn't always win out in the end."

"I thought you dated Mom, and that the mayor just liked her, Dad. What do you mean she was dating James first?"

"It doesn't matter." His eyes looked away from mine. "I need another beer."

"Dad, we need to talk about this."

I watched as he picked up the remote control and started switching the channels. He lay back down on the ratty couch, and I watched as he kicked some potato chip packets onto the floor. I surveyed the room and all the dirt and knew that I needed to make changes in here as well. I could no longer sit by idly, and let my dad wallow in this mess. I couldn't be scared of him anymore.

"Dad, I'm going to clean this room tomorrow."

"Just make sure you get me some beer."

"Dad, we need to talk about—"

"Get me some beer." He reached down and grabbed another beer can from the floor, and this time he threw it at me.

"Night, Dad," I sighed and walked out of the room. There was no point trying to deal with him right now. As I walked up the stairs, I thought about what Maddie had told me and about what my dad had just said about my mom and the mayor. What was going on? The story was changing rapidly, and now I was beginning to question everything.

***

"We're really getting it." Jared grinned at me as we arrived back home after spending the afternoon practicing how to break in to different types of garages. Joey's friend was some guy from Russia or some Eastern European country, and he was one of the biggest criminals in the world. He had stolen a Picasso from some museum and had been trained by some of the best thieves in the world. We were definitely learning a lot, but I still wasn't quite happy with everything that was going on. We didn't know the name of the buyer, we didn't know who Joey's contact was, and the teacher told us to call him Tolstoy, which I was almost certain wasn't his real name. There were so many unanswered questions, and I was starting to worry about everything. It all seemed a bit convenient that Joey would find out about this Bugatti and we would be the ones approached to get trained and to steal it. And the owner would be out of town and we would get one million dollars. But Jared vouched for Joey a hundred percent and I was trying to give him the benefit of the doubt, seeing as he really seemed to be trying with the whole Maddie situation.

Maddie hadn't contacted me and it had been about a week since I had seen her, and I was growing antsy. The house was spic and span and had been for a few days, but it seemed like it had all been for naught as she hadn't called me. I had been planning on surprising her with the invite once she called me, but now I was starting to wonder if she hadn't already given up on me. At first, I had been shocked that it was taking so long. I had assumed that she would be in contact and apologizing to me within a day or so. But then no call had come through, and I realized that she must have been a bit more upset than I thought. But now it had almost been a week and nothing. I had been unable to sleep well, and Maddie was constantly on my mind, and I was irritable.

"Yeah, as long as everything goes according to plan, we'll be fine," I snapped, and I saw Jared and Vincent exchange a glance. I ignored them and ran up the stairs and to my room. I pulled out my phone for what seemed like the hundredth time that day, and saw no missed calls or texts. I called my voicemail to make sure I hadn't missed a call or a voicemail notification. I threw the phone on the bed when I heard I had no new messages.

"What the fuck, Maddie," I muttered under my breath as I fell to the bed. "Where are you?"

I looked up the ceiling and felt my heart sink into the mattress as I wondered if she had finally decided that I wasn't worth it. She was gorgeous; she didn't need to put up with my crap. Maybe she had met a new guy, someone who had a real future, who wasn't a criminal. Someone who could take her out and have a good time, someone her parents would be happy for her to date, someone who would invite her over right away. Maybe she was done with me. I thumped the mattress as I thought about her sweetly kissing someone else. I felt murderous inside. She was my Maddie. I couldn't bear to think about her with anyone else. Not now.

I hadn't admitted it to anyone, not to her and not to myself, but Maddie was fast becoming my world. When I was with her, I felt like a man, like I could do anything. I felt like she saw the person inside me, the person only my brothers knew. She laughed at my jokes, and when we were together, I felt like I could be anyone, do anything, and I wanted .to change. I wanted to be a better man for her. I wanted to climb mountains. I wanted to build ships. I wanted to show her that the man she was falling for was a man that was worthy of her love and affection. Because I had believed her. I had allowed a small part of me to believe in her girlish dreams and jokes. A part of me had pictured Maddie as my wife and as the one I spent the rest of my life with. I would never have admitted it to her, but when she had told me I was the man she was going to marry, a part of me had lit up. I had laughed off her comment, but it had made me feel special and delighted inside. I had begun to hope that perhaps there was a possibility of more in my life. Maybe I wasn't going to be tied down to my lonely existence. Maybe with her I could achieve something I had never allowed myself to believe was possible. I had believed her when she had said she was willing to wait and be patient for me, but she had lied. She had already given up. I grabbed my phone and stared at the screen again, feeling like a foolish schoolboy. The screen displayed the time, and even though I stared at it, willing it to ring, it never did.

"Fuck it." I pressed the numbers I had memorized from looking them up on the computer screen the day before and waited for the phone to ring.

"Hello," a lady answered the phone and my mouth dried as I realized that it must have been her mother.

"Hi, is Maddie available, please?" I spoke slowly, hoping she wouldn't ask who was on the phone.

"Sure, one moment please." I heard her put the phone down. "Maddison, there's a call for you."

"Who is it?" I heard Maddie's voice in the background and my heart skipped a beat.

"A guy, maybe Joey?" her mom answered and I froze, pissed. Why would Joey be calling her?

"Hello." Her voice wasn't its usual vibrant self, and I was immediately worried that something had happened.

"Maddie, it's Logan."

"Logan?" Her voice changed slightly, and I grinned as I realized she was happy to hear from me.

"Yeah, how are you?"

"I'm okay, you?" Her tone changed back to one of nonchalance, but I didn't let it bother me. I had heard the initial happiness in her voice.

"I've been better."

"What's wrong?" Her tone immediately changed to one of concern. "Is everything, okay?"

"You didn't call me."

"I was waiting on you to call me."

"I thought you would call me."

"I'm the girl, Logan. I don't want to be chasing you."

"You weren't chasing me." I shook my head and laughed. "I wasn't running anywhere."

"I didn't want to keep coming after you if you weren't interested."

"What are you talking about?" My jaw dropped. "Why would you think I wasn't interested?"

"Are you joking, Logan Martelli?" Her voice sounded shocked. "You have never come after me; it's always me coming after you."

"I told you that I liked you. That we were dating."

"You also don't want me to get to know your brothers better, and you won't tell me why you hate my dad. You don't call me. I haven't seen you in a week, you never initiate hanging out. You always seem like you're angry with me half the time."

"I'm not angry with you at all."

"Then why are you so mean to me?" Her voice cracked. "A girl can only take so much. I know Jared and Joey said to expect you might not be very nice to me at first because that was your personality, but it's hard."

"I'm sorry, Maddie. I never meant to hurt you. I didn't realize that you were that upset."

"You didn't realize I was upset?" She laughed gently. "Are you joking?"

"I mean, I realized you were being emotional, but you know, I just thought that was your personality." My voice trailed off. I didn't think it was a good idea to tell her that I thought that was just how girls were, up and down all the time.

"Oh, Logan. What am I going to do with you?" She giggled.

"Come over for dinner tonight and hang out with my brothers and me."

"Are you sure?" She gasped. "I don't want you do to something you're not comfortable with."

"I'm sure." I laughed. "I've been waiting to ask you all week."

"So why didn't you?"

188

"Because you haven't called me," I admitted, realizing how weak that sounded now. "I know, I'm a bit of a doofus. I've never really been in a relationship before. I'm a bit of a mess."

"I thought you said you'd had girlfriends before?"

"Well, I mean, I use the term 'girlfriend' loosely." I laughed. "Have I dated girls and had some fun? Yes. Have I been in a real relationship, per se? Maybe not. At least not with someone I like so much."

"You like me." She giggled.

"Don't you like me?" I needed to be reassured that she still cared for me. I wasn't sure why it was so important but I needed for her to tell me. I needed to know that the feelings that were building up were there for both of us.

"Of course I like you, Logan." Her voice was soft and sweet, and all I wanted was to have her there with me so I could hold her close to me.

"How much do you like me?"

"How much do *you* like me?" she questioned me back.

"I like you a lot," I whispered into the phone. "A whole lot."

"I like you a whole lot, as well." She laughed. "So what time should I come over tonight and what should I bring?"

"There's my eager beaver." I grinned into the phone. "Just bring yourself. Come over as soon as you can."

"I have to get ready."

"Come as you are. You always look beautiful."

"What should I bring?"

"Yourself." I laughed. "And maybe you can spend the night as well?"

"You're asking me to spend the night?" She sounded surprised.

"If you want to."

"Well, duh." She laughed, and I could hear her running up the stairs.

"How long will you be?"

"A few hours."

"That long?" I frowned. "I want to see you now."

"I'll try and be as quick as possible."

"Good, hurry." I hung up and jumped off the bed. "Jared, Vincent, where you guys at?" I shouted as I ran down the stairs.

"What's up?" Vincent called out to me from the kitchen where he was eating some carrots.

"Maddie's coming over tonight."

"No way." Vincent grinned at me and Jared looked up with a surprised expression. I knew he had thought it was over between us.

"Yeah, and she's staying the night, so don't be wise guys, okay?"

"Okay." Vincent laughed. "Whatever you say."

"What do you expect from us?" Jared cracked open a beer and stared at me as he drank slowly. "Shall we line up like some sort of welcome committee meeting the queen?"

"You're such an ass, Jared." I glared at him. "You're the one who told her where to meet me in the first place. Don't go getting upset because it didn't go as you planned."

"You better not tell her about the plan." Jared leaned forward. "No talk about the Bugatti tonight."

"Of course not." I didn't tell him that my reasons for not

190

wanting to tell her were different. I was worried that she would look at me differently if she knew I was planning on breaking into a house to steal a car.

"So what are we going to do?" Vincent stood up and walked over to us quickly. I knew he was scared that Jared and I would get into another argument and possibly start fighting.

"I figured we could order a pizza and a salad or something and play some cards." I looked at them both casually. "Do you think that's okay?"

"Sounds fine." Jared shrugged. "Get ham and pineapple on the pizza."

"What are we going to do about Dad?" Vincent looked worried. "He's going to want to know who she is. What if he comes out of the living room?" He chewed on his lower lip and I could tell he was nervous.

"I figured we could play upstairs in my room or something." I took a breath. "I don't want to involve Dad right now."

"Yeah, no point getting him upset over nothing." Jared made a face. "It may not even work out much longer."

"What does that mean?" I glared at him.

"You know what it means. Do you really think little Ms. Perfect is going to date you forever and Daddy is going to accept you?" He rolled his eyes. "But whatever, I'm not trying to be a jerk. Bad things come to those who wait."

"What the fuck does that mean?"

"Her and her dad will get what's coming. Whether you do something about it or not."

"You better leave her alone, Jared." I moved closer to him and I could feel my blood boiling. "I swear to God, if you do anything to her, you will no longer be my brother." The kitchen went silent and Vincent and Jared looked at me with shock in their eyes. I felt sad that I had said the words, but I wasn't going to take them back. Maddie was very important to me, and I wasn't going to let anyone say or do anything to her that could cause her hurt or pain. I didn't care why they were doing it. It wasn't going to happen on my watch. I hated her father with a passion, but I loved her more than I hated him. My vision seemed to go blurry as the realization hit me. I loved Maddie. This was about more than like or a summer fling or crush. This was about more than seeing where a relationship could go and getting to know each other. I already loved her. I knew without a doubt in my heart that she was the one I would dream of until I was old and gray. And I wasn't scared or worried. I was just happy and excited. And all I wanted to do was to see her and kiss her and hold her tight. I wanted to stare into her beautiful violet eyes and kiss her sweet luscious lips as her soft fingers played and tugged in my hair. I could lie next to her and stare at her for a million years and never feel bored or tired. I had missed her something rotten that week, and I knew that I didn't want to spend my lifetime without her.

"Wow, you're so far gone," Jared finally spoke. "I sure hope it doesn't blow up in your face."

"Let me worry about that." I ran my hand through my hair and sighed. "I just need you to be here for me and give her a chance."

"Okay." Jared looked away. "But only because I love you, brother."

"Thanks, dude." I choked up and looked at Vincent, who was laughing. "What's so funny?"

"You guys have both gone so soft." He shook his head. "What has happened to the Martelli brothers?"

"Whatever." I rolled my eyes and turned away. "I'm going to go sort out my room." I walked out of the kitchen. However, my lightheartedness was filled with worry. What Vincent had said was a joke but in fact, the opposite was true of what was happening to us. We weren't becoming softer; we were becoming harder. Pulling off the Bugatti theft was going to be the biggest, most dangerous thing any of us had ever attempted to do. Just today, Tolstoy had asked us

192

what we would do if someone with a gun were to appear. I froze as I remembered him asking if we had bulletproof vests. This was serious business. And there were so many potential things that could go wrong. But I knew we were in too deep; this was our big chance to change our destinies. If we pulled this off, we could stay out of the crime life forever.

***

"This is delicious pizza." Maddie grinned at me as she took a big bite and licked her lips.

"Isn't it great?" Vincent grabbed another slice. "This is absolutely the best pizza in River Valley." He smiled at Maddie, and I tried to ignore my jealousy as she beamed at him. I knew she was just happy that Vincent seemed to like her, but it annoyed me to see her looking so happy at someone else.

"Yeah." She leaned towards him. "So Logan tells me you want to be a lawyer?"

"That's the goal." He laughed, slightly embarrassed. "But I've got a long way to go if I want to see that happen."

"You can do it," she grinned at him. "And kudos to you, I'm not sure I would be able to make it as a lawyer."

"That's not a surprise." Jared mumbled under his breath and I gave him a death look.

"Sorry, what, Jared?" Maddie looked up at him questioningly and we all paused. "I hope you don't think I'm out of line here, but I'm not sure what your problem with me is? When we were both at Joey's, you seemed quite excited that I wanted to get to know Logan, but now you seem to have an attitude, and I'm not sure why." She spoke slowly, directly, and without hesitation, and once again I was reminded why I loved her. I saw Jared's face turning red and I could see that he was surprised at such a direct question as well.

"I don't know what …" He glanced at me and faltered.

"I'm not trying to make this uncomfortable for you. I know you guys don't like my dad, for whatever reason. Logan won't tell me." She gave me a quick face, before turning back to Jared. "But I don't want you to make any judgments as to my character until you get to know me. Logan and I, well, we…" she stumbled a little bit and blushed. "I just don't want you guys to hate me, before you get to know me."

"I like you already, Maddison." Vincent rubbed her shoulder. "You have put both of my brothers in their place, what's not to love?"

"Thanks, Vincent. I really like you a lot as well." She gave him such an appreciative look that I was grateful that she hadn't met him first. We all waited for Jared to respond, and he gave me a look and then sighed.

"Okay, okay. Maybe I've been a bit rash in my assessment of you." He gave her a weak smile. "If my brother likes you, you can't be all that bad."

I reached over and held Maddie's hand and squeezed it, letting her know that she had my support. I knew it was important to Maddie that they liked her, but I wanted her to know that it didn't matter to me how they felt. I was still going to be here for her, no matter what.

"Good, can I kick your asses at poker now?" She winked and we all burst out laughing. We hadn't known what we were going to do with Maddie; none of us really had friends who were girls and we had all felt a bit awkward when she had arrived. But she had been effortless, cracking jokes and really trying to get to know them. She really cared about my brothers and I could see her becoming a real part of the family.

"Oh, there is no way you're going to beat me." Jared pulled some notes out of his wallet. "Let's play with large blinds, I feel like making some money tonight."

194

"You wish, Martelli." She smiled at him, and I started shuffling the cards with a content and happy feeling in my heart.

Chapter 10

Maddie

"I'm so excited for you to come and meet my friends and family." I couldn't keep the excitement out of my voice as I whispered into the phone.

"Yeah, yeah," Logan mumbled sleepily and I knew that he wasn't as excited as I was. But I didn't mind; I had finally convinced him that this was a good thing. I was still pretty giddy inside at how much he had done to make me comfortable in his home, and I was still pretty shocked at how far he had gone to show me that he liked me and that he was trying to open up to me as much as possible. I truly loved both of his brothers and I felt like I had been welcomed with open arms by both Vincent and Jared, even though I knew Jared didn't particularly care for me.

"Aren't you excited?" I pressed on with the conversation. "And didn't you just love the invitations?"

"The invitations?" Logan's voice sounded even drowsier, and I wished that I was in bed with him at that moment, caressing his sleepy face and tousled hair, while snuggled into his warm body.

"Yes, my mom helped me choose them. We love to get fancy invitations for my end-of-summer party." I yawned involuntarily and stretched out, closing my eyes as I lay there. My heart felt light with happiness and I snuggled into my pillow pretending it was Logan's chest. I hadn't seen him since the night I was at his house and we played cards, but we had spoken on the phone every night before bed.

"Sounds good."

"Are you even paying attention to me?"

"Sorry, Maddie. I'm just so tired."

"What have you been doing?" I had been trying to keep my hurt feelings to myself, as Logan hadn't told me what had kept him so busy all week.

"Vincent and I have been learning some new skills."

"What skills?"

"Don't worry about it."

"Did you ask Vincent if he can make it to the party? I know Jared said no, but Vincent said he would check. Did he let you know if he can come?"

"I think one Martelli at the party is fine, Maddie."

"So he's not coming?" I was disappointed. I had hoped to spend more time with Vincent. I had hoped that he could come to look at me as a sister. We had really seemed to connect on poker night, but I had to keep reminding myself that nothing was going to happen overnight.

"I'm sorry, Maddie, but I don't think this is the right time. I mean, I think your family is already in for enough, what with me being introduced as your boyfriend. I can't imagine that's going to go down super well."

"Well." I bit my lip, not sure of what to say. "Just read the invite properly, okay? Maybe Vincent will want to come then."

"Unlikely." Logan laughed lightly. "I miss you, Maddie."

"When will I get to see you?" I pouted into the phone. "Before the party I hope."

"Once again, unlikely."

"No fair." I took a deep breath and pulled the covers up over my head. "I wanted to talk about us."

"What about us?" Logan's voice sounded weary.

"What we're going to do when I go back to school." I waited for him to say something. "What we're going to tell my parents."

"I don't know what we should tell your parents. That's up to you." His voice trailed off and silence filled the air as I waited for him to acknowledge and answer the first part of my question.

"So you're not going to say anything?"

"I just said you can decide."

"I mean about us."

"Maddie, can we take it one day at a time please?" Logan sighed. "My head is really full right now. Let's get past the next two weeks and then we can see where we stand."

"Fine." I bit my tongue. I didn't want to push the issue, but I was worried. What if he wanted to break up at the end of the summer? It wasn't like we had been dating for a long time, and Logan was so new to relationships. Yes, it was a feat that he and I were even in this space, but I needed more. I wanted to know that this was going somewhere. But I knew how crazy I would sound if I pushed the issue. Logan didn't want to hear about my silly dreams and hopes for the future. I knew he still didn't even think he was good enough for me. I knew that he would never move forward with me unless he felt that he could provide for me. I'd been shocked to see how meager his house had been. I'd expected it to be a lot different. More opulent, and full of cool gadgets. But it had been pretty barebones, and I hadn't seen anything of real value. The Martellis didn't have any money, of that I was sure. I wished I understood why they were the crime family of the town when they didn't really seem to be criminals.

"I'll talk to you tomorrow, yeah, Maddie?"

"Yes, Logan."

"Sweet dreams, beautiful."

"Sweet dreams, handsome," I whispered into the phone.

"Of course, they'll be of you." And with that we hung up. I

stared at the phone for a few minutes, upset that I still didn't know what was going on with Logan and how he was spending his days. I thought about pushing the issue like I had meeting his family, but I didn't want to do that again so soon. It had been a very long week ignoring him, and I'd been so scared that I was going to lose him. When he had called and invited me to dinner with him and his brothers, I had started crying in relief. I didn't want to put either of us through the hell of that week again. And I knew he was trying, and I knew that he liked me a lot. He had said as much the night that I stayed over. He had made love to me so sweetly and tenderly that I had almost wondered if it was the same guy who slammed me against the wall in Victoria's Secret. Just thinking about that day was enough to turn me on. I closed my eyes and tried to fall asleep. I didn't want to push anything. I was just happy that he was coming to my party and would finally be able to meet my parents. My mom was so excited to meet him; I had been so surprised at how supportive she had been when I had told her I was dating him. Not that I would have stopped dating him if she hadn't been, but it made it that much easier. Logan Martelli was my boyfriend and it was all I could do to stop from pinching myself. I couldn't believe it. But still, I wanted more. I needed to know more. I could still sense his slight hesitation and worry, and I was scared that he was going to talk himself out of dating me. He was so worried that he wasn't good enough for me and that he was going to bring trouble or drama into my life. I didn't know how to tell him that none of that mattered to me. I just wanted to be with him. I was planning to have a conversation with him on the night of the party. I figured we could get everything out in the open and I could see exactly where this relationship was going.

***

I stared at my reflection in the mirror, amazed at how different I looked in my midnight blue silk dress and flowing locks. I had brushed my hair to a shining luster and my eyes sparkled as I took in my appearance. I stared at the blatant red on my lips and swallowed hard. I looked like a seductress or vixen, and I wasn't sure what my dad or Logan was going to say. I was hoping Logan would be blown away by my appearance. That he would stare at me and think I was the most beautiful woman in the world.

"Maddison, guests are starting to arrive." My mother stopped by my room and peered in. "You look beautiful, my darling."

"Thank you, Mom." I smiled at her gratefully.

She kissed my cheek. "I love the woman you are becoming, Maddison Wright." She ran her fingers across my cheek. "You are beautiful and strong and caring. Don't ever let anyone make you change, you hear me?"

"Yes, Mom." I tried not to roll my eyes at her, and she laughed.

"I'm excited to meet Logan." Her eyes saddened. "I heard he has mother's eyes."

"He's gorgeous, Mom," I paused. "I think I love him. I mean I know I love him. He's the most wonderful man."

"Just remember what we decided." She smiled at me widely. "I think tomorrow will be a lot better, it will just be the four of us, and it will mean a lot more."

"I know, Mom." I nodded in agreement. "I put a note on Logan's invite so he knows as well."

"Good." She pulled my hand. "Now go downstairs and greet your guests."

"Yes, Mom." I ran down the stairs to see who had arrived and laughed at my disappointment when I realized Logan wasn't one of the first to arrive. I walked over to Lucy and some other girls I knew from the neighborhood and grinned to myself as I remembered I wasn't wearing any underwear. These girls had no idea that I was dating Logan and that he was hands-down the best lover I had ever had in my life. Add to that, he was the nicest, most sincere, and most generous man I had ever met.

"Hey, Maddison." Lucy looked up at me with wide eyes. "Wow, you look hot. Who are you expecting to show up—Bradley Cooper? Ha, ha, ha."

"No, silly. I just wanted to dress up."

"Celebrate your last weeks of freedom before school starts back?" She laughed.

I groaned. "Don't remind me, I've got to write my thesis this semester. It's going to be killer."

"I've got to take the GREs," she whined. "I really need to take a refresher course in math because I have no clue how to do half of those problems."

"Which ones?" I asked, slightly distracted. I couldn't keep my mind off of Logan, and I was having a hard time reining my excitement in.

"Fractions, algebra, stats." Lucy laughed. "If it's slightly related to math, then I need help."

"Oh, Lucy." I laughed at my friend. I had no idea how she had gotten admitted to Dartmouth with her intellect, but I supposed it didn't hurt that her father had connections and a lot of money to donate. The doorbell rang again, and I froze as the hairs on my arms stood up. Intuitively, I knew that Logan had arrived and my heart started beating fast. "Excuse me, girls, let me go get that." I walked away from the group quickly, without waiting for an answer. I groaned as I saw my dad walking to the front door from the other side of the room. This wasn't good. I didn't want my dad to be the first person Logan saw as he walked into my house.

"Maddison, darling, you look beautiful." My father walked over and gave me a big hug. "You look like a woman and not my daughter." He sighed and shook his head. "Where did the time go?"

"Well, I'm a woman now, Dad." I rolled my eyes and took a deep breath as he opened the door. It was like I was watching a movie, and I noticed my dad's nostrils flaring as he saw who was on the other side of the door.

"May I help you?" His voice was polite, but I could hear the hint of a threat in his tone.

"I'm here for Maddie's party." Logan's tone was smooth as silk, and my heart skipped a beat as I heard his voice.

"And you are?" My dad's voice was slow, but we all knew his question was a farce. I could tell from the arch of his back that he was very much aware that this was Logan Martelli at his front door.

"Dad, don't be silly." I pushed past him. "Let my guest in." I gave Logan a huge smile. "I'm glad you were able to make it." His eyes looked slightly confused as he looked at me, but I turned to my father quickly, wanting to get Logan away from him as quickly as possible.

"Dad, this is my friend Logan. Logan, this is my dad." I introduced them to each other, and they stared at each other for a moment before shaking hands.

"Come in, Logan." I ushered him inside and frowned as I noticed the hurt and slightly angry look in his eyes.

"Logan, is it?" Dad looked him up and down and paused. "Are you new to town?"

"No." He shook his head. "My brothers and I were born and raised in River Valley."

"Oh?" My dad raised his eyebrow. "Do I know your parents?"

"I think so." Logan smiled bitterly. "I think you were pretty good friends with my dad."

"What's the name?" My dad pretended to be interested, but I saw his eyes narrow as he controlled his breathing. I was glad that I had told him that Logan was my friend and not my boyfriend. I wasn't sure what would have happened.

"Martelli." Logan's tone was deadly as he stared at my father.

I touched his arm lightly. "Logan, let me introduce you to some of my other friends."

"Yes, you should do that, Maddie." My dad smiled at me. "Maybe one of the girls here will take a liking to your new friend."

"Yeah." I nodded and gave him a weak smile. Logan reached over to grab my hand, and I walked away from him quickly. I didn't want my dad to see any physical contact between us. "Logan, have you met Lucy, Marie, and Joanna?" I turned to him with a smile, and his eyes looked at me vacantly. He was standing stiffly, and I frowned at him.

"No, but it's a pleasure to meet you all." He gave them all a sexy smile and kissed each of their hands. "I haven't seen women as beautiful as you in a long time." I noticed Lucy's face reddening, and I tried to smile at her, even though I was upset that Logan was being so friendly to them.

"Logan, let me introduce you to everyone else." I tried to grab his arm, and he flinched at my touch.

"It's okay. I'd love to spend some time with these gorgeous young women." He avoided eye contact with me and I felt crushed, wondering what I had done for him to treat me this way.

"So, Lucy." He walked over to her and put his arm around her shoulder. "You're Joey's sister, right? You're even more beautiful than my brother Jared told me."

"Jared said I'm beautiful?" Lucy's eyes lit up and I wasn't sure if it was because Logan was touching her or because of what he said.

"Logan, come. I want you to meet my—"

"Not right now, Maddie." His eyes made contact with mine, and he looked me up and down, stopping to stare suggestively at my partially exposed bosom. "Nice dress, Maddie. Very *classy*." He laughed and turned back to Lucy. "So, Lucy, tell me. Are you dating anyone?"

"No, no, no," she giggled. "I'm single. You?"

"Oh, I'm very single and looking." He leaned down to whisper in her ear suggestively. "You know anyone who would be interested in going out with someone like me?" He stood up straight and all four of us stared at him. He looked absolutely gorgeous, his hair looked blonder than I remembered and it complimented his golden tan nicely. His green eyes sparkled dangerously and he had a smug look on his face as we stared at him. He was wearing a pair of khaki pants, with a nice shirt and jacket, and all I wanted to do was go to him and touch his chest and kiss him. But I knew that now wasn't the time. I didn't want my dad to see me with Logan.

"I sure do." Joanna leaned towards him and winked. "In fact, my boyfriend and I broke up a few weeks ago and I've been feeling horny as hell."

"Joanna." My voice was loud and shocked. "That's not appropriate."

"Why not?" She giggled and leaned into him. "He's single and I'm single."

"Logan and I wanted to tell you something." I smiled at them widely and walked over to him. "We are actually …"

"I don't think you really want to say something you don't mean, do you, Maddie?" Logan interrupted me. "It's funny how things change, isn't it?"

"Logan." I grabbed his hand and frowned. "We need to talk."

"Yeah, I guess we do." He glared at me, and we walked away from the other girls. I looked back and saw them staring at us, and I gave them a quick smile.

"Can we go upstairs and talk?" I pulled him to the side.

"Why can't we talk here?" He looked around the room with a deceptive smile. "Don't you want everyone to see us standing here?"

"Logan, please. I don't understand why you're upset."

"You don't understand why I'm upset?" He looked at me with slanted eyes. "I thought you were different, Maddie. Out of everyone, I thought you were the one person I could always count on to be proud of me."

"What are you talking about?"

"I guess I was wrong." His eyes hardened. "I suppose Jared was right all along."

"Right about what?" I shook my head, confused. "What's going on, Logan? I don't understand why you're so upset with me."

"It doesn't matter." He shook his head. "What the fuck ever, I was the idiot who thought you were different."

"Logan, I don't know why you're upset."

"I'm not upset." He smiled at me. "I have nothing to be upset about."

"Are you sure?" I bit my lip, unsure if things were really okay between us.

"Yeah." He leaned in towards me and kissed me on the lips quickly. "Let's go upstairs."

"What?" My lips tingled from his brief touch and I looked up into his eyes.

"I said, let's go upstairs."

"You want to talk?"

"No." He licked his lips. "I don't want to talk."

"Oh." I felt my body tremble as he stared at me with unadulterated lust. "I don't know."

"I've missed you," he whispered in my ear. "You look fucking hot tonight, Maddie. I want to fuck you while everyone is downstairs wondering where you are. I want to lift that sexy dress up and have you screaming my name while you come for me, and then I want to watch you come back downstairs smiling because you just had the best fuck of your life."

"I don't know." I swallowed, incredibly turned on by his words.

"Let me show you how much you mean to me." He ran his hand through his hair and turned to look around the room quickly. He spotted my father and then turned back to me with a smile. "I've missed you this last week. I need to feel myself inside of you, please, Maddie."

"Okay," I whispered. "Let's go." I ran up the stairs quickly and heard Logan behind me. As soon as we reached the top of the stairs, he pulled me towards him, and kissed me, his mouth pressing down on mine hungrily, and I responded to him just as passionately. "Let's go in my room." I grabbed his hand and pulled him towards the room, and he shook his head.

"No, let's go the bathroom." He grinned at me. "I want you bent over the bathtub."

"Oh." I blushed as he fucked me with his eyes, and I pulled him to the bathroom a few doors away. We hurried in and I made sure to push the door closed. As soon as we walked in, Logan pushed me against the door, and I felt his hands on my breasts, caressing them roughly. He pushed the straps of my dress down and pulled the front down so he had access to my naked breasts. He bent down and took my nipple in his mouth and bit down on it so hard that I cried out in pain and pleasure. He nibbled lightly and I felt his hand on my other breast, rubbing my nipple lightly. I put my hands through his hair and closed my eyes, groaning as I felt the wetness in between my legs.

"I missed you, Logan," I moaned as he kissed his way back up to my lips. His eyes locked into mine as he kissed me roughly and pushed his erection against me, crushing my breasts against his chest. I reached under his shirt and ran my hands across his stomach, relishing of the feel of his naked skin against my fingers. I then ran my hands down to his pants and undid his button and unzipped him. I reached my hand down into his pants and held his erection in my hands, delighting in the feel of him growing as I squeezed it. He gasped as my fingers ran up and down his shaft, and he looked down at me with a devious smile.

"Suck me." His voice was coarse as he commanded me.

"What?" I looked up at him with a slight smile.

"Suck me." He raised an eyebrow at me, and I couldn't read the expression in his eyes. I kneeled down on the floor and took him into my mouth. I heard him groan as I sucked on the tip of his hardness and licked along his shaft. I took as much of him into my mouth as possible and moved my mouth back and forth on him as quickly as possible. "Fuck, Maddie, I'm going to come," he groaned as I continued sucking him off. I looked up at him and smiled and he shuddered as he came hard and fast into my mouth. I swallowed his cum quickly, relishing the taste of him in my mouth. I laughed as I felt his cock hardening again after his orgasm.

"You're still horny?" I stood up and he grinned at me.

"I'm never satisfied until I hear you screaming out my name." He winked at me and pushed me towards the bathtub. "Bend over." He bent me forward and I felt him lift my dress up. I heard his intake of breath as he realized I had no panties on. "You really are a bad girl, aren't you, Maddie? You've been waiting for me to show up all night so I could fuck you."

"I…"

"Shhh." He growled and I felt his fingers running across my wet slit. "I don't want to hear you saying anything until I hear you screaming out my name." I whimpered as I felt him slip a finger inside of me and I rested my arms on the bathtub. I then felt the tip of him running up and down my slit, and I tried to push myself back into him so he would finally enter me, and put me out of my misery.

"Please."

"What?" He growled into my ear, as his tip teased me.

"Enter me," I whispered slowly.

"What? I can't hear you."

"Fuck me, Logan," I groaned, unable to take the incredible pleasure he was giving me with his fingers and manhood. "Please."

"What?" He slipped the tip of himself into me, and I moaned in relief but groaned as he withdrew from me again.

"Fuck me, Logan," I cried out a little louder.

"What?" He started to slide into me again.

"Fuck me, please!" I cried out.

"What's my name?"

"Logan," I moaned.

"Tell me again."

"Fuck me, Logan!" I screamed as he slid into me fully. I felt him slide in and out of me quickly, and he held onto my hips as he filled me up completely. He slowed his pace and I moaned out, wanting to feel all of him again. "Don't stop."

"What?" He growled.

"Don't stop, please."

"Don't stop what?" He started to increase his pace again, and I was lost to the pressure building up inside of me.

"Don't stop fucking me, Logan!" I screamed out as he intensified his pace. He slammed into me and I cried out, not believing just how wonderful it felt to have him filling me up. It was even more wonderful than I had remembered.

"Say it again." He paused for a second, and I moaned out. I was so close to orgasm that I couldn't stop myself from screaming.

"Don't stop fucking me, Logan!" I screamed out even louder this time, as I felt myself climaxing. I looked around briefly to smile at him, and I was shocked to see that he had opened the door. He stared back at me with a closed off look as he orgasmed into me, and I shuddered as he grabbed my breasts and I felt him filling me up with his warmness.

"What the fuck?" My dad's voice boomed into the bathroom, and my eyes widened in shock as he stared at the two of us in the bathroom. I froze and tried to stand up, but Logan held my hips as he finished coming into me. He released me after a few seconds and I stared at him in shock and anger. "Get off of my daughter, you fucking piece of shit." My dad walked into the bathroom, shouting. His fist was up, as if he wanted to punch him.

"I was just leaving anyways." Logan stared at me. "I think I got what I came for." He smiled at me cruelly and walked out of the room. He paused for a moment and looked back at me with cold eyes. "It was nice being friends with you, Maddie." And with that, he turned around and walked away.

Chapter 11

Logan

I walked down the stairs slowly. I could feel the stares of everyone at the party on me and I wondered if they had all heard Maddie screaming out my name. I kept my head high and looked straight ahead. Fuck these people. They weren't anything to me. I couldn't wait to leave this godforsaken town. They were all just as bad as each other. Anger and sadness ran through my blood. How could Maddie have done this to me? I was still in shock and disappointment that she had introduced me as her *friend*. After everything that had happened and everything she had said. She had told me that she was proud to be dating me, that she was so excited for me to meet her family as her boyfriend. It had taken a lot for her to convince me to even come. I was the one who told her I didn't think it was a good idea, but she had convinced me that my ideas were antiquated and that her father would respect her opinion and choice and that she wasn't embarrassed about dating me.

I guess she had lied. Jared had been right. I wasn't good enough for her, and even she knew that. I walked past Maddie's mother, and she stared at me with shocked eyes and a tight smile. I gave her a twisted face and walked out of the front door. As I walked to the main street, I stopped and turned to look back at the familiar house. It seemed so foreign to me now. I looked at the house and all I could feel was pain inside, and this time it wasn't the angry, bitter pain of my father, but the sad, heartbreaking pain of despair and lost hope. As I walked down the street, I realized that Maddie had used me. I had been her teenage crush, and she had made that crush a reality. She had come onto me with abandon, getting me to fuck her and fall in love with her and then she had crushed me with no care. What did I matter to her? My feelings were just part of the game. Now she could go back to school and tell all her stupid, spoiled friends that she had a summer of fun, taming the town's bad boy, and once she got him, she left him.

I was a bigger fool than I had ever thought I would be. I walked down the street and towards the bus stop and shook my head at how eager and excited I had been to see Maddie. The evening had started with me thinking that this was the start of my new beginning and transition to a new life. Maddie had inspired me to become a new man, and I wanted to prove myself to her. The fact that she had trusted me and believed in me made me want to become a better man for her. I clutched the necklace in my pocket and held onto it tightly. How could I have been so stupid? My father was right: the mayor and his entire family weren't to be trusted. My head was spinning as I stood waiting for the bus. Maddie's rejection of me was hard to accept and I stared blindly into the lights of the passing cars. I pulled the necklace out of my pocket and studied it, glad I hadn't given it to Maddie before I realized just how much of a liar she was. The small dainty pearl shined up at me, and I held the necklace gingerly in my hands. It had belonged to my mother. It was one of the only pieces she had owned, and I had been planning on giving it to Maddie that evening as a token of my love to her. I knew that she had been upset that I hadn't told her what I had been doing all week, and I knew that she had wanted to talk about what the plan was when she went back to school. I was worried that she thought that I didn't care because I hadn't been able to see her for the last week. We had spoken on the phone every night, but I had been so tired most nights that I had fallen asleep on the phone. I had wanted her to know that she was my everything, and that I wanted to be with her every night. Everything I was doing was so that I could be a man who could provide for her, a man she could be proud of and rely on. I wanted to be a better man for Maddie, and I wanted to give her the most precious thing I owned to show her that she was now the most precious thing in my life. But the joke was on me, because it didn't even matter. I didn't matter. And now it was all over. I could still see the look in her eyes as she realized I had opened the door and her father had witnessed her screaming out my name as she orgasmed. I don't think I would ever forget. It was bittersweet, and I knew one person that would be happy about what had happened. Jared would be exhilarated to hear that we had finally gotten some revenge on the mayor. My heart constricted as I realized that the revenge had been at the cost of Maddie and her self-respect, but I tried not to think about that. She was the one who had played me. She had hurt me more that she would ever know. And the pain she had inflicted on me had turned me into a man I never wanted to be. I still couldn't quite believe I had concocted that plan so quickly and carried it out. It was as if I couldn't help myself. I couldn't think past the blinding pain and hurt. I wanted her to see how I felt.

I was happy to see the bus arrive, and I got on, paid my fare, and sat down at the back of the bus, vowing to never come to this part of town again. My days visiting Manor Road were officially done forever. I never wanted to see that house again. It was all part of the nightmare that I wanted to put behind me. I arrived home about an hour later, and I was grateful to see that my father was asleep on the couch for once. I ran up the stairs to my room and closed the door quickly before Jared and Vincent realized I was back. I really wanted to go to my field but I had no way to get there, and I didn't want to take Vincent's Mustang.

I lay on the bed and turned on some music and I stared at the wall, wondering where it had all gone wrong. Was I forever damned to a life of unhappiness? What had I done to deserve this life? I wasn't that bad of a person. I didn't even want to be a bad person. I just wanted to pursue my dreams like everyone. I wanted to love and be loved. I wanted someone to look at me for me and not judge me because of what they heard about me. Maddie's face flashed in my mind; I had really thought she was different, but when it all came down to it, she had been just like all the rest. She had gotten to know the real me, I had opened up my home to her, and yet it still wasn't enough. I flinched as the scenes from the night kept replaying in my mind. This wasn't how our story was meant to end. I pulled out my mother's necklace again and placed it on my night table before turning off my light and allowing the darkness to take me to a better place.

***

"Logan, you up?" Vincent knocked on my door the next morning, and I groaned and rolled over, keeping my eyes closed. "So, how was last night?"

"Vinny, I didn't say I was up." I glared at him. He was staring at me with a worried expression, and I sat up in the bed. "What do you want?" I snapped.

"Joey got the call." Vincent's eyes were excited. "Tonight's the night."

"Tonight. Fuck." I jumped out of bed, unblinking. "We're not ready."

"We're ready." Vincent's voice was calm and sure. "We got this, bro."

"Tolstoy hasn't gone through shutting off the alarm yet."

"It's the garage." Vincent shrugged. "Most garages aren't connected to the alarm system."

"We don't want to take that chance." I pushed past him. "Where's Jared?"

"He went to check the mail." Vincent followed me down the stairs. "The address is supposed to be in a letter."

"Are you fucking joking?" I walked out the front door. "It's in the mail?"

"Yeah, that's how they do it." He shrugged. "We're ready for this, Logan."

"I don't know." I shook my head and winced. I felt like shit, my head was pounding, and I was filled with trepidation, sadness, anxiety, and anger. Not the best combination for the biggest theft of my life. "I think we should drop it."

"What?" Vincent looked at me in shock. "What are you talking about?"

"I don't think this is a good idea."

"Where is this coming from?" Vincent looked at me thoughtfully. "What happened last night? How's Maddie?"

"It's over with Maddie." My tone was final. I didn't want to discuss it with anyone.

"It's over?" Vincent sighed and looked away as Jared approached us.

"What up, bros?" Jared said excitedly and held up the letters in his hands. "Did Vinny tell you that today was the day? The day we become millionaires."

"We need to talk," I snapped. "I don't think this is a good idea anymore."

"Why not?" Jared looked at me like he thought I was crazy.

"Logan and Maddie broke up." Vincent made a face. I glared at him.

"What?" Jared looked at me with a shocked expression. "How'd you guys break up?"

"You were right," my words were light. "I realized she was a bitch and so I got my revenge."

"Oh my God, Logan." Jared looked worried.

"I don't wanna talk about it. It's done." I clenched my fist. All I wanted to do was punch the wall. I still couldn't believe Maddie had done that to me.

"Well, this is for you." Jared handed me a letter, and I looked at the envelope in irony. It was from Maddie, and it looked like the invitation she had been going on about the other night. I'm not sure why she felt she needed to send me a formal invitation to a party that she had already been begging me to attend for a week.

I was about to throw it in the trash but decided to open it first. I guess I wanted to relive the misery and memories of the night before.

I ripped open the envelope and pulled the invitation out. I rolled my eyes at the formality of it all; you would think she was getting married, not just having a summer party. A dart of pain flashed through me at the thought of Maddie getting married. I didn't want to think about her anymore. She'd find a nice guy now, one that Daddy approved of. That would make them both happy. She'd find a guy who didn't have issues and had a lot of money. Someone in her class. I was about to rip the envelope up when I saw a small post-it note stuck in the envelope. I pulled it out, and the blood ran from my face as I read it. I dropped the invitation onto the ground and read the post-it note again to make sure that I had understood it correctly. As I read it again, time seemed to stand still, and I looked up at Jared's and Vincent's faces in shock.

"I messed up." I stared at them and then the note. "She attached a note with the invitation. It makes sense now. Oh my God, what did I do? She wrote a note." I paused and read from the paper. "*My darling Logan, I'm so happy that you have agreed to come to my party and meet my friends and parents. It means so much to me. I told my mom that we are dating, and she thinks that we should wait to tell my dad about us the day after the party at lunch. She thinks he will take it better in a more personal setting. I hope you understand and will come to the lunch as well. I'm so excited for the two of you to get to know each other. I know he will come to love you as I do. See you soon. Ever yours, Maddie.*" I stopped reading and stared at my brothers unblinkingly. "She thought I knew. I didn't know. I didn't know. I thought she was ashamed." I stood there frozen, with my stomach in knots. "I have to call her, I have to explain."

"I don't know what you're talking about, Logan." Jared looked at me with a frightened expression. "What's going on?"

"I have to go and call her." I walked out of the kitchen quickly.

"But we need to talk about tonight," Vincent called out after me.

"I have to call Maddie!" I shouted down the stairs. "I have to fix this." I ran into my room and grabbed my phone and called her number with my heart pounding. I cussed as the phone went to voicemail and tried calling back again. It went to voicemail again and I left a message. "Maddie, it's Logan. Please call me back. I fucked up. I know that now. Please forgive me, please call me back. I love you. I thought you were ashamed. I brought my mom's necklace. Please call me back," I rambled on and hung up and called her number back again, but it kept ringing and ringing and going to voicemail. What had I done? Had I just cost myself the love of my life because I was so down on myself? Why had I listened to my heart? I knew who Maddie was. I had been so hurt and quick to jump to conclusions and wanting to shame her for hurting me. And I had been wrong. If I had just listened to my rational mind and thoughts, I would have known that Maddie would never use me, would never be embarrassed by me. She had risked everything for me and for her feelings for me, and once again I had screwed it up. I had fucked it up royally and I wasn't sure if she would ever forgive me. I knew that no matter how much someone loved you, there was a point of no return. There was a point where the love didn't matter anymore. That was a point my mother had reached with my father. His behavior had been so destructive that all she wanted to do was leave him. The love she had felt for him had faded, and she hadn't wanted to be with him anymore. She had wanted to leave, only fate hadn't been kind to her. I had let my mother down, and now I had done the same thing to Maddie. I had to go to her. I had to explain. She had to understand. I ran back down the stairs with my phone and into the kitchen.

"I need to borrow the Mustang," I charged up to Vinny. "Where are the keys?"

"You can't borrow it right now." Vinny shook his head.

"I have to go to Maddie!" I yelled at him in anger.

"We need to go pick up the rental car and get the tools at Lowe's," Jared interrupted me in a hard tone. "You know we have to drive two hours away to get this stuff. We don't have time for you to go to Maddie."

"You don't understand." I frowned at him. "I need to go to her now. She is all that matters."

"No." Vincent grabbed ahold of my shoulders. "She isn't all that matters. We are what matters right now. We need to do this for us. This is our chance."

"I need to go to Maddie." I pushed past him. "Give me the keys."

"Logan, listen to me. She will still be there." Vincent raised his face and grabbed me, pushing me against the wall. His blue eyes bore into mine seriously. "This is not the time, you hear me? This is not the time." I stared at him, unblinking. Jared stared at us both with his mouth agape, his face reflecting the shock in my mind. We had never seen Vincent be the dominant one in our relationship.

"I don't want to lose her," I mumbled and pushed him off of me. "I really fucked up."

"I'm sorry." His eyes looked sad for me. "But we have a dad in the living room who is a few weeks from the point of no return. I have tuition due in a few weeks, and we have rent. Right now, we have to do this for us. If it's meant to be, it will work out with Maddie."

"What if she never talks to me again?" My eyes blazed but my words were soft.

"She'll talk to you again." Vincent nodded at me in assurance. "You'll see."

I stared at him and at Jared and realized that no matter what I wanted to do, no matter how badly I needed to speak to Maddie, I couldn't just walk out now. I had a responsibility to my brothers and to my family. I would never put myself before them.

"Let's go." I nodded at Jared. "You have the details?"

"We're going to go to Sawyerville to get the rental car, a white Honda Accord. Then we'll go to Lowe's and get the tools. Then tonight we'll go eat at an Olive Garden and talk about how we're going to play pool. Instead of going to play pool, we will drive to the address in this envelope. Vincent will get out of the car and pretend to go to ring the doorbell. You will also slip out of the car and go work on the garage door. If anyone is looking, they will see Vincent at the front door and won't be paying attention to the garage. After five minutes, Vincent will go back to the car and we will pull away.

We will stop around the corner and park the car. By that time, you should have gotten into the garage. Vincent and I will run back to the house, and Vincent will stand watch at the garage door. You will break open the car door and work on getting the ignition started. I will use the special paint we get from Lowe's to spray the car while you are working, and I'll change the license plate as well. We should be able to leave the garage within thirty minutes max. Once we are out, Vincent will run back to the white Honda and drive it home. We will follow and go home. We'll call Joey, and he will call the buyer and set up the sale." Jared grinned. "Easy-peasy."

"I just hope it will all go according to plan." I sighed. There were so many different things that could go wrong. I didn't want to voice any of them out loud. I knew we were all worried about a million things, and now I was a loose cannon who was even more frightened.

"It'll be fine. This time next week we'll be millionaires." Jared laughed and I gave him a weak smile. It all sounded like it was going to be too easy. Nothing in life was ever this easy, nothing. But what could I say? We had come this far, and on paper, it seemed like nothing could go wrong. But I hadn't foreseen last night happening, either.

"We need to make a contingency plan in case something goes wrong." I thought for a moment. "If anything happens, like if the cops come, or the family is home, or a neighbor shows up, I want you both to run. I will stay in the garage and take the heat." I put my hands up and glared at them. "And there will be no debating this, I will call this whole thing off if you don't agree. You got it?"

"Logan, you can't go down by yourself." Vincent shook his head. "That's not right."

"We're not all going down if it goes wrong." I was emphatic and my voice was loud. "I know you guys will roll your eyes and groan but I'm the eldest and I'm in charge. Mom asked me to take care of you guys. I don't even want you guys to be involved with this, but I know I need your help. I will never forgive myself if anything happens to either of you."

"Fine," Jared sighed. "But only because nothing is going to go wrong. We got this, bro, and once we arrive home tonight, you can call Maddie, and you guys can make up."

"Yeah, like you care." I turned away from him with my face red. I was sure he was happy at how this had turned out.

"Of course I care." Jared shook his head and stared at me for a moment. "Anyway, I need to call Joey and let him know I got the package."

"Okay." I looked down at my half-naked body. "I'm going to go shower. I'll be back down in a bit."

"Try not to call her too many times, bro." Vincent patted me on the back and I ignored him as I ran back up the stairs and tried calling Maddie again. I kept calling and calling, hoping she would pick up the phone. I called one last time and left another message. "Hey, Maddie, it's Logan. I'm sorry. Please call me. I fucked up. I know that. I've been a bit of a dick. I want to tell you everything. Please call me. I miss you." I hung up and went into the shower. My stomach was in knots and my brain was cloudy with misery and regret. I had a bad, bad feeling about everything, but out of all of my worries, I was most worried that I might never see Maddie again.

***

"We did it!" Jared high-fived me as we drove out of the driveway. I checked the rearview mirror and made sure that the garage door was closed. I grinned at him, unable to believe how smoothly everything had gone. Everything had gone according to plan, and we had gotten into the Bugatti in record time. Vincent was already on the way back home, and I was enjoying the smooth ride of the expensive sports car.

"Joey was right, the key was exactly where he said it would be." Jared sounded surprised. I didn't want to ask him why he was surprised his friend had told the truth, if he had trusted him so much.

"I'm glad Tolstoy told us that we wouldn't be able to hotwire this car." I shook my head, not believing that we had almost tried to steal a car that wouldn't start without the key, due to the chips used in the design. "Could you imagine what would have happened?" I sighed. "Thank God, Joey's connection had more detailed information or we would have been screwed. And this is exactly why we don't steal super-expensive cars."

"I nearly had a heart attack you know." Jared grinned at me. "Damn cat."

"I know." I checked the rearview mirror to make sure no one was following us. "When you screamed, I thought that was it."

"I felt him on my back, and thought for sure this was someone catching us in the act. Never again."

"I know." I looked at him with thoughtful eyes. "I used to get such a thrill from stealing cars. It was such an adrenaline rush, but today I was just scared. I was nothing other than scared about what would happen to us if we got caught."

"Yeah." Jared nodded. "But we did it, bro. We're home free."

"We still have to make it home, but it looks like we did it." I grinned back at Jared, hardly able to contain myself. Maybe everything in our lives was finally changing for the better. I only hoped that the one person who mattered to me aside from my brothers would be able to share it all with me.

"I'm going to call Joey and let him know." Jared whipped out his phone. "Oh, and when we get the money, I figured out where we can send Dad and how we can get there."

"Oh?"

"There's an alcohol rehab I found that I think will really help him." Jared nodded and then held his hand up as his call connected. "Joey, you there?" He laughed into the phone. "We got it. Yup, everything was smooth. Let the buyer know. Oh, you're busy? On a date? What? With who?" Jared looked at me with a grin. "He's

220

getting laid," he mouthed to me with a grin and I shook my head in exasperation. "Maddie? Maddie Wright?" Jared's voice dropped and he turned away from me. "You're with her now? Did she say why?"

"What's going on?" I slowed down and looked over at Jared. "Maddie's with Joey?"

Jared shook his head and kept his eyes averted from mine. "Well, just call us tomorrow with the information for the drop. Tell Maddie I said hi."

"Maddie's with Joey?" I glared at him. "She's fucking him already?"

"No." Jared shook his head slowly, and I could tell he was thinking furiously. "She's not fucking him."

"So what then?"

"I guess they're on a date?" He bit his lip and stared out the window. "Something must be up." He mumbled under his breath and he cursed. "Fuck it." He took a deep breath. "Hurry up and drive home."

"What's going on, Jared?" I stared at him angrily. "Did you know Maddie was seeing Joey? Is that why you didn't want me to fall for her? Because you knew she was involved with your friend?"

"It's complicated, Logan." He looked at me with a frazzled expression. "I can't get into this right now, I need to sort some stuff out."

"What stuff?" I looked at him with narrowed eyes.

"I don't know." His looked panicked. "Just drive home."

"What the fuck is going on?"

"I don't know, okay? I don't fucking know." He slammed his fist against the glove compartment. "Let's just say that you may have been right."

"Right about what?" I felt like I wanted to shout. "So she is dating Joey?"

Jared stared into my eyes and I was scared. I had never seen such a look of fear in his eyes before. He closed his eyes and sat back in the chair and rubbed his temples. I concentrated on the road ahead and didn't say anything else. I went as quickly as I could without going over the speed limit, and I breathed a sigh of relief as we made it back home and I saw the white Honda in the driveway. I drove the car and parked it on the grass, and we jumped out silently and pulled the sheet that we had left on the grass over the car, so that it wasn't completely visible from the road.

We walked into the house and into the kitchen. Vincent was sitting at the table, and he stood up to give us both a big hug. We were all relieved that part one had gone so well, but I think we all realized that we were far from in the clear. Jared and I exchanged a look, and I knew that there was something else going on, but I kept my mouth shut. I didn't want to frighten Vincent, but I was scared. But I wasn't scared about what might or might not happen with the Bugatti. I was scared that I had lost Maddie forever, and I knew that if I had, my life would never be the same again.

Chapter 12

Logan

I tried calling Maddie about ten more times that night, but I didn't leave any more messages. I was too scared I would say something that would make her not talk to me ever again, though that was already a real possibility. She hadn't answered any of my calls or returned any of my text messages. I was full of worry and stress, and I knew that Jared and Vincent were avoiding me because they were scared I would go off on one of them. They were right to avoid me because I was just looking for an argument. They were still riding high from the thrill of stealing the Bugatti, and while I was happy that we had been successful, I was gutted that Maddie wouldn't speak to me. I tried calling one more time before I jumped out of bed and pulled on my shoes.

I ran down the stairs and into the kitchen, where Jared and Vincent were playing cards. "Hey, where are the keys to the Mustang?" I held my hand out. "And don't even say no or I will take the Bugatti, and I don't think either of you want that to happen."

"Let it go for the night." Jared grimaced at me. "Just let it go."

"Let what fucking go?" I turned towards him with a hiss.

"Let Maddie have some time to think about things," he continued in a steely tone.

"You're happy about this, aren't you? You don't want me to be happy with Maddie. Did you tell Joey? Was he waiting to poach her away from me?"

"You sound crazy, Logan." Jared shook his head. "Trust me, I'm not happy about this."

I turned away from him and back to Vincent. "Are you giving me your keys?"

"Logan," he began and I glared at him. He closed his mouth,

sighed, and handed me the keys from his pocket. "Be careful with her."

"I always am." I grabbed the keys away from him. "I've never gotten a single scratch on her."

"I mean with Maddie."

"I'll see you guys later." I turned away from them and ran to the front door, ignoring the shouts of my dad from the living room. I jumped into the Mustang and drove as quickly as possible. I needed to apologize to Maddie in person, I needed to look into her eyes and tell her that I fucked up and wanted to make it up to her. I needed her to see the sincerity in my eyes, and I needed her to know why I hated her dad. It was time for Maddie to find out the full story behind my hatred of her father. I needed her to understand that I while I hated him, I could never hate her. I only hoped that it would be enough to warrant her to give me another chance. Because if it wasn't, I didn't think I would ever feel whole again.

I parked in my usual spot and pulled out my phone and sent her a text message. "Maddie, I'm outside your house. I will be slamming the door down in ten minutes if you do not call me back or come out. I'm not leaving until you come out or the police escort me away." I hit send and waited. I stared at the house I had sworn I would never visit again and prayed that I would see her walking out the door to come and see me. Just as I was about to text her again, a car pulled up in front of the house. I peered over my steering wheel and watched in shock as Joey jumped out and walked around to open the passenger door for Maddie. She got out slowly, and I saw her laughing about something. My heart constricted as I watched her smiling at Joey. She looked beautiful and happy. She was wearing a white summery dress, and her long dark locks were flowing in the breeze of the night. My fingers gripped my cellphone so tightly, I thought I was close to breaking it as I watched them standing there, talking. I thought I was going to murder someone when I saw Joey lean down and give her a kiss on the lips. It wasn't long, but those few seconds were like the cruelest torture. I felt as if the world was ending, and I was getting to see my worst nightmare play out in slow motion. I let out a huge breath as I saw Maddie pushing him to go in the car, and I grinned to myself. *That's my girl*, I thought. I wasn't sure what I would have done if she had let him go into the house that night. I might have committed murder, and then he'd never have been able to orchestrate the sale of the Bugatti. Jared and Vincent would be stuck with a stolen Bugatti in the front yard and a brother in jail. And I still wouldn't have Maddie.

I jumped out of the car as soon as Joey passed me in his vehicle, and I ran up to Maddie as quickly as possible so I could intercept her before she went inside. "Maddie," I called out as she was opening the door. She looked at me with a frown and paused.

"What are you doing here?" she hissed, and all I wanted to do was swoop her into my arms.

"I need to talk to you." I smiled hopefully. "I've missed you."

"I don't want to talk to you." She shook her head and made to open the door again. "Just leave me alone."

"Listen to me, please, Maddie. Give me five minutes, please?" I pleaded with her.

"No." She shook her head and she avoided eye contact with me. I walked closer to her, and stopped right in front of her.

"Look at me, please, Maddie."

"No." She shook her head and looked over my shoulder.

"Look at me, please." I sighed and I reached my hand over to her face and lifted her chin up, so her eyes would look directly into mine. "Maddie." I said her name slowly, as she finally made eye contact with me. I froze as I stared into her hurt, wide eyes. My heart felt as if I had just run a marathon and emotions ran through me as I took in her appearance hungrily. She was the most beautiful woman in the world. "Maddie." I said her name again. "I've missed you."

"You don't get to say that." She bit her lip and turned away from me. "You don't get to come here and pretend everything's okay."

"I came to apologize." I took a deep breath. "And I came to explain."

"I don't care. I don't want to know." She shook her head, and looked away from me again. "I don't trust you anymore."

"I love you, Maddie." The words tripped out of my mouth and I saw her jaw drop as she looked at me uncertainly. "I love you." I said the words again and laughed. "I didn't think I'd ever say those words."

"I don't care." She shook her head, but I could see her lips were trembling.

"Please, Maddie." I reached down for her hands. "Can we just speak?"

"No," her voice broke. "I can't do this anymore, Logan." She shook her head vehemently. "I knew it was going to be hard, getting to know you and trying to break through. But I can't deal with this anymore. I can't deal with you. You don't trust me and you never will."

"I didn't see your invitation until the day after the party," I interrupted her. "I didn't know, Maddie. I thought you were just—"

"It doesn't matter." She pulled away from me and shouted. "It doesn't matter when you saw the invitation. You should have had faith in me. You should have trusted me. You should have known me better than to think I was ashamed of you. You broke my heart, Logan. Not because you fucked me and set me up so my father, my own father, would hear and see. But because you did it because you didn't trust me."

"I wasn't thinking, Maddie. Please." I looked at her with distraught eyes. "You have to understand, I was just so hurt, I couldn't think straight. I messed up, I know. But I do trust you. I love you. I will never doubt you again."

"I can't just forgive you, Logan." She shook her head and there were tears rolling down her face as she looked at me. "You betrayed

226

me and my feelings."

"Don't you love me, Maddie?" I grabbed ahold of her and pulled her towards me. "Don't you love me?" I crushed my lips down on hers and tried to kiss her. She pushed against me, but I continued, trying desperately for her to remember the connection we had. Our chemistry was unbeatable and I hoped that the feel and taste of me would awaken her from her numb state.

"Stop it." She pushed me and broke her face away from me. "You can't just kiss me. It's over, Logan. I don't want to do this anymore."

"You told me once that I was the man you were going to marry."

"I got it wrong."

"You told me that our story was like that of a movie."

"So?"

"So the guy always gets the girl in movies." I stared at her. "That much I know."

"Well, maybe it's a different guy who gets the girl."

"No." I shook my head. "When two people are fated for each other, no one can break them apart."

"We aren't fated for each other." She shook her head. "It's over, Logan."

"You don't mean that." I ran my hands through my hair. "You can't possibly mean that."

"I'm just a silly, spoiled schoolgirl, Logan." She sighed. "You knew that when you first met me. You were right. I'm fickle, I'm capricious. I don't want you. I don't need you. I don't love you. I'm over you."

"Liar." I shook my head, refusing to believe it.

"I'm over you, Logan." She shrugged carelessly. "I don't care if you believe me. You need to go. This is not a good place for you to be."

"I love you." The words came out bitterly, and I laughed. "Ironic that now that I've met the love of my life, she doesn't want me. Seems to be the story of my life. Once a loser, always a loser."

"Get over yourself, Logan Martelli." She grabbed my hand and pulled me away from the front door. "You need to leave, and I need to go in, or my parents will wonder what's going on."

"Come talk with me in the car."

"I have nothing to say." She made to go in the door, and I grabbed her arms and held them up so she couldn't move.

"I won't let go until you come to talk with me in the car."

"Let go of me, or I'll scream." Her eyes bore into mine.

"Scream then."

"The police will come."

"I don't care."

"You'll get arrested."

"I don't care."

"Fine." She squirmed away from me. "Just let go of me. I'll give you five minutes." We walked to my car quickly, both of us breathing rapidly. My head was a flurry of emotions and I felt as if I was going to break down and shout. I had to get her to give me another chance or there was a real possibility that I was going to do something stupid. We got into the car in silence, and I turned to face her with a weak smile.

"You look beautiful tonight."

"Thank you." She nodded without smiling.

"You're dating Joey now?"

"No." She shook her head and looked away. "Kind of."

"I see. That was fast." I couldn't keep the hurt out of my voice.

"He asked me to dinner, and I said yes." She shrugged her shoulders. "I've known him all of my life, our dads are best friends, they always hoped we'd date. I figured it couldn't hurt. I needed to figure out some stuff."

"I'm glad you decided to date someone in your league," I spat out bitterly.

"We're not dating, and I don't know what you're talking about when you say 'league.'" She sighed, and I watched as she played with her fingers.

"I don't trust him." I leaned towards her. "I don't want you to date him."

"Are you joking?" She laughed. "You don't get to tell me who I can and can't date. And trust me, I know who I can and can't trust." She rolled her eyes and said something under her breath.

"Maddie, I love you. I made a mistake. A big mistake, and I hurt you. Please give me another chance." I leaned forward to kiss her again, and for a moment I felt I had gotten through to her. Her lips melted against mine, and she kissed me back. My tongue slid between her lips eagerly, anxious and happy to taste her again. I felt like I was inhaling manna from heaven, and I moved closer to her, so I could run my hands through her hair. I felt her fingers in my hair, tugging on the strands as she kissed me back. I slid my hand to her breast to caress it, and then she jumped back and broke the kiss. Her eyes looked at me feverishly and my heart dropped as she shook her head and grabbed my hands.

"Listen to me, Logan." She spoke slowly and steadily, and I sat there staring at her, wondering how I had could have ever doubted her. "You are a special, wonderful, brilliant man. You're not less than anyone. You are handsome, and kind, and funny, and you are loving and sweet. And my heart will always have a place for you, but I'm not the one for you." She shook her head slowly. "I love you, but I can't do this."

"Give me another chance," I begged her, my head caught up in the wonder of her words. "I fucked up. I know. I will do anything to prove myself to you."

"I can't do this, Logan!" she shouted at me, and the tears ran down her face more quickly this time, smearing her mascara. "I just can't do this. Please. You hurt me. You are so quick to think the worst of me. I will do anything for you. But I just can't do this. What you did to me the other night, it hurt me more than I've ever been hurt in my life. You crushed me. Do you understand that? You *crushed* me!"

"Your dad used to be best friends with my dad." The words coming out of my mouth sounded robotic. "Your dad was upset because my dad was smarter and got my mom. Your dad set my dad up with the police. My dad's life was never the same." I knew I was mumbling and not making sense, but I couldn't stop myself. I wanted her so badly to understand. "I grew up hating your dad because my dad hated him for ruining his life. We came to this house every week for years and just sat outside, and my dad would tell us about his dreams and his goals before your dad screwed him over. And then we would go home to our squalor, and we'd lay in bed hungry and cold, and we hated the family that lived on Manor Road." I paused to see if she was listening, and I saw the dismayed shock on her face as she stared at me. I continued and lifted up my shirt, "You see this scar? My dad stabbed me one day when I asked him to take us home. I was fed up of hearing the story about what your dad had done. It consumed his life. He was a drunk. He is a drunk." I paused and banged my fist against the steering wheel, unable to look at her as I spoke. "I hate him so much, I hate who he is. He's a sorry drunk who hit his wife and his kids, and I hate your dad for making him that person. I'm a jumble of emotions and I don't even know what to say." I turned to look at her to see how she was reacting, and she ran her hands down my chest and over my scar. She looked up at me with more tears welling in her eyes and I continued, this time, grabbing her hands and talking. "My whole life has consisted of

230

hating your dad, stealing cars, and trying to make a better life for my brothers. I never wanted to meet a girl and fall in love, and I certainly never wanted to meet you." I rubbed the tears away from her face as she cried. "When I saw you that night, I wondered who you were, this calm, cool and beautiful car thief, and I took you to the field because we had instant chemistry and I just liked how I felt when I was around you. And then you were so spunky and confident, and I was intrigued by you. When we made love, I felt like my body was on fire. But then you told me who you were, and I hated you. I hated myself for being with you."

"That's why you hurried me home." She spoke softly, and I nodded. "I think I understand it now." She sighed. "I'm glad you're finally opening up to me. I guess I understand why you wanted to hate me."

"But I couldn't stop thinking of your sweet smile and confident manner. And you kept coming back for more, and you seemed to get me, to understand me, to know and like me. You saw the real me. The me inside of the shell. You saw the real Logan Martelli, and I couldn't stop myself from falling for you."

"I thought it was the sex." She made a little joke and I felt my heart leap as she finally cracked a smile.

"Well, the sex was amazing, but that was just a bonus. You made me start to believe that there could be a happy ending for someone like me."

"But you didn't really believe it." She shook her head, sad again.

"No, a part of me didn't believe it." I sighed. "And when I got to the party, with my heart in my hand, and you told your dad I was a 'friend' after everything, I thought to myself, it was all a lie. She doesn't love me, she's not going to always be there for me. And I just couldn't take it. I needed to make you hurt, as you had hurt me." I paused and closed my eyes. "And I regretted it as soon as I saw the look in your eyes when you realized I had opened the door."

"You wanted to hurt me."

"No." I shook my head. "I have never wanted to hurt you."

"And you didn't trust me." She bit her lip. "I would do anything for you, Logan, and my heart is broken about my father. I'm shocked and devastated, but I—"

"Do you love me?" I interrupted her, not wanting her to reject me again. She nodded and my heart soared. "Do you think I would hurt you on purpose?" She stared at me for a long time and shook her head. "Do you believe I love you?" My voice cracked as I said 'love' and she nodded, her eyes darkening. "I think we deserve to give each other another chance." I stared at her, hoping to convince her to give me one last chance. "For the sake of love, give us one last chance."

"Okay." The sound was so low, I wasn't sure that I had heard her properly.

"What?" I asked, not daring to believe the words I had heard.

"Okay, I'll give you another chance."

"No more dating Joey." I grinned at her and she rolled her eyes. "And no more kissing him either."

"I didn't kiss him." She laughed and I pulled her towards me.

"I saw him kiss you tonight." I frowned at her, as I started to get jealous again. "You didn't say no."

"He pecked me, Logan." She giggled. "That's hardly a kiss."

"Don't let him do it again."

"Okay." She smiled and stared into my eyes. "I'm sorry about my dad."

"You believe me?" I looked at her with a worried expression, scared she doubted what I had said.

"Yes." She nodded. "I know you wouldn't lie to me. And from some things my mother has said recently," she sighed, "well, I think she was trying to tell me that my dad wasn't or isn't the man I think he is."

"What did she say?" I looked at her curiously.

"You can ask her yourself." She smiled at me. "We'll go to lunch and she can tell you everything she knows, if you think that would help you."

"I'd love to know more." I nodded. "I feel like I don't know everything. Maybe she can help me piece it together."

"I don't even know what to think about my dad." She bit her lip and looked at me sadly. "I still love him, and it makes me feel so guilty. I just don't know what to do."

"I don't want to talk about him." I kissed her. "I still hate him. I don't think I'll ever stop hating him, but I'm not going to let that stop me from loving you with all my heart."

"Do you really love me?" She grinned happily.

"If you love me." I laughed easily now.

"Tell me again," she whispered against my lips, almost shyly.

"I love you."

"Why?" She looked at me in wonder.

"I love you because you're spunky and brave. I love you because you're the first person I think of in the morning and the last person I see before I go to bed at night. I dream of you and live my days thinking about how I can be a better man for you. I don't know how I lived without you in my life, Maddie Wright."

"I love you, Logan Martelli."

"Why?" I held my breath as I waited for her response. A part of me still didn't feel worthy of her love.

"I love you because you're the most handsome man I've ever seen in my life. When you smile at me, a part of my heart explodes with happiness. When you look at me, I feel like you are seeing every part of me, and you care about what I have to say and what I do. I love that you appreciate that I'm a smart, loud, confident woman, but you also allow me to be your special someone, and you protect me, and keep me warm. I love that you like to take charge and dominate me, and when I feel you inside of me, I feel as if the world has stood still and there are only two people left." She gasped as I slipped my hand up her dress and caressed her inner thighs. "When you touch me, I feel like my skin is on fire and only you can quench me." I licked her lips and grinned against her mouth, laughing softly at her low moan as my fingers slipped into her panties.

"I love how wet you are for me, Maddie," I whispered against her lips. "I love that I can feel your body trembling slightly as I touch you lightly. I love the way you press into me and kiss me back passionately. I love that when I am inside of you, I am on top of the world, and when we climax, I feel like we are on top of a cliff, jumping into the waves together. And I never want to let you go. Not even if I have to drown. I want to be with you and in you at all times. I want to touch you and feel your heart race against mine. I want to see your big violet eyes light up with happiness when you see me, and I want to feel your soft kisses against my lips, waking me up in the mornings."

"Oh, Logan," she groaned as I continued rubbing her wetness and then slipped a finger inside of her. I groaned as I felt her tremble against me and clench against my finger.

"You're mine, Maddie Wright." I looked into her eyes possessively. "You're mine and I am never letting you go." I felt my phone vibrating as I spoke, and I pulled it out quickly with a frown. I saw Jared's name flashing across the screen and put it back down without answering it. "I want to make love to you," I leaned over and whispered in her ear, and she turned to me with a brief smile.

"Not in the bathroom." She winked at me and I laughed. I laughed because I was happy to have found the love of my life, and I was happy that she was forgiving and had a sense of humor.

"Can I make love to you, Maddie?"

"Yes." She grinned at me and I pushed my seat back as far as it would go. She climbed over the gearstick and straddled my lap, reaching down to unzip my pants, she pulled out my hard, throbbing erection and grinned as she leaned towards me and kissed me. I grabbed her around the waist and pulled her down on me. I lifted her dress hastily and slid her panties to the side roughly before positioning myself at her opening. She moaned as I pushed the tip into her slowly and moved her hips so she was now in charge. She kissed me as she started riding me slowly, and I grabbed her butt and caressed it as she moved back and forth quicker and quicker. We kissed passionately and with abandon, and I tried to make her move more slowly as I felt my orgasm building up quickly.

"Slow down, Maddie," I groaned. "I'm going to explode."

"So am I." She grinned and continued rocking back and forth, and within a few minutes I was exploding inside of her as she continued her movements. I felt her trembling and moaning as she starting to come, and I sucked on her tongue as she climaxed on me. We sat there for a few minutes grinning at each other, and then her phone started ringing. I looked at her with a frown and she shrugged her shoulders as she reached over to look at her phone. She glanced at it quickly and stuffed it back into her bag, her face looking at mine anxiously. I was pretty sure it was Joey, and I kept my mouth shut, not wanting to ruin the moment with my anger and jealousy. I was still upset that she had gone on a few dates with him, even though nothing had happened, but I knew I just had to get over it.

"Do you want to come over?" I played with her hair as she lay on top of me.

She shook her head slightly. "I have to go in."

"You can stay with me," I persisted. "I don't want to sleep without you tonight."

"I want to sleep with you as well, but not tonight." She looked at her bag distractedly. "In fact, I better get in before my parents start looking for me, and my dad catches me *in flagrante* with you again."

"I'm sorry." I bit my lip, and she shook her head.

"No. It's the past. I don't want to relive it." She leaned forward and kissed me again before getting off of my lap. "Call me tomorrow?"

"You're leaving now?" For some reason I was reluctant to let her out of my sight. A part of me was scared that she would change her mind and decide that she didn't want to be with after all.

"Yes." She nodded, and opened the car door. "Call me tomorrow."

"Let me walk you to the door." I jumped out of the car to escort her, and she smiled at me sweetly.

"You're such a gentleman, who would have figured it." She laughed and shook her head. "But no, this is fine." She wrapped her arms around my neck and kissed me one more time. I felt myself growing hard again and pulled her into me and she pulled away laughing. "Not again."

"Please?" I winked at her and she giggled.

"No." She shook her head and I tickled her. She started laughing and twitching and her handbag fell to the ground, and her wallet and phone fell out. I helped pick up her phone and as I passed it to her, I decided to check out who had left her the missed call. I looked at the screen as I passed her the phone, and I nearly dropped it again when I saw Jared's name.

"Why is Jared calling you?" I frowned.

"I don't know." She shrugged. "Maybe looking for you?"

"Yeah." I nodded slowly, not believing it but not wanting to question her. "Dream of me tonight?" I traced my finger along her palm as we walked back over to her house.

"Of course." She smiled back at me sweetly.

"Then I'll meet you in my dreams tonight." I smiled at her. "You'll be naked and in a field."

"And you'll have some whipped cream." She winked back at me, and my heart ached as I realized I wouldn't be with her tonight. I hadn't even left yet, but I already missed her.

"I can get some whipped cream now and come back," I offered eagerly and she laughed.

"I'll see you tomorrow, Logan."

"I love you." I kissed her and she nodded.

"I know." She hurried away from me and I watched as she walked through the front door with my heart in my hand. I wanted to shout out and stop her. I wanted to hear her tell me she loved me as well. I needed to hear it again. I walked back to the car slowly and happy. I hadn't lost her. I couldn't quite believe how lighthearted I felt. I hadn't lost her.

I got in and started the car but for some reason, I didn't want to leave. A part of me felt that something wasn't quite right. There was an uneasy feeling in the pit of my stomach. I still didn't really understand why she had dated Joey so quickly after we had fallen out or why had Jared called her. I didn't believe he was calling her looking for me. How would he even have her number? I chewed on my lower lip and frowned. My stomach started churning, and an odd feeling of foreboding filled me. Something wasn't quite right. I knew that with every fiber of my being. Maddie wasn't telling me something. She hadn't even really asked me any questions about our dads. Something was off, and I was scared that I wasn't going to like the truth.

***

I tried calling Jared as I drove home, but he didn't answer the phone. As I pulled into the driveway, I saw Vincent waiting for me and my heart started pounding.

"Where's Jared?" I jumped out of the car, and ran up to Vincent.

"He left." Vincent looked at me with a scared expression.

"What do you mean he left?" I shouted at him.

"I don't know." Vincent spoke hurriedly. "He was pissed when you left to go meet Maddie. He said you were going to fuck up everything. He called Joey to find out about the sale and when it was going to go down. I don't know what happened, but he got really angry and hung up."

"Why was he angry?" I questioned, my brain going a hundred miles a minute.

"I don't know." His tone was tense. "Then he tried calling you, and you didn't answer."

"I was busy."

"With Maddie?"

"Yes, with Maddie."

Vincent looked away and mumbled something, and I pushed his shoulder. "If you have something to say, tell me to my face."

"Why don't you just leave her alone?"

"I love her," I bit out harshly.

"She's bad news."

"I thought you liked her." My voice announced the betrayal I felt at his words, I had always known Jared hated Maddie, but I thought Vincent liked her.

"I do like her, but she's the mayor's daughter, Logan." He sighed. "This isn't the time to be focusing on her. We need all our wits about us."

"Don't worry about it." I tried calling Jared's number again, and I heard the phone ringing in Vincent's pocket.

238

"Why do you have his phone?" I shouted at him.

"He left it with me." Vincent looked scared. "He said there was something he needed to take care of. He told me that we were to do the exchange together without him. We just needed to wait for the call."

"What the fuck? Where did he go?"

"I don't know." Vincent looked at me with wild eyes. "But he was crazy. He told me that now was the time to make everything right. He said if you weren't going to do it, he would."

"Do what?" I felt a chill run through my bones. "What is he going to do?"

"I don't know." Vincent grabbed my shoulders. "But he told me to tell you to trust him. He said that no matter what happens, remember that he is your brother and he loves you."

"What the fuck does that mean?" I broke away from Vincent and paced up and down. "We need to find him." I grabbed hold of his shirt and pulled him towards me. "If you know where he is Vincent, you better tell me. By God, you better tell me."

"I don't know." Vincent pushed me away from him. "I know you're anxious, but threatening me is not going to help anything."

"Give me his phone. I'm calling Joey." I took the phone from Vincent and dialed Joey's number. He answered on the second ring and started talking.

"Dude, you need to chill, okay? I'm only fucking with Maddie 'cause her dad wants me to, I told you that. I told you before, she is not my type. I like them skinny and blonde. She's got big tits, but her ass is too big for me as well." He laughed and I gripped the phone tightly, not saying anything. I wanted to see if he would say anything of importance and I didn't want him to know that I wanted to knock his front teeth out. "Jared, you can be such a baby sometimes, stop being a pussy. Do you want her or something? Does Logan even know you've been talking to her? I bet she wants to suck on your cock. Her dad would be pissed if she caught her with another

Martelli. I wouldn't do it, bro, he'll fuck you up. Trust me. Let Logan fight that battle. Ha, ha, ha. Jared?"

"This is Logan." My voice was tight and I wished I was with him so I could thump him so hard that I had him crying. I knew he was a piece of shit.

"Oh," Joey paused. "Where's Jared?"

"That's what I want to know."

"I was joking about Maddie." Joey laughed uncomfortably. "Jared's not fucking her or anything. He hates her guts."

"I see."

"He just told me tonight," Joey continued quickly. "In fact, he encouraged me to go on another date with her."

"You were out with her before tonight," I growled.

"You mean the other night, when you guys stole the car?" Joey laughed. "That was her dad's idea." He laughed. "But tonight was all Jared's idea. I guess he wants to make sure you're out of the picture."

"He wouldn't have done that." My voice is deceptively soft, but all I wanted to do was cuss.

"He hates her." Joey was matter-of-fact. "He should be careful who he tells that to. I know her dad well, and he will fuck him up if he hears that."

"When is the exchange going to happen?" I changed the subject, not wanting to discuss my brother and Maddie anymore.

"I was just about to call you guys. Bring the car to the pier tomorrow morning at seven a.m. We'll be waiting with the money."

"You'll be there?"

"Yeah." Joey's voice was low. "I gotta get my cut as well."

"The buyer will be there?"

"I guess so."

"Joey, who is the buyer?"

"I don't know everything." He sounded nonchalant. "And who cares? It's a million bucks. For nothing. Just be there."

"It's not for nothing, and this better not be some stupid setup."

"Look," Joey sighed. "I honestly don't know who set it up. My dad told me about it, 'cause he knows I'm friends with Jared. And he told me to approach you."

"So you have no idea who the buyer is?" My heart started pounding. "That is not how you made it seem."

"It's fine." Joey sounded unsure of himself. "Look, I gotta go. Be at the pier at seven."

"Wait a minute, I want to—" I stopped talking as I realized he had already hung up the phone. "Something's going on." I frowned at Vincent. "I don't know what, but I have a bad feeling." I shook my head in worry. "I fucking knew we couldn't trust Joey."

"It'll be okay, Logan." Vincent's eyes blazed. "It has to be."

"We have to take the Bugatti to the pier at seven a.m." I sighed. "With or without Jared."

"And we'll get the money?"

"I guess." I bit my lip nervously. I had a bad feeling that we were never going to see the million dollars. "Listen to me, Vincent. You need to drive the Mustang to the pier. And if anything shady goes down, you deny everything. You don't know anything about the Bugatti. If the cops show up, it was all me."

"No." Vincent shook his head. "I can't do that."

"Vincent, listen to me. You need to take care of dad and Jared if anything happens to me. Okay?"

"Okay." We stood there silently for a few moments and then walked back into the house. We stopped by the living room door and we watched as my father slept on the couch, snoring his head off. I wanted to go and talk to him. I wanted to go to him for advice. I wanted him to tell me everything was going to be okay. I wanted him to be better. I took once last look and turned away to go up the stairs.

"You coming?" I looked over at Vincent, who was still standing at the door.

"No." He shook his head. "I'll go up in a bit."

"I love you, bro." I gave him a quick smile and walked up the stairs, worry making every step heavier. Just an hour ago, I was the happiest I had ever been in my life and now I was the most stressed. I tried to remember Maddie's smile as I lay down on the bed, but all I could think about was the missed call on her phone from Jared. And what Joey had just told me. I closed my eyes and tried to stop analyzing everything. I didn't want to jump to any conclusions. I would talk to Maddie after all this was taken care of. I'm sure there had to be a reasonable explanation. I drifted off to sleep, but all I could think of was how much Jared hated Maddie. I really hoped he wasn't out there doing anything stupid.

***

Vincent and I arrived at the pier at six-thirty a.m., and we walked to the shore and stared at the waves in companionable silence as we waited. We didn't bring up Jared's name, but I knew that both of us were worried about where he was. I tried to ignore the worries in my mind. The drive to the pier had been smooth and there had been no cop cars around. So far everything was going smoothly. Jared's phone rang, and I looked at Vincent as I answered it.

"Hello."

"Hey, it's Joey."

"Where are you?"

"I just got to the pier, where are you?"

"Down by the jetty."

"Come to the parking lot. That's where he is going to meet us."

"Who is he?"

"The guy who set it all up."

"Who is it?"

"Just come to the parking lot." And with that he hung up on me again. I put the phone in my pocket and looked at Vincent with a brief smile.

"This is it, bro. Joey's here and said the guy who set it up will be in the parking lot."

"So we're doing the deal in the parking lot?" Vincent frowned, and I knew he felt as I did, that something seemed off.

"Yeah," I shrugged. "Remember what I said last night."

"I don't like this, Logan."

"There's nothing we can do right now." I took a deep breath. "Hold on a second." I pulled out my phone and called Maddie quickly. I sighed when it went to voicemail, but decided to leave a quick message. "Maddie, I just wanted to tell you I love you. I'm doing a deal right now, and it doesn't seem right. I just wanted to let you know that I love you. If anything goes wrong, please know I did this because I wanted to be a man you could be proud of. I love you." I hung up quickly and Vincent and I walked to the parking lot in silence.

"Over here," Joey called out to us as we walked into the almost empty lot.

"So where is he?" I stared at Joey with cold eyes. I took in his appearance and it took everything in me not to deck him. He looked so cocky and carefree, and there was something in the glint of his eyes that made me shiver. Something seemed off and I wasn't sure what it was. Maybe it was because he didn't seem to have any nerves. But it was more than that. It was almost as if he knew something that gave him great pleasure. Like he had a surprise. A big surprise that he couldn't wait to share. But it didn't feel like a good surprise. All of a sudden I felt very apprehensive. "Where the fuck is he?" I growled at Joey with intense eyes, warning him that I wasn't here out of fun and I could blow up at any moment.

"He's coming." Joey looked at me with a slightly scared look.

"This better not be a setup."

"Look, dude, I'm just here for my money." Joey shrugged. "I didn't do anything."

"Where is Jared?" I got up in his face. "If you did anything to him, I'll fuck you up."

"I don't know what you're talking about." Joey looked at me with an apprehensive look. "Believe me when I say I didn't set this up. I just approached him because everyone knows you are the guys to steal a car."

"So where is he?" I muttered.

"I'm right here, Logan." I heard the familiar voice behind me, and I froze. I turned around slowly, and there standing behind Vincent, was Marty. He looked at me with a short smile, his eyes looking beady in his fat face, and I wanted to punch him. I should have known that something was up.

"You. Fuck it," I cursed as I realized that Marty was behind it.

"Nice to see you as well." He grinned at me evilly. "It's been a while."

"What do you want?"

"I thought I warned you that if you steal cars in River Valley, they go to me or you don't steal. I even had my man tell you when he bought the Toyota to not fuck with me. I thought you understood what the deal was."

"I didn't agree to that." I squared my shoulders.

"I think you need to learn a lesson." He laughed. "You don't mess with me."

"Why? You messed with me and my family!" I shouted at him. "Why should we let you get away with not paying us properly? Do you think I'm going to steal cars and take a quarter of the money? This is a free market, Marty, I can do what I fucking want."

"You're costing me money, Logan. I don't like it when that happens." He stepped towards me. "And neither does my boss. You have screwed us over one too many times. Your dad knew the deal. He stole the car, brought it to me right away, and took whatever money he got. He was grateful and happy. You're just a greedy little boy. You've been causing way too much trouble. I tried to give you a warning, but you fucked up one too many times, and now my boss is ready to take you down."

"Huh?" I looked at him puzzled. "What are you talking about? What boss?"

"Logan," Vincent hissed at me, but I was too busy staring Marty down to turn towards him.

"You're a bully, Marty. Give me my money and fucking leave us alone." I walked towards him, ready to take him by the scruff of his collar. I was surprised that he didn't have his henchmen there. There was nothing to stop me from beating him up. And after him, I would beat up Joey. I knew he was a sorry motherfucker. I would get both of them so black and blue that they wouldn't pull this shit again with anyone, then I would steal the money and leave town. "Where the fuck is the money?" I shouted at Marty. "Give it to me now before we take this down a very bad road."

"I'm afraid that's not going to be possible, Logan." Another voice came from the left of me, and I turned around to see who had spoken. The voice sounded slightly familiar but I couldn't place it. As I turned and saw who was there, the blood drained from my face, and I couldn't say a word.

"It's nice to see you again," he cackled while staring at me with evil eyes. "Well, I can't really lie, it's not that nice seeing you again."

"The feeling is mutual," I finally spoke up, and took a deep breath as my head started spinning. What was the mayor doing here? I looked at Vincent and his face reflected the shock that was on my own. I tried to move, but my body wouldn't cooperate. I felt like I was in a bad dream and there was nothing I could do to escape the impending danger I saw coming.

"You can go now, Joey." The mayor smiled at the traitor casually. "Thanks for your help."

I turned to look at him and he shrugged. "Traitor," I hissed at him, wanting to kill him. My brain was screaming at me, *I told you not to trust him. I told you not to trust him.*

"You brought it on yourself." He looked back at me with a hard expression.

"What do you want?" I turned back to the mayor, unable to stop the hatred spewing from my eyes. In that moment, I wished I had a gun because I would have shot him without thinking of the consequences.

"I want you and your family to leave River Valley. I don't want you to call my daughter again, and you must never see her again." His voice was cold, and I saw his upper lip twitch slightly. I realized that more than anything, he was mad about me seeing Maddie. This wasn't about the cars or selling them to Marty; this was about me not being good enough for his little girl. As I stared at him, I realized that we had one thing in common. We both loved Maddie with all of our hearts. The only problem was that he was an evil bastard as well.

"That's not going to happen." I stared back at him, not moving. "I love Maddie, I will not stop talking to her or seeing her, unless she

246

tells me not to."

"Then I will call the police and tell them to come and collect you and your brother." The mayor pulled his phone out of his pocket. "I will have you arrested for grand theft auto and for assault."

"You won't do that," I called his bluff. "You have no leg to stand on. I haven't assaulted anyone, and you set up the theft. I'll have you go down as a co-conspirator. I will tell them that you knew what Marty has been up to."

"I don't think you get it, Martelli." The mayor looked at me pompously. "Marty isn't up to anything. He works for me. I run this town. How do you think you were able to steal so many cars without the police coming after you?"

"Marty has connections?" I frowned and looked at Marty, who stood there looking small and insignificant. Why hadn't it struck me before? It was unlikely that Marty was in charge of the whole endeavor. I had never questioned what my dad had said about Marty having the police connections. "You have no connections, do you?" I felt my shoulders slump as I looked at him. "You've been working for the mayor from the beginning." I shook my head as it all started coming together. My dad had started stealing cars because he had no other options and Marty had approached him. But if Marty had been working for the mayor this whole time, it meant that it was the mayor who had told Marty to contact me dad. "So you set my dad up on purpose?" I frowned as I realized the truth about the situation. I stared at the mayor as I spoke to him. "You set this whole thing up from the beginning, didn't you? From when you were kids? That was your whole plan."

"I'll tell you this, you're a lot smarter than your dad." The mayor laughed heartily while he stared at me with cold eyes. "My father was in this business for years. He told me I needed to recruit someone to help with the business. I was friends with your dad. He was poor. I figured I had the perfect guy. I didn't anticipate him becoming a loser, though. How is your drunk of a father, by the way?"

"Don't you ever—" I moved forward to go and hit him, but Vincent grabbed my arm and stopped me.

"It wasn't easy." The mayor looked at us with a baffled expression. "I thought he would have jumped at the chance to make some extra money, what with him having none. But he wasn't interested in hearing about any of my schemes. He just wanted to go to college, get a degree, and find a good job.

"So why did you have to take that away from him?" The words fell out-of-my mouth. What sort of evil person would deliberately do that to someone else?

"He stole the woman I loved." His expression changed. "From the moment, I laid eyes on your mother, I knew. She was the one for me. She was my everything. And then your dad stole her, and I begged her to take me back. I told her I'm rich, I have the money, I can take care of you. And she said to me she didn't care. Money meant nothing to her. She loved your dad and wanted to see where it went with him. Well, I took care of that." He laughed bitterly. "She never had to worry about having too much money or that she was with him for anything but love."

"How could you do that? You had Maddie's mother."

"Ha, I never loved her." He shook his head. "She gave me Maddie, who is the light of my life. But I've never loved her or felt the same passion as I did for your mom."

"You're an evil man." I stepped towards him unseeing but ready to hurt. My heart sagged with pain and the thirst for revenge and I wanted to make him cry out. I wanted to hear him scream for my forgiveness. I wanted to make him pay. Vincent must have seen the look in my eyes because he reached forward and grabbed my shoulders. I tried to push him off of me, and he tightened his grip. "Let me go," I growled at him and his eyes pleaded with me to stop.

The mayor looked at us both in disgust and was about to step forward when his phone rang. He frowned and pulled it out and answered it.

"Hello, dear, what is it? I'm busy." His face paled and I saw him look at me quickly. "They took Maddie? What? How much? Don't call the police yet." He hung up and faced me, his face as white as a sheet. "What have you done with Maddie?"

"What are you talking about?" I felt faint as I stared at him. All my worst fears were coming true and I was scared to hear what he was going to say. All of my anger and hatred faded as worry seeped into my heart. I was scared that he was going to tell me that something bad had happened to Maddie.

"Maddie has been kidnapped." His voice cracked. "They want me to deliver a million dollars for her safe recovery. They called my wife." He looked away from me. "They said they would kill her if I didn't give them the money."

"Who took her?" I heard the words but they didn't seem like they were coming out of my mouth. I had a bad feeling that I knew who had taken her. Everything around me seemed like it was spinning out of control, and all I could think was, what had I done?

"I was hoping you would tell me that." His eyes narrowed as he looked at me and Vincent. "Where's the third brother?"

"Home." I swallowed hard, not wanting to believe Jared had anything to do with it. He was my brother. I knew he hated Maddie, but he also knew that I loved her. I didn't want to believe that he could do this to me or to her, but as I thought back to the last few conversations we had had, I started to think that maybe he thought this was the only way. The mayor's phone rang again and he answered it quickly. "Hello." He spoke quickly and then he put it on speakerphone so we could all hear it.

"I have your daughter. I want a million dollars by eight p.m. tonight or I will kill her." The voice sounded calm, and Vincent and I exchanged a worried look.

"Where is my daughter?" The mayor shouted into the phone. "I will have you arrested."

"You can't do anything to make my life any worse than it is. But I can make yours a lot worse. Trust me." There was a sudden noise and then a high-pitched scream. "I will call you back in a few hours.

Do not call the police or get anyone else involved, or you will not see Maddie alive again." And then the phone went dead. We all stood there in shock and fright and I stared at Vincent wordlessly. I didn't know what to say or do. I had to find Maddie and save her. There was no way I could live with myself if anything happened to her, but I was also scared about what would happen to her kidnapper. I knew I would do anything to get her back safely, but I also knew that it could cost me everything. Because I knew the voice on the phone. I knew who had kidnapped Maddie. It was Jared.

Chapter 13

Maddie

I shivered in the cold room and tried to keep my eyes open, though it was really hard because I hadn't been to sleep as yet. I pinched myself in an attempt to stay awake and tried not to scream when I saw something scurry across the room. I took a deep breath and tried to calm my nerves. I saw Jared pacing up and down in the corner with a gun in his hands and I looked away quickly. I was scared and frazzled, and I knew I was out of it. I really needed to sleep for a few hours to refresh my brain, but I hadn't been able to.

Jared had called me twice last night. The first two times I hadn't picked up the phone as I had been busy with Joey and then with Logan. But when I saw his second missed call, I knew something was up. And then he called a third time, about five minutes after Logan had left, and he had asked me to come down to meet him outside, and now here I was. I looked around the sparse room and thought that it was straight out of a movie scene. I almost smiled to myself at just how surreal everything felt. I felt like I was an actress playing a role, though I'd never practiced being kidnapped before. All my senses were working in overdrive, and I buried my face in my lap for a moment, while I tried to gather my thoughts.

"Do you have any water?" I asked him quietly. My throat was dry and I really needed something to drink.

"No." he shook his head. He stared down at the gun, and I shivered at the sight of the metallic weapon. "Sorry, I didn't think about that."

"It's okay." I looked away from him quickly, as I felt my eyes welling up with tears and I didn't want him to see how upset I was. I couldn't believe that it had all come to this. Everything I thought I knew about the Martellis was wrong. They weren't the men I thought they were, and my heart broke at my complete and utter naiveté. My life would never be the same again, and I wasn't sure how I would ever get past this, and that was if everything went well. I felt like this summer I had grown from a girl to a woman. I'd been so naïve when I had gone to meet Logan at the pier, my only hope had been to impress him and get to know him. I'd been thrilled and excited to finally meet him, and I hadn't been scared of anything. It had been like one super-duper rollercoaster ride, and now I was starting to worry I was going to fall out and go crashing to the ground. It had been a mistake for me to pursue Logan like some psycho. I had convinced myself that all was fair in love and war, and that he liked me too, but now that everything had happened, I realized that I had messed up. All I had done was ruin people's lives. And I had gotten hurt in the process as well. Every fiber of my person was crying inside at this moment. For everything I thought I knew that was wrong. For all the love and joy inside of me that had been captured and tied up. I felt tears welling in my eyes, but I wasn't going to allow myself to cry. I couldn't allow myself to cry.

"Your father better love you as much as you say he does." Jared's voice was harsh. "I sure hope you really are the apple of his eye and he loves you so much, he will do anything for you."

"He does." My words were short and simple. That was one thing I was sure of, my dad would do anything for me. "He'll pay."

"He better pay." Jared sat down and I could see the strain in his face. He looked up at me with tired eyes, and I thought of Logan as he stared at me. "He better pay or there will be hell to pay." He looked worried and tense. "And it won't be just me who goes down, it will be Logan, and Vincent as well."

"Logan doesn't know anything, does he?" I whispered, scared to hear the answer. My heart raced as I thought of him. How I loved him. How I wished I could replace every worry and fear and hatred in his heart with love, joy, and happiness. I wished I could kiss away all the hurt he had gone through in his life. It killed me to know that someone I loved could have done this to him.

"Of course not." He shook his head. "You know that."

"He'll be worried." I bit my lower lip.

252

"Yes, he will." Jared sighed. "I really wish you wouldn't have spoken to him last night."

"I didn't want him to think that I wasn't willing to give him a second chance. I love him and he loves me." I sighed. "I know we agreed that I shouldn't talk to him until everything was done, but he begged me, Jared. I saw the fear in his eyes, and the love, and I just couldn't turn him away. I was so angry after the party. I hated him with everything in me. But I understand why he did it. And he finally opened up to me. I just couldn't send him away. I needed to see him and be with him. I know now that was a mistake. I should have waited a bit."

"I know." Jared shook his head, and rolled his eyes. "What a mess."

"Love isn't a mess, though." I smiled briefly. "At least he knows I love him, no matter what happens. And I know he loves me."

"This is all a hot mess." Jared jumped up and started pacing again. "I just hope it works. I want this all to work out for everyone, but for you and Logan especially. I want this to work out for him. He's always been there for me and Vincent. I'm glad he has someone like you, who loves him as much as you do."

"It'll work out." I jumped up as well and walked over to him slowly. "You need to hurt me." I stared into his eyes thoughtfully, trying to think of how we could escalate the situation.

"What?" He looked at me in shock.

"You need to punch me or scratch me. Then send a photo to my dad so he knows you mean business."

"I'm not doing that." Jared stepped away from me and shook his head vehemently. "I'm not going to hit you."

"It's not a request, Jared." I stared at him wildly. "He needs to know you mean business. We can't let anything happen to Logan."

"What do you think he's planning to do?" Jared looked at me, and for the first time, I really saw just how scared he was.

"I don't know. I honestly don't know." I looked down. "If you had told me a few months ago that this was who my father was, I would have laughed. I never would have believed any of this, but now, well, now, a whole lot of things are making sense."

"He better not hurt him." Jared gripped the gun in his hand I saw his fingers on the trigger. "If anything happens to Logan, I don't know what I will do."

"You need to be careful with that. Is the safety on?" I touched his shoulder gently.

"I don't know." His finger moved away from the trigger quickly. "How can I tell?"

"Give it to me." I took my father's gun from his hand and checked it. "Let's just put it down for now. I don't want anyone getting hurt."

"I don't know why you brought the gun." He trembled as he looked at it.

"I'd rather we have it than him." I shrugged. "I couldn't have let Logan go to that meeting this morning if I had known Dad had the gun available."

"You really love Logan, don't you?" Jared looked at me in amazement. "I've never met anyone, asides from Logan, who thinks about others as much as you do. You're a real gem, Maddie."

"Yes. You know that I would do anything for Logan." This time I couldn't prevent the tears from falling. "It's like he's my other half. He just gets me and I just get him. It's like we were fated for each other. I know that sounds kooky, but I feel like he was made for me, and I was made for him."

"Yeah," he laughed. "I mean, I knew you were sprung on him when we first met at Joey's, but when you came over to play cards that night, well, that's when I knew you loved him and he loved you." He shook his head. "Only God knows why he put you two together. It couldn't have been a worse match. The two children of two men who hate each other."

"Come on now." I tried to laugh. "We were made for each other. And really my dad has no reason to hate your dad, and your dad has every reason." I sighed. "I just wish that none of this had ever happened."

"I am glad he has you." He nodded weakly and gave me a quick hug. "I'm sorry for everything in the beginning."

"It's okay, I know why you hated me." I smiled up at him, genuinely at that point. "My dad is and was an ass."

"I just can't believe he was in charge of the whole car theft business all this time." Jared's eyes were wide.

"Yeah," I sighed. "I guess my grandfather started the 'family business.' My dad had been trying to recruit your dad all through high school, but your dad just never showed interest."

"I wonder why my dad never mentions that." Jared looked confused. "All these years, he's told us about everything, but it's like he didn't even know."

"I don't know." I took a deep breath. "My mom didn't really know everything that went on between them. Though she said there was a lot of competition between them. And it all blew up when your mom decided to date your dad. My dad was gutted. My mom knew, you know. She knew what happened. But she had been in love with my dad for years and so she never said anything. She was just so happy to be with him, even though he never loved her." I felt sad as I thought about what my mom had let happen with her silence. "I almost feel like she is just as bad, she was so weak. But she said she used to think that the best thing that happened in her life was your dad stealing your mom away."

"He never told us he stole her from your dad, either."

"I guess he didn't want to look like a bad guy?" I shrugged. "But really it's my dad who is the bad guy. People steal girlfriends all the time. You don't ruin someone's life because of it. My mom thinks that he has just always been plain evil. And now she realizes that a lot of it was her fault for letting it happen without saying a word. That's why she is helping with the plan now."

"When did you realize your dad may be involved?"

"When I went with Logan to sell the Toyota. The guy who came to buy it was someone I'd seen my dad with. My dad had said he was a business associate. And when I heard Marty was involved, I knew he did a lot of work for my dad." I bit my lip and turned away. "It all just seemed to click into place. When I was over at Lucy's, I heard you and Joey talking about stealing the Bugatti one night, and I was confused as to why Joey was involved. That's why I pulled you to the side and told you I thought something may be up."

"I can't believe I ever trusted that motherfucker." Jared's fist curled into a ball. "But thank you for reaching out to me."

"Yeah, so when Joey invited me to go out on the night of the robbery, I was suspicious. Especially because when he picked me up, my dad said something like, 'Make sure you stay out for a long amount of time.' It just struck me as weird. And that he wouldn't take me home until he spoke to you on the phone, and I realized he was trying to use me as an alibi." I tried not to cry again. "I just can't believe my dad had him use me as an alibi. I just don't know who he is."

"I'm glad you called me that night. I knew something was up when I called him and he said he was with you. I knew there was no way you would be out with him, unless something was wrong." Jared spoke slowly. "Logan always said Joey was trouble, and I always kind of knew. But I didn't want to believe it."

"I called you because I just knew that somehow my dad had to be involved. And I was certain when Joey dropped me off and he told my dad that it was all done and winked at him." I played with my fingers as I remembered the smug and satisfied expression on my father's face. I could still remember how my heart had dropped as I realized that my father was not the man that I thought he was. "I wanted to accuse him right then and there," I sighed. "But then I figured I should tell you first and we could figure out what to do."

"Yeah, I'm so glad you called me. That wasn't the right time. We really needed more info. I'm glad I convinced you to go out with Joey again."

"It was awful, but I knew that I needed to find out what the plan was for the Bugatti. I had a bad feeling, and I was right."

"I was calling you all night," he sighed. "And then stupid Logan had to go and see you. I thought he was going to ruin everything."

"He knows you called me."

"Shit, what did you say?"

"I said you were most probably looking for him."

"Ha." Jared rolled his eyes. "He didn't buy that, I'm sure."

"I wanted to tell him." I looked at Jared with a sad expression. "But I wanted to tell you first."

"I'm glad I came over so we could decide what to do." He laughed. "Only you could come up with such a perfect plan."

"It's the only solution I could think of." I shivered. "After Joey told me that I should forget Logan because he was likely going to jail for a long time, I knew my dad had something shady planned. And so I went to talk to my mom. And she cried. She cried and cried and asked me to forgive her. She knows how much I love Logan, and she didn't want me to suffer because of my dad and his hatred of the Martellis. So we came up with the plan together."

"It was ingenious."

"You can't give me all the credit. I got the idea from a movie on Lifetime, and it still hasn't worked yet." My teeth chattered in the cold. "But I figured the only thing that would get my father to relent was if something were to happen to me or somehow threaten my life. This was the perfect scenario, me being kidnapped. And my mom called my dad to tell him, so now he thinks it is really legitimate. And Logan doesn't know that we're friends now, so he would be believable in his behavior." I bit my lower lip. "I hope he's okay. I'm sure he is pissed and worried."

"I'm sure he wants to kill me right about now. I'm sure he is thinking about how he can take me and your dad down." Jared joked but I could see the worry in his eyes. "I just hope he forgives me."

"We had to do this. It was the only way to ensure that my dad didn't get Logan sent to jail, and that you guys would get the money. Kidnapping me was the only solution. At least, it was the best solution my mom and I could think of."

"I don't even want the money from the Bugatti." Jared shook his head. "It feels dirty. I know Logan won't want it, either."

"Don't think of it as money from the Bugatti. Think of it as money for everything my father has done to your family. He owes you." I froze as the phone rang. I watched it as Jared answered it on speakerphone.

"Hello." His voice sounded a lot more confident than he looked.

"Where is my daughter?" I heard my father's booming voice and swallowed hard. I still wasn't sure how my father could be this person. He was the man who had loved me and protected me my whole life. But he was the worst person I had ever met.

"She's here."

"Let me talk to her." Jared looked at me questioningly and I bit my lip, unsure of what to do. "Let me talk to her or the deal is off."

"Hold on." He passed me the phone, and I held it for a second before talking.

"Daddy," I whimpered.

"Maddie, oh my God, Maddie, is that you?"

"Yes, Daddy," I cried. "Please come and get me."

"Where are you?"

"I don't know!" I cried out again. "Do whatever they ask, Daddy. He has a gun."

"He has a gun." My father's voice was loud and I heard someone in the background saying something.

"Wait, what are you doing?" My dad's voice sounded angry.

"Maddie, Maddie, are you there?" Logan's voice sounded hoarse and worried.

"Logan," I said his name softly. "What are you doing?"

"I know Jared kidnapped you, Maddie. I'm so sorry. I know he hates you, but I never thought he would do this."

"Logan, please—" I bit my lip and looked at Jared's anguished expression. This was not going according to plan at all. "Please just give my father the phone."

"Tell Jared I told him to release you now. Tell him I said if he loves me, he will let you go now."

"He can't do that, Logan," I cried, hoping he would realize that there was something else going on.

"I love you, Maddie. Please, please tell him that. I won't let anything happen to you. I promise."

"Logan, I—"

"Give me back the phone, you piece of scum." I heard my father's voice in the background. "Maddie, it's me again. Where are you?"

"I don't know, Daddy," my voice was louder this time. "Please just do as he asks."

"I'm going to get the cops," he breathed into the phone. "Try and find out where you are."

"No cops, Dad. He'll kill me!" I screamed out. "No cops. Just get the money."

"I can't just let them—"

"Noooooo!" I screamed and hung up the phone. I turned to Jared with a panicked look. "He said he's going to call the cops."

"You said he wouldn't do that. You said he would just pay so he could get you back." Jared's eyes looked wild.

"That's what I thought."

"What are we going to do?" He looked at me in fright and I grabbed the phone again.

"I have to call my mom." I grimaced. "I have to call her and trust her to help me."

"Fuck." Jared sat back down on the ground with his head in his hands. "It's over."

I didn't answer him, because I felt the same way as well. What had I done? What had seemed like a way out now seemed like it had only made the situation worse. The penalty for kidnapping was going to be a whole lot worse than it would be for stealing a car.

***

"My mom said not to call him or answer his calls again." I looked at Jared. "She's going to bring them to us."

"What does that mean?"

"She's going to tell them the address here. She'll say this is where the dropoff is supposed to happen. She's going to call the police from a neighboring town and have them waiting outside while everything goes down. She knows the chief of police in Sawyerville and so she has told him what's going on. She trusts him and knows he won't interfere with anything. I sure hope it all goes well. All we need is for my dad to bring the money and give it to you and let you and Logan go." I shivered again. "I'm cold."

"Come here." Jared called me over, and I picked up the gun and went and sat next to him. I put the gun down and then huddled next to him. He put his arms around me and I wrapped my arms around him so we could stay warm. I closed my eyes, and we must have fallen asleep because the next thing I knew we were lying flat on the ground and I could hear his heartbeat against my ears. I cuddled into him to stay warm, and then I heard the footsteps. Everything seemed to happen so quickly, and I was even able to jump up before Logan and my father burst into the room with Vincent and Marty behind them.

"Logan!" I cried out as I saw his distraught face. Jared and I sprang apart and Logan looked back and forth at us furiously.

"What the fuck is going on?" My dad charged towards us and Jared grabbed me.

"Stay back!" he shouted and grabbed the gun on the ground. "Stay back or I'll fucking shoot."

"What are you doing, Jared?" Logan screamed furiously and I tried to make eye contact with him so that he could see that everything was okay.

"You fucking Martellis, I should have—" My dad ran forward and pushed Jared back into the wall, he stumbled back and dropped the gun, and my dad and Logan both jumped to the ground to get it. Everything seemed to happen in a blur but before I knew it, a shot had been fired and I was screaming. I looked to the ground to see who had been shot, and my screaming intensified as I saw Logan just lying there. My father stood up with a shocked look on his face, and I gave him the most venomous look. I ran to Logan and fell to the ground, kissing his cheek. "Please, Logan. Please be okay!" I screamed at him, but he didn't answer me. And then I saw the blood seeping out of his body onto the ground and the next thing I knew, I had fainted. It all seemed like a bittersweet poetic justice. After all that I had done, I still hadn't been able to save my darling Logan.

***

I woke up in a hospital room. There were white lights all around me, and I could see my mom whispering to a nurse in the corner. I tried to stretch but my limbs screamed out in pain, and I tried not to moan.

"Where's Logan?" I cried out, and my mom looked over at me with a pained expression before walking over to me slowly.

"How are you feeling, Maddie?" Her eyes flashed in sympathy and my stomach dropped.

"Where is Logan?" I screamed out in fear.

"He's in the ER." She grabbed my hand. "I don't know what—"

"I need to go and see him, he needs me," I started crying. "How could Dad have shot him? You told me that everything would be okay."

"I'm so sorry, Maddie."

"It's all my fault, if I would have just left him alone," I mumbled. "This is all my fault. If he dies, oh my God, what am I going to do if he dies?"

"Maddie, none of this is your fault." She sighed. "Your father is a bad man. I'm so sorry, Maddie. I never should have let things go this far. I knew when you told me that you were falling for Logan that something bad would happen. I had hoped that we could talk to your dad, that hopefully his love of you would change him. Make him a better person. He's a very evil man, Maddie."

"But you love him." I looked at her in confusion.

"I was blinded by love, and it cost me everything. That is why Logan's mom left him. She saw him for who he was, and she tried to

262

warn me. But I was so jealous I didn't want to hear it, so I pretended that she was the enemy." She shook her head. "Look at what I did. I ruined so many lives. I'm not sure how I can ever make any of this right."

"Oh, Mom." I cried into her shoulder as she hugged me. "I don't understand but I'm sorry. I still love you. Where is Dad?" I looked into her eyes, worried. I was scared that he was at this moment trying to think of a way to ensure he ruined the Martellis' lives even more than he already had.

"He's at the police station," she paused. "In a cell."

"What?" My eyes popped open. "How come?"

"We'll discuss it later. For now we should go and see how Logan is. He should be coming out of surgery right about now."

"Surgery?" I frowned. "How long have I been here?"

"Four hours." She smiled at me gently. "You hit your head quite hard."

"Where are Jared and Vincent? Are they okay or—" I couldn't say the words out loud. Were they in jail as well?

"We're here." Jared smiled at me weakly from the door, and they both walked into the room, looking dazed and traumatized.

"Hey." I sat up and stared at them both with love filling my heart. "How's Logan?" I chewed my lower lip.

"They haven't said yet." Vincent kissed my cheek. "He'll be okay."

"He has to be okay." Jared took the words right out of my mouth.

"I'm so sorry." I started crying again and they both looked at me in dismay.

"It's not your fault." Jared stared at me with passionate eyes. "We know that. It's not your fault. It's your evil dad's." He looked over at my mom, and his face turned red. "Sorry."

"Don't be sorry." My mom's voice was loud and clear. "It was his fault, and I'm sorry for everything. None of this should ever have happened. It has to stop here." She pulled out her phone and walked towards the door. "I need to make some calls, please excuse me." She left the room, and I stared at Logan's brothers in silence. What could I say to them to make it better? It seemed to me that I, or everything that I represented, had ruined their lives.

"Maddie," Vincent began. "Jared and I want you to know that no matter what happens, you will always be our sister."

"Oh." I felt overwhelmed with emotions and looked down at my hands. How could they be so sweet and loving to me? After everything.

"You're a part of the family now, Maddie." Jared gave me a warm smile and took my hand. "It's what Logan would want."

"I want to go and see him." I attempted to get out of bed but fell back slightly because I felt woozy. Both Vincent and Jared rushed to my side, and I smiled at them thankfully, my heart filled with warmth and love once again. I just didn't understand how anyone in River Valley could have judged these boys so unfairly. To know each and every one of them was to love them. They were the most loving and courteous men I had ever met.

"Lean on me." Vincent smiled at me as he offered his arm. "We can go and see if Logan is out of surgery."

"Take my other arm." Jared smiled down at me from the other side, and they both helped me as we walked to the ER.

"I'll die if anything happens to him," I whispered. "He has to be okay."

"He'll be okay." Vincent's voice was confident. "He's Logan Martelli, he will always be okay."

I looked over at him, and I saw the strain in his smile, even though his words were positive. He was as worried as I was, and he was trying to convince both of us that our worlds weren't about to end. We stopped in the ER waiting room, and we all sat there in silence, waiting for someone to come and give us the word.

"Are you a relation of Logan Martelli?" A middle-aged man walked into the ER with a clipboard and we all jumped up.

"Yes, I'm his brother," Vincent spoke up, and we waited for the doctor to speak. I felt myself going weak and I held onto Jared's arm tightly. He looked at me with concern, and held onto me with a tighter grip.

"Logan just got out of surgery. I'm afraid that—"

"Oh my God, no!" I screamed, and I felt like my heart was being pulled out of my body. "No, please, God, no."

"Ma'am, calm down." The doctor gave me a harried look. "I was just about to say I'm afraid he is still under due to the drugs we gave him. However, his prognosis is good, the bullet only grazed him, so he is very lucky."

"But he was unconscious, the— the blood," I mumbled incoherently.

"It is likely he fainted from the shock," the doctor continued. "He did lose a lot of blood, but we were able to contain it."

"So he's going to be okay?" I asked in disbelief.

"Yes, he should make a full recovery." The doctor nodded and then turned away. "He should be up and able to talk in a few hours."

"Thank you, doctor." Vincent grinned as the doctor walked out of the room, and I felt him envelop me and Jared. "He's going to be okay. I'm going to kill him for scaring us like that."

"Not if I kill him first," I laughed shakily. All of a sudden, my world seemed like it was going to be okay again. I felt some of the tension leave my shoulders and I felt lightheaded.

"Trust me, guys, I will get him first." Jared joined in our laughter and I squeezed his hand.

"I'm going to go to his room. I want to be there when he wakes up." I walked to the door. "Do you guys want to come?" I watched them exchange a look, and Jared shook his head.

"You go. We'll be here. Come and get us when he's up."

"Thank you." I smiled at them both lovingly and went to go and find Logan's room. I walked into the room slowly and walked to Logan's bed with my heart in my mouth. I stared down at his handsome face, and I leaned down to kiss his cheek and run my hands through his hair. I couldn't stop myself from touching him, and I was tracing his lips with my fingers when he opened his eyes slowly.

"Maddie," he whispered up at me with a smile, and I grinned back at him.

"Hey, you." I gazed into his loving green eyes, and felt my stomach flip-flop with butterflies.

"What happened?" He tried to sit up, but winced in pain and stopped.

"You were shot." I held onto his hand. "My dad shot you."

"Jared kidnapped you." Pain flashed in his eyes. "I'm sorry, I've been nothing but trouble to you and your life."

"Logan Martelli, are you joking?" I cried out. "It's me, it's me and my family. All this time, you've been so worried that you haven't been good enough for me, but it is me who hasn't been good enough for you. All I've done is bring drama and trouble to your life. My mom told me everything. She knew, you know. What my dad had done. The poison he put into your lives. I feel like I've made your life even worse. I have been the deadliest poison ever."

"No," he shook his head. "Never say that."

"Logan, you're in a hospital bed because of me." I looked away from him. "What if you had died? I never would have forgiven myself."

"Maddie, I didn't die." He smiled. "Unless I'm in heaven right now." He laughed. "Then thank you to God, because as long as I have you by my side, I don't care where I am."

"Logan," I groaned, though I was delighted at his words. "You were right about my dad and about everything."

"I'm sorry, Maddie." He sighed. "I know it must hurt to know your father is this person."

"I don't want to talk about him." I shook my head. "I just want to talk about us."

"Oh, yes?" He sat up slightly. "Do you want to tell me how much you love me?"

"Yes." I leaned forward and kissed him lightly. "I love you with all my heart, Logan Martelli."

"I love you, too, Maddie." His eyes sparkled at me and he reached over and ran his fingers down my cheek. I held his fingers in mine and kissed him again, and he groaned.

"Oh, no, did I hurt you?" I pulled away from him in concern.

"Not at all." He winked. "I was just wondering if you were trying to seduce me in this hospital bed."

"Logan Martelli." I giggled at him. "You're too much."

"That's why you love me."

"I love you for many reasons, silly."

"You can tell me all of them."

"Well, I love you because you're you. You're the man of my dreams, the man of my heart, the light in my life, and I've known this all from the start."

"Are you trying to dazzle me with your purple eyes, my darling?"

"What?" I looked at him in confusion.

"When I look at you, Maddie, I feel as if I'm being transported to another world. A world of good, a world of wonder, a world that makes me believe in good and right. A world that makes me believe in love."

"When I look at you, Logan, I feel as if I am finally home. Never leave me, Logan. I never want to be apart from you."

"I will never leave you if I can help it." He yawned, and my heart melted.

"You're tired." I broke away from him. "I don't want to tire you, let me go and get Jared and Vincent. They are waiting for you."

"About Jared—" His eyes looked pained and I held up a hand.

"It was my idea, Logan. I told Jared to pretend he had kidnapped me. It was all my idea. I did it because I found out my dad was trying to set you guys up. I'm sorry. I—"

"Shhh." He shook his head. "You have nothing to be sorry about. Never."

"I love you, Logan Martelli."

"I love you, too, my very own bad girl." He laughed and we stared at each other for a few moments, allowing the love to flow between us, before I went to go and get his brothers.

Epilogue

Logan

I like to clear my head at night, so I usually go for a long walk down by the pier. There's something about being in a mass of people that makes you feel like you're a part of something, even if you're not noticed. Even the most solitary person needs to be reminded that there are other people in the world. That's just the way life goes. That's what it means to be a human being. I stared out at the water with a tinge of sadness. I would miss coming to this pier, listening to the people talk about their mundane lives, and watching them go back and forth, never seeing but always seeing. I watched the waves as they crossed into the rocks, and it seemed to me that waves were like life, they seemed to be so calm, and then out of nowhere, they would come crashing down, bringing destruction in their wake.

"I don't want to go to Applebee's," I heard Bella whining to Roger as they walked past me, and I smiled. I could remember the last time that I had seen them. It was the night that changed my life. The night I met Maddie. I turned away from them and turned back to the waves in sadness. That seemed like such a long time ago now; so many things had changed, and I was scared. I was scared that I didn't know who I was anymore, or where I was going. I was still Logan Martelli, but I wasn't *the* Logan Martelli. And while that was great, it felt as if a part of my identity had been stolen away from me. People still looked at me in awe and whispered about me, but it was different now. It was different because they weren't whispering about me being a bad boy, they were whispering about my entire life.

Sometimes, I just wanted to grab my leather jacket and go and steal a car, just for the fun of it. I wanted to give people something to talk about. I wanted to stand out. I want to be the invisible-visible man. But that was only sometimes, when things started feeling overwhelming. I listened to the sounds of the seagulls and breathed in the salty air, and I felt sad. This was it. My life as I knew it was over and I wasn't sure how to feel. I started to walk down to the beach, when I felt the hairs on the back of my neck stand up. I turned around slowly, and I was immediately struck by her purple-blue eyes, such unusual and beautiful eyes, and my heart stopped. She grinned at me and ran towards me, and my heart once again ran a marathon as she jumped into my arms and kissed me.

"Hey," she whispered, her eyes sparkling. "I missed you."

"Hey, I missed you as well." I kissed her back, enjoying the sweet taste of her lips. "You smell good." I buried my face in her neck. "I've missed your smell."

"It's only been a few hours." She laughed happily. "How are you feeling?"

"Good." I nodded at her and took her hand. "Let's go for a walk."

"You feel crappy, huh?" She gave me a teasing smile.

"You can always read my thoughts." I gave her a smile. It was true; Maddie always knew how I really felt inside, no matter what I said. It was one of the things I loved most about her. I wasn't sure how to tell her how much I appreciated her paying attention to the small things. I'd never had someone care about me that much before.

"I know you love the pier." She cuddled into my side. "We can always come back and visit."

"No." I shook my head. "We need a clean break. I don't want us to relive this."

"But it's also where we met." She squeezed my hand. "It's special."

"We're special." I led her down to the beach. "What we have is special, the place doesn't matter. We could be anywhere, and it would be magnificent."

"Right." She laughed. "That's true."

"I wanted to give you something." I reached into my pocket and pulled out the necklace. "This was my mom's." I handed her the silver necklace with the small pearl and the M, and she held it in her hands carefully.

"I love it. Thank you." She grinned at me, and kissed me. "Thank you, I love it."

"Do you want to put it on?" She nodded and I clasped it behind her neck. "Beautiful."

"And it even has the M for Maddie." She smiled at me, touching the letter gingerly.

"Or Martelli," I said softly, staring into her eyes. "I'd love for the M to stand for Maddie Martelli, if you'd like that." I heard her gasp, as her eyes widened in shock, and she squeaked out a reply. "What's that?" I laughed.

"Yes, yes, one hundred times yes."

"I'm sorry I don't have a ring." I brushed her hair away from her face. "I thought we could make a ring from the pearl if you wanted."

"That would be wonderful." She smiled at me. "That way we can always have your mom in our lives."

"You're so wonderful, Maddie." Tears sprang to my eyes, and I her brought her towards me and held her tight. I was overwhelmed with emotion and I felt as if I was the happiest man in the world, yet I still couldn't quite believe it. Maddie pulled away from me and she smiled at me shyly. "I have something for you as well."

"No," I groaned. "You don't have to give me anything."

"No, you need to have this." She smiled up at me through tears. "It's a necklace as well." She reached into her handbag and pulled out a chain. There was a heart with a key and I choked up at the words. The heart read: "He who holds the key can open my heart." And then on the key, it read: "Logan."

"I love you, Logan Martelli, from the tips of my toes to the hair on the top of my head. I love you with every fiber of my being. You are everything to me. You will always hold the key to my heart."

"Thank you for trusting me, Maddie. Thank you for trusting me from the very first moment we met."

"Thank you for what you did for my dad." She took a deep breath. "I know how hard it was for you to decide to not go forward with the gunshot charges. That would have been the ultimate revenge."

"I realized that revenge on him wouldn't have been worth it if it hurt you in any way. Plus he's going to be in jail for a long time anyways, with his fraud charges and his theft ring." I took a deep breath. "I know he's your dad, but I finally felt like justice was being served when he got imprisoned for twenty-five years without a chance of parole."

"I hate him, you know," she sighed. "But I love him as well. He's my dad, and he was always there for me, and I can't just stop loving him, but I'll never forgive him for what he did to you and your family. I'm glad he was imprisoned for what he did to your dad. I wish I could go back in time and change everything. Make it so none of this happened. I wish he hadn't ruined your dad's life, and your mom's. I wish that you and Jared and Vincent had been able to grow up without those harsh conditions. I wish that—"

"Maddie, stop. It's not your fault. I'm sorry that all of that happened as well, but it has nothing to do with you." I rubbed her back. "I know how hard it must be for you."

"It's okay." She smiled weakly. "And it's easier now, I have you and my mom and Jared and Vincent."

"I love your mom, she's great." I smiled at her. "I know that she knew what was going on, but I understand how love can be blinding. I forgive her for her role, and she is so supportive of me and my brothers. She has really taken on a mother role and gotten them sorted out with their applications to college and scholarships. She even got Vincent a math tutor." I laughed. "Now I just need to concentrate on my own studies. And I can't believe she is helping to finance our car shop. We will finally be able to make our own money, the legal way. Jared and I will work there fulltime and go to school part-time, and Vincent will work part-time, as he is closest to getting his degree. I just love her so much for all she is doing for us."

"She loves you, too. How is your dad doing in rehab, by the way?"

"They say he's doing better. He's been there for two weeks now and hasn't had a drink. He is still angry, but with therapy and counseling, he should make some sort of recovery. Please tell your mom thank you for paying for his rehab. We're going to go and visit him in two weeks, that's when they say we can take our first visit. I would love for you to come with me. I've spoken to him on the phone, and he would like to meet you." I smiled at her, with overwhelming emotion. "He told me that he knew I had found love, even though he was too lazy to appreciate it. He wants to thank you. I truly think he may get better." I squeezed her hand, wanting to convey through my touch as well just how much I loved her.

"Logan, of course I will come with you. And you know it's my mom's pleasure. She still wants you to take the million dollars, though."

"No," I shook my head. "I've taken enough in my life. I'm not going to take any more. I'm going to prove to myself and to you that I can make it on my own. Without breaking the law. I'm going to do this. Don't get me wrong, I am so-o-o thankful for her help and support. I wouldn't have known what to do next if she hadn't offered to get us all into college and allow us to start this business."

"I know she is only doing what she thinks is right. My family owes you a whole lot more." She smiled. "I still can't believe we're moving in together. We'll be living in sin. I'm so excited that I just can't contain how happy I am."

"We'll be living in fiancé sin." I grinned. "And Jared and Vincent will be in the house as well, so it won't be a picnic, trust me."

"It'll be great. I've always wanted brothers." She clapped her hands excitedly. "This is going to be a real adventure. I'm so excited to shop for furniture, and cook, and do regular couple things."

"You mean no more stealing cars?" I winked at her. "You've never done that with a previous boyfriend before?"

"I've never had sex in a changing room before either." She snuggled into me. "Or at the pier."

"You naughty girl," I laughed. "I can make one of those things happen now if you want." I whispered into her ear.

"I want." She winked at me and then hugged me. "Thank you for being you, Logan Martelli. I can't wait for us all to live together."

"It's going to be crazy." I laughed.

"No, it's going to be beautiful." She poked me.

"Okay, it's going to be crazy beautiful."

"That's love," she leaned in to kiss me again. "It's going to be a house filled with crazy beautiful love."

Thank you for reading *Crazy Beautiful Love (The Martelli Brothers)*. I hope you enjoyed it. Please leave a review if you liked the book. There will be two more books in the series, one about Vincent and one about Jared.

Join my <u>mailing list</u> so you are notified about my new releases.

Like my <u>Facebook page</u> so that you can see new teasers, covers, and giveaways.

And you can find all <u>my other books</u> here!